The Bridge
on Beer River

Terry Tierney

The author expresses his warm appreciation to the following literary journals where several of these stories first appeared: *The Fiction Pool, Big Bridge, Fictive Dream, Doubly Mad, Potato Soup Journal, Spank the Carp, Bridge Eight,* and *Blue Lake Review.*

Thank you to the talented and tireless editorial and production team at Unsolicited Press for sticking with me and making this book possible. And to Michaelyn and John for making everything possible.

Contents

WAKE

THE END

THE END OF THE WORLD

I hear about the end of the world from my landlady. Chelsea wakes me up on Saturday morning with a knock on my door, standing there smirking with an ironic, detached look in her eyes, the expression she wears when she collects the rent.

She leans against the door frame with one hand behind her head like Betty Grable in a World War II pin-up, except she has thick dark hair and round steel-rimmed glasses. Her massive gray sweater flows down her shoulders and torso until it dams up on her hips. The sweater is large enough to fit a much taller person like me, and it makes her look Bohemian, a beatnik Betty Grable.

Fresh out of bed with my overnight beard, I look like a furloughed soldier on a victory binge.

"Come on, Curt, I have something to show you upstairs." Chelsea steps over the threshold and waits while I pull on my blue jeans and sneakers.

She scales the stairs to her apartment as if she's on a mission. I follow closely, running my hand along the rail like a climber feeling the edge of a cliff.

"It's the African violets," she says, unlocking her door and pointing across the room.

A strange red tinge emanates from the edges of the petals. I tiptoe across the room and lean over for a closer look.

"Wow, they seem radioactive." I say, drawing back at the thought and pushing my crouched frame into Chelsea who's standing directly behind me. "But if they're radioactive, they'd be dead already."

"Maybe it's Agent Orange or volcanic ash from St. Helen's," she suggests.

"Binghamton's pretty far from St. Helen's."

The mention of St. Helen's makes me wonder about local volcanic activity, unlikely but plausible. The red rims on the delicate petals pulsate and the African violets swell, inflated by some unknown power. Mesmerized by the pink glow, I begin to sweat, and my muscles contract as if I'm going into a fit. A shiver runs up my spine.

Chelsea hums Chopin's "Etude in E," her favorite melody, while stroking the inside seam of my blue jeans. I turn to face her and drape my arms over her shoulders.

"Have you tried phosphorus?" I ask.

"Phosphorus has nothing to do with it."

"Maybe it is a volcano," I suggest.

Chelsea responds with a coy smile and pulls my head down for a long kiss. "I think it's your Celtic good looks," she whispers, inserting a warm tongue in my ear.

Through a wash of seductive white noise, I recall the running banter we carried on for weeks about my girlfriend

Mona whom Chelsea compares to Lolita. She claims Mona suffers corruption in the flower of her youth because of me. Chelsea even read the novel to sharpen her barbs. I lean back into the long nails she drags along the base of my spine, dipping under my thermal undershirt. Catching my eye, she blinks with the perky wide-eyed gleam she often uses to imitate Mona, and I shake my head, securing a lock of her hair behind her ear.

"You might cure me of younger women," I say in self-defense. "I haven't been to the playground in weeks. Days." I glance sideways, momentarily distracted by the pink petals on the edge of my vision.

"Such a martyr," she says.

"What about the African violets?" I ask quietly, as if they might be listening.

"Oh. They're that way because the world's coming to an end." She guides me toward the bedroom.

"How do you know?"

"It's just something I know from looking at them. A feeling that something significant is about to happen. Don't you think something's about to happen?" She pulls off her sweater and smiles in an odd way that suggests a measure of seriousness.

I eye her navel as we flop on the bed. "Aren't you afraid of the world ending?"

"No, should I be?"

During the past few weeks, we often talked about making love, but our conversations always remained in the third person. We talked about characters making love in movies and love-making episodes in each of our past lives as if they were movies. We talked about Bridget Bardot seducing an Olympic athlete in her French chateau and Robert Redford cornering Katherine Ross in a shack in Arizona. We even discussed high school kids dry humping at the drive-in and me seducing Mona in the back seat of my old Ford Galaxie, which I never did. After we considered everyone making love in every position, it became obvious it would take a natural catastrophe to break through the third person barrier we had constructed between us. We avoided each other for several days, until the African violets intervened.

Making love near mutated African violets on the last day of the world was a possibility we never discussed. After our weeks of lengthy dialog, we embrace quietly and intensely, the thrill of our first encounter enhanced by a sense of deep recognition, like a reunion after a long separation.

Afterwards we recline with exhaustion and relief that our talking about sex has finally been resolved. I feel the glow of the African violets spreading to my skin. But with it I begin to wonder if I should have paid more attention to their warning. As much as I wanted this moment to happen, I might not be fully prepared for the implications.

"Since this is our last day on earth, there are some things I should take care of," I whisper, staring into a tangled strand of her hair.

Chelsea props her head on an elbow. "What could be so important?"

"A mission of mercy." My joints crack as I stand up and dress. "Maybe I'll see you later."

"Maybe I won't be here. Who knows what will happen?"

I watch her bounce up on her toes to pull up her jeans and adjust the fit as I walk over to the door. "Call me?"

"No," she says in a drawn out, seductive tone. "You're coming back, right?"

"I guess that depends."

She playfully pushes me out the door.

Descending the stairs, I pause on the lower landing before striding past my door and knocking on Allen's across the hall.

My neighbor cracks it open, admiring my red socks.

"Did you know this is our last day on earth?" I ask him.

Allen knits his eyebrows and ushers me in.

"The landlady told me," I continue. "Do you have any African violets?"

Allen's known for his green thumb and the jungle-like environment of his apartment. If anyone knows what's affecting Chelsea's plants, he will. "No, it takes a special breed to grow African violets," he explains. "I have a personality conflict with any plant that's not green and leafy."

"Her African violets have developed this strange red tint. They look radioactive."

"Has she tried phosphorus?"

"That wouldn't help."

He nods. "I heard Chelsea come down and fetch you this morning."

"She wanted me to look at her flowers."

"It's about time she did. I can always tell when you fall in love because you shut yourself up in your apartment. It was the same with Mona."

"No, it was different with Mona." I look my friend in the eye. "The world's coming to an end."

"I don't think it will be that bad. Think of it as another dimension or a different phase of your life."

"I think we should do something," I insist. "A mission of mercy."

Allen studies my face, decoding my intention, and retrieves the key from his bedroom. "You better hurry. The bank closes at one on Saturdays."

I pocket the key and turn to leave.

"Wait a minute," Allen says, taking my arm. "Mona's on her way over. We're going out to breakfast and you're welcome to join us when you finish at the bank."

I examine Allen's deadpan expression. Sure, it's only breakfast, but when I think about him and Mona my emotions twist like spliced wires, sparking with jealousy, relief, or some combination of the two. I never suspected Allen, though I encouraged Mona to take his poetry class. Shorter than me, Allen is stockier, but his curly black hair and thick beard are his primary assets. When he holds his hands together like a monk and chants poetry before his classes, he transports his students to an alternative beat universe. Some must think he's Allen Ginsberg in the flesh.

"You were avoiding her," Allen continues, "so I didn't think you'd care. I feel sorry for her." He expresses his concern with a straight face, but I know him well enough to know his intent is not that saintly.

"We were slowing things down," I admit, suddenly unsure if I'm doing the right thing. Mona's leaving for nursing school downstate at the end of the semester, which is reason enough even if it's not the only reason.

Before I can escape, Allen greets Mona at the door. I stand in the center of his living room with my hands in my pockets, feeling oddly uncomfortable. Though I planned to talk to her today, this is not the meeting I had in mind. I quickly shake her hand.

Mona smiles, rising on her toes to plant a warm kiss on my unshaven cheek. She glances sideways at Allen. She might think he's a genius because at one time she thought I was a genius. She might be right about Allen, not me. Any apparent difference in our intelligence is more likely a function of the difference in our ages.

Although she's well past puberty and soon graduating college, Mona's the perfect subject for a Lolita complex. A small woman, she has dark languorous eyes and wavy black hair falling to her waist. She has a voluptuous figure seldom covered with more clothes than necessary and an unconscious habit of touching her cheek and full lips when she talks.

I first saw her on a muggy day sitting on a park bench with her legs tucked beneath her pale blue gym shorts. A book rested on her tanned thighs. She might have just finished exercising because her breasts heaved against the thin veil of her white tank top, and a strap had fallen from her shoulder. Watching her gave me an immediate fever. Her intelligence and the unconscious lilt in her voice sealed my desire.

As she stands next to Allen, her pointed little tongue darts along the edges of her lips. She might be the most beautiful and alluring woman I've ever known. I must be crazy.

"You're joining us for breakfast, aren't you?" she asks with a blink of her brown eyes.

"Sorry, I can't," I explain. "The world's coming to an end, and I have some things to take care of."

Mona scans me and Allen with a questioning slant of her head.

"Bound to happen sometime," Allen says, shrugging his shoulders.

I shuffle toward the door.

"Nothing surprises me anymore," Allen continues, increasing his volume. "I wouldn't be surprised if Reagan's been dead for years--a servo-operated cadaver and a tape machine. Or Anita Bryant's pregnant by a gay Cuban. Or a volcano erupted in Binghamton. Mount St. Helen's on Church Street."

Mona rewards his tirade with a soft smile. He's about to continue when I remind him I have to leave.

"Okay," Allen relents, "but if we're still here tomorrow, will you help me move some books out of my office on campus?" My friends often appeal to me for manual labor, something I'm good at. Chelsea says I should charge for moving services.

"Remind me in the morning," I reply as I step out the door.

"Hey, Curt, it won't be as bad as you think," Allen calls after me.

The brisk air smells more like late spring than the end of the world, and I'm glad to have a few hours to ponder the implications. If the world survives the catastrophe, I must figure out what to do about Mona and Chelsea, not to mention Allen and me, given his interest in Mona. My life would be simpler if the world ended. Maybe this is the way the world ends, with unresolved dilemmas. Why should it be easy?

I recheck my pocket for the key as I walk up Front Street toward the First National Bank of Chenango. Ever since a druggie living in the basement apartment broke into Allen's place and stole a chunk of hashish, Allen insists we keep our mutual stash in a safe deposit box. I came home from work early that day and found Justin holding Allen's door, trying to fit it back on its hinges. When he saw me, he leaned the door against the frame like it fell off by accident and ran down the stairs.

Later I convinced Chelsea to change the hinges of her old converted Victorian house so the apartment front doors all open inward. She paid me to rehang the doors, knowing I was between jobs and needed cash to pay the rent, but that's how our meandering conversation started. Despite our months of close contact, I know little about her other than her pending PhD program and her real estate business. When I asked how she came to own our building, along with two others, Chelsea cocked her hips and patted the back of her head, suggesting a wealth of unrevealed talents.

I push through the bank's whirling glass doors and walk past the guard. While I wait in line, I spy a pot of wilted African violets sitting on a computer terminal behind the teller. The terminal also supports an "Out of Order" sign.

"Your African violets don't look very well," I say to the teller when she leads me to the vault.

"It's the lights," she replies pleasantly.

"I think it's more serious than that."

The teller pauses and looks me directly in the eyes. "You're right. The plant was a present from my ex-husband." She rests her hand on my forearm and smiles cynically. "I'm letting it die a slow death. I give it a few drops of water on Mondays." Pivoting on her spiked heels, she leaves me alone among the rows of safe deposit boxes.

Inside our box I find a pound of Colombian reefer. I lift out the zip lock storage bag and gather a couple handfuls into a baggie and shove it in my pocket. After I secure the box the teller signs me out.

That night my sparsely furnished apartment becomes the scene of an End of the World Party with two sawhorses, an unfinished desk, and the pillows off my bed all supporting guests. Some bring food and drinks, including a carrot cake and a plate of brownies. Three bottles of wine, two Bordeaux and one Cabernet, appear during the evening, along with a six-pack of Coca-Cola. I'm the only one drinking beer, dipping into my emergency supply of Genesee Cream Ale.

Mona arrives about the same time as Allen who carries a gift African violet with gold foil wrapped around the plastic vase. I place it gently on the orange crate in the center of my living room where the petals emit their curious glow, causing the revelers to gather around.

Someone behind me says, "Maybe the end of the world will be a mystical event like Don Juan dreaming in the desert."

"I'd rather see a political revolution," a hopeful voice replies.

"You're too late, the world has ended already," Allen asserts. "No one's noticed it." He launches into a rant about zombies driving cars, buying groceries, and watching television evangelists. Mona agrees with everything he says, though she keeps glancing at me for approval.

When Allen pauses for a breath, I interject, "Look at the pink tinge on the violets. The world must not have ended yet." The petals glow even brighter under the Colombian haze, but it's hard to refute Allen when he's on a roll.

I hear Chelsea walk down the stairs just as Mona squeals at one of Allen's jokes, followed by footsteps back up to her apartment. Her piano erupts with Jerry Lee Lewis, faintly pounding over the din of Bruce Springsteen on my stereo. No Chopin for her tonight. She returns about a half hour later and I pull open the door before she knocks. Chelsea enters cautiously and surveys the room until her gaze catches on Mona leaning toward Allen as he continues his lecture. Chelsea relaxes, pausing to admire my new African violets and holding up a bottle of Vouvray, which I quickly open and pour into two paper cups.

"Glad you came," I tell her.

"I thought we agreed you were coming back upstairs." She eyes me accusingly, only half serious.

"The world doesn't end every day."

"That would be impossible."

Soon after Chelsea arrives, the party begins to disperse, most expressing a desire to spend the last hours of earth in their own apartment, until there are just the four of us left standing around the orange crate like wrestlers in neutral corners.

"Nearly midnight," Allen says to me, glimpsing Chelsea. "I'll talk to you tomorrow if we're still here. Don't forget my books."

Mona's eyes follow Allen as he edges toward the door. She sends me a yearning look, her eyes blinking sleepily. She raises a finger and runs it around the edge of her lips like she's checking her lipstick, though she's not wearing any, the gesture I find so appealing.

Chelsea's cool touch brushes my arm and I rest my hand on her shoulder, feeling self-conscious, knowing I still need to talk to Mona. Before I can articulate a sound, Mona's face flashes muted surprise at my gesture, followed by annoyance, and finally acceptance, raising her eyebrows to signal I'm making a mistake. Allen observes the brief interplay with amusement. Mona takes his elbow, and they glide out the door.

"You wanted her to stay," Chelsea says.

"I wanted you to stay."

"Some part of you wanted her to stay."

"Maybe," I admit, "but she's leaving after the semester. Allen's leaving, too." I swivel to face Chelsea, our arms winding together. "And you're leaving."

She snuggles her head against my chest. "I'll be here longer than they will. My classes at NYU don't start until August."

Combing my fingers through her thick hair, her warm breath on my T-shirt, I spy the pink petals shimmering behind her. I've seldom tried to raise plants, certainly not ones this portentous. I know animals can also predict storms and earthquakes, sense their inevitability. Maybe that's what I'm feeling.

"Where are you?" Chelsea whispers.

"Just wondering how often I should water."

BALLOONS

In mid-August, the last wave of Binghamton University graduates begins its migration back to New York City. Yard sales sprout on every street, piled with furniture, books, old clothes, and discarded lovers, a time for decisions.

I help Chelsea pack her Datsun, and at lunchtime we take my car to Otsiningo Park, the site of the annual Speidi and Balloon Festival. Over the campus radio station, we hear that the authorities canceled the hot-air balloon launch this morning due to thunderstorms. They'll try again tomorrow. But the food and beer booths are all open despite the Arctic cold front, their wet canvas and plastic tarps shining in transient sunbeams.

"This is fun!" Chelsea exclaims. She wears a green raincoat and a flat-brimmed cowboy hat, resembling a Mexican outlaw queen with her long dark hair pinned up and her orange umbrella tucked under her arm like a riding crop. Her sarcastic smile is contagious.

"Never ate a speidi," I admit.

"Here's your big chance." We pick our way across the soggy grass to the speidi tent just as a lone customer squishes away. Chelsea waits for me to order, then asks for a soft pretzel with extra mustard. "I can't do the spiedi thing," she says.

Wiping off a steel picnic bench with a wad of napkins, we sit close together. The damp cold seeps through my jeans as I huddle over the speidi for warmth. Chelsea studies my face when I venture my first bite.

According to speidi lore, the delicacy is marinated lamb grilled on a skewer and served on Italian bread, but it's hard to identify or chew the fatty cubes of undercooked meat. I spit them into my napkin and look around for a dumpster.

"I tried to eat a speidi a couple years ago," Chelsea confides.

"You could have warned me."

"It's an experience you can't miss." She slides her pretzel between us to share. "They're usually much better than this."

"I'll never know."

Chelsea cracks a smile. "You like it here, Curt. Now you can say you ate a speidi." She eyes my beer can, another sign I'm transforming into a townie.

"The bread is okay." I toss my wad of half-chewed fat and grizzle into a cardboard trash bin stenciled with the festival logo, hoping to avoid another discussion about our pending separation. Chelsea and I are good at talking. We discussed the topic of sex for weeks before we slept together, and lately we talk about her graduation and her plans as if they're happening to someone else, even as we packed her car. I always knew this day would come. Her ambition of teaching and earning a doctor's degree in education at NYU was never a secret: our summer romance had a shelf date.

We dodge puddles back to my old Ford and drive across the Exchange Street Bridge to the south side. Swelled with rain, the Susquehanna River flows in the wrong direction. It should drain downstate like everything else, but the current runs west, defying logic.

Chelsea packs a few last-minute boxes, always the slowest chore, while I cart my meager possessions upstairs, starting with my coffee pot and an armful of books. I agreed to manage the building along with her other two converted Victorians for reduced rent. Her apartment comes as part of the deal, twice the size of my cramped rooms downstairs.

She sold her bed so I lug mine up the narrow stairway along with my orange crate and my African violet, its plastic pot wrapped in gold aluminum foil, the gift from my friend Allen, who has already left for his new teaching position downstate. As always, the African violet seems to glow with premonition, its fuzzy leaves brushing in whispers.

When she carefully unwraps the flowerpot from my grasp, Chelsea eyes my other memento from Allen, a black and white photo of Allen Ginsberg wearing hippy beads.

"It's supposed to be Ginsberg, but it really looks like Allen," she says.

"Hard to tell them apart."

"Except for their sexual orientation."

"You mean Mona?"

"The real Allen Ginsberg would never put up with her."

"She has her own poetry," I reply with an exaggerated leer. Chelsea never took to my former girlfriend, now Allen's.

She tosses a stray sock and watches it drop harmlessly in mid-flight.

After I drive out to fetch a Nirchi's pizza, best in town, with mushrooms and peppers, we sit at her aluminum kitchen table and share a joint. Chelsea's leaving the table and three matching chairs along with the threadbare armchair in the living room, doubling my array of furniture if you count the orange crate and my two sawhorses. When the weed smolders to ash we munch quietly.

"You can't drive a forklift forever," Chelsea says, clearing her throat with a swig of Diet Coke.

"I like that job. Moving pallets takes precision. And I get free milk." I stand and reach into the refrigerator for another Genesee Cream Ale.

"You liked your old job. You're built for construction."

"The machines were bigger."

"I wish I had more work for you," she says. "I wish I had machines."

After I was wrongfully fired from my construction gig, maintaining her buildings helped me fill the gap, and now I can return the favor. I'm not looking for money. "I like your lawnmower. You could buy me a riding one."

She shakes her head. "This isn't about my machines or your holy forklift."

Parmesan flies across the table as I tear open one of the tiny packets. I sweep the grains off the edge and drop them on my pizza slice. Chelsea pretends not to notice.

"You say you want to learn computers," she says.

"They have a computer at the dairy."

"Why don't you go back to school? You have the GI Bill."

"I'm a terrible student," I reply through a mouthful of Nirchi's. "You know that."

"Just take a computer course."

"You like school and you're good at it." I stare at my green beer can, having heard all this before, but then she surprises me.

"I can teach here as well as New York." Her moist eyes gleam under the dull kitchen light. I stare at the fluorescent bulb, both ends black and the tube faded to yellow, thinking I should replace it. Over the past few days Chelsea hinted I might be better off leaving Binghamton, breaking out of my rut and trying my luck downstate. Part of me knows she might be right, something about this place feels unhealthy, and it's not just her pending absence. I evaded her nudges, knowing how alien I'd feel in New York and how she was sure to sense my dissonance eventually, and blame our relationship rather than the place. My reluctance aside, I was never sure she wanted me to accept her offer.

Today's the first time she mentioned forsaking her life in New York and remaining in Appalachia, as the students call the vast, sparsely populated region west of the Tappan Zee Bridge.

"You already shipped your piano," I reply, "and you complain there's no Bloomingdale's."

She flashes a quick grin. "There's a Bloomingdale's three hours away."

"What about your PhD program?"

"You won't ask me to stay, will you?"

"I'd love for you to stay, but you'd be miserable." I sit back and sip my beer. My face warms with the strain of not asking her to change her plans, even though our long weeks of discussing the separation make a final appeal easier to resist.

Chelsea dabs the olive oil off a wedge of pizza with a paper towel. Her eyes clear as she returns my gaze, curling her mouth playfully, treating her offer like a trial balloon, another flight of the annual festival. She bends her neck over the table. "I know you're right," she says, "but you're not the typical townie."

"You mean I'm not inbred?"

"You're too Celtic looking." She pushes away a strand of hair hanging above her pizza slice. "You have that sinister mustache, and your eyes are too smart."

I raise my can in an Irish salute, acknowledging her apparent compliment and her unstated concern about what will happen once we're apart, a concern I share. We've been careful to avoid promises. "You know I only date women who are leaving town."

Shaking her head, she drops her paper towel on the table, careful to keep the oil off her fingertips. "I think you're serious."

The next morning we sit at the table one more time. I lap up Rice Krispies with free milk, Chelsea following each spoonful while the percolator hisses on the gas stove. She never eats breakfast. The fluorescent bulb flickers and hums.

When I drop the dishes in the sink, I hear her retreating down the stairs. I follow a few beats later, balancing my coffee cup. Down at the curb Chelsea leans toward her car, her back to me, frozen in place. She turns with a flowerpot cradled in her hands.

"I forgot to leave room for my African violets. What an idiot." She presses the plant into my chest and rests her head on my shoulder. I hold her close, squeezing the pot between us and extending my coffee behind her back.

As our hug relaxes I stare down at her African violets, knowing she wants me to adopt them. I imagine the flowers spying on me, their plant network with pollen and spores hitchhiking on insects, broadcasting my secrets. Or maybe it works both ways, a purple antenna.

"They can stay with their cousins until you visit. Plenty of room on the orange crate." My voice quavers, sounding like an echo. I lift the flowers from her cold hands and set them on the porch.

Trailing Chelsea's Datsun down the hill in my Ford, the scent of her exhaust whisks through my open window until she turns toward Highway 17. I find myself fighting the steering wheel, my mind drawn toward her tail lights as if on rails. The traffic light changes between us, and I jerk to a stop, inhaling the fog rolling off the river to clear my lungs, the sun cresting razorback hills. I twist my head away from the highway and drive toward Crowley Dairy. Cows never take the weekend off.

My tires buzz across the corrugated steel bridge over the Susquehanna, and the morning sky fills with hot-air balloons--green mint swirls, barbershop stripes, blue and yellow bursts, Easter egg dyes on inverted tear drops, all floating free below the white puffs of scattered clouds.

MUSEUM

"I can't wait to get there," Chelsea says in an even tone, unchanged from our discussion of a new hot water heater a moment ago. Since she moved from Binghamton to New York City the frequency of our phone calls has declined, and we focus more on my part-time management of her apartment buildings, the three converted Victorians, and less on our long-distance relationship.

"You'll love it," I reply. "Round and gray, a masterpiece of nineteenth-century engineering."

"I don't believe you, Curt," she says, sounding a bit warmer. "You're not that old and fat." Normally her voice has two settings, business and suggestive, but seldom tentative like this, a quarter of the dial.

"You might be surprised," I reply. This will be her first visit since she relocated. Our previous plans ended up canceled, the pressure of her doctorate program always to blame.

"We have a lot to talk about." She pauses. "How are my African violets?"

Sorry she asked. When I first brought my violets upstairs and set them next to hers, the pink glow on the petals resonated between the plants, their energy multiplying in proximity, the way I feel around Chelsea. "Frankly, not so good." I confess.

"They could be past season, whatever their season is."

"I think they miss you." The phone line fills with silence and a background of static. "Are you okay?"

She clears her throat. "I'll bring some phosphorus for the violets."

"Never worked before."

"Yeah, I know."

Soon we hang up and I sit back and stare at the wilted plants, trying to decode the phone call. As much as I want to see Chelsea, the intervening months since her departure feed my anxiety. She might stroke my shoulder in greeting, the gesture that always fans my anticipation, sure to erase my concerns. Or maybe our romance is destined for the trash bin, another old flowerpot not worth saving.

My mind hovers like a ghost in my own apartment that used to be Chelsea's, just like the armchair where I'm sitting. A museum diorama. At least the bed and the orange crate are mine, along with the used stereo, a small collection of tattered record albums, and a photograph of Allen Ginsburg in hippie beads that looks like my friend and former neighbor Allen. I find myself talking to it late at night when I smoke the weed from the diminishing stash he and I once shared.

Allen has kept closer contact than Chelsea. Just this week I received his latest book, "Dystopian Dharma—the Beats and the Bomb," which won him his new job at Columbia. Brilliant and obscure, the literary treatise is way over my head, though I detect the rhythm of Allen's throaty rant when I try to read it. He asked me to send him a cube of hashish, since he's still feeling out of place and unconnected in New York City.

With most of my friends moving back downstate, I share his sense of dislocation. So, I agree to meet some fellow workers from Crowley Dairy for an evening at Pearl's, a country-western joint downtown that transforms into a disco bar on Thursday nights. I pull on my one pair of non-jeans and a cheap sports coat, glad for the distraction.

When I arrive at Pearl's the repetitive beat promises a headache, and the dance floor teems with white John Travolta suits and eager partners, just as my friend Renee promised. I hardly recognize her without her spattered smock from the dairy, but her blond curls give her away. She bounces across the floor and plants a kiss on my cheek. Wearing a light blue sweater with a silver studded necklace, she emits a warm smile and a whiff of jasmine.

"Is that Anton?" I ask, projecting my voice over the Bee Gees and catching the cold stare of a husky guy with oiled hair. Renee and I often meet in the coffee room when my break time matches hers. I've heard a lot about her boyfriend Anton, his short temper, and his rich family who own a trucking company, Binghamton nobility.

"Want to meet him?"

"Maybe later." A few stools down from Anton another set of eyes burn through the shadows. Dark with heavy eyelashes set in a mass of auburn curls, the sharp gaze cuts through me like a witness might examine a suspect, accusing but entranced. A small woman, she reminds me of my one time girlfriend Mona, now Allen's, though Mona is more innocent in demeanor.

"Bar snipe," Renee chuckles. "Bar snipe with a nasty boyfriend."

"You know her?"

"From high school. Her family owns Mother's, that dive on Court Street."

The bar snipe's boyfriend raises his head from the bar and elbows their pitcher, nearly knocking it over. The dark eyes shoot back in time to save the beer from disaster, and she refills his glass. His face looks angry, a permanent twist of mouth, likely there when he sleeps, making Anton's angular mug appear angelic. Anton hasn't moved, still glaring at me over Renee's shoulder.

"Good investment, a family bar. Cheap way to keep her boyfriend," I reply, unsure if my words survived the din around us. Raising my voice, I change the subject to the dairy. "I talked to Sherman about learning computers."

"I like him," Renee says. Everyone at the dairy likes my boss because he's the only one who knows what to do. He acts like he does anyway, and people believe him.

"He looked at me like I wanted to pitch for the Yankees."

"You'll win him over." Renee nods goodbye and brushes my hand, sliding across the raised wooden floor to Anton who winds her in his arms. The strobes flash to announce the next song and they swing out to dance.

I sip my beer and search for other Crowley people. Renee made the evening sound like a dairy convention, but I see no familiar faces other than the bar snipe, her radar sweeping over me as she half carries her sodden boyfriend out the back door to the parking lot. I chug my beer and head out the front, not wanting to watch the snipe couple trying to crawl into their car. Again I wonder if I should have taken the offer Chelsea made before she left in August and moved downstate. I always thought I'd regret that decision. Now I'm not so sure.

Friday night I slouch in the armchair with my <u>Blonde on Blonde</u> album scratching in the background, waiting for Chelsea's Datsun to putter up the street. Bob Dylan carries me closer to Chelsea's place near NYU, though I only imagine it, never visited, never invited. She says her apartment's too small and crammed with roommates, all fighting grad school deadlines, and she'd rather come up here. She must be nearing Binghamton by now. Maybe we'll pass one other on the psychic Highway 17, somewhere near the Roscoe Diner.

When the record ends I find myself watching the pair of African violets as if a surge in their resonant glow might signal her approach, reflecting my anticipation and apprehension, even if their pink tinge has faded over the past three months, each bloom paler than the one before. Maybe it's the flowers or the faint rumble of Chelsea's muffler, but I look out the front window just as she pulls up under the yellow streetlight.

She hops out the passenger door and tosses a quick wave toward my silhouette. I raise my hand, waiting to see who's driving. Maybe it's her sister. Chelsea didn't mention anyone else joining her.

Allen slides out and salutes toward the window. He pulls on a leather jacket as he and Chelsea pace up the cracked walk to the front door. I flop back in the chair, wondering why Chelsea didn't say he was coming. I should be happy to see Allen, though the timing is wrong.

A syncopated rhythm announces their arrival, Allen's two-fisted knock. Chelsea hugs me quickly, wearing a worried expression, her hair trimmed to her shoulders, her red beret in its customary perch. She scans my eyes, hugging me again. I kiss her forehead. "Sorry we're late," she says. "It's been too long."

"The Binghamton time warp," I reply, stepping back, sensing her anxiety mirroring mine.

I turn to Allen with a firm handshake. "You look so Ivy League," I gibe. All that remains of his wild beard is a thick mustache matching his styled haircut and brown sweater.

He taps my biceps. "I thought you'd grow soft working at the dairy. Guess not."

"More books to move?" I ask, recalling how I helped stack and pack Allen's substantial personal library when he took the Columbia job.

"I'd like to move a few more copies of my new book. Even Chelsea read it."

Her soft eyes tell me she read about as much as I did. My host reflex kicks in, so I take their coats into the bedroom and throw them on the bed. I check the closet for my old sleeping bag and camping cot, thinking I'll pull them out later for Allen.

When I return they're still standing fixed in place as if hesitant to enter further, afraid to touch anything. I ask, "Coke or beer? A pebble of hashish? Should I order a pizza?"

Chelsea spies the African violets. "Poor things." She approaches the orange crate, bending over and lifting a limp leaf.

"I tried, no response," I tell her.

"I'm sure you did everything."

"Cycle of life," Allen chants, launching his pedantic voice. "Birth and dirt. Nothing to mourn, no souls, but their lives were fulfilled, living out their African violetness."

"I feel remorse," Chelsea counters.

Allen nods. "You're not a plant."

Chelsea turns to me.

"I'm not a plant either." I grin, though I feel less remorse than she does.

She straightens and crosses the room to Allen, leaning her long fingers on his shoulder. "This is making me crazy," she says. Her gesture is one I remember too well, only it used to be my shoulder.

Seeing them together explains the timing of Chelsea's visit, her mystery driver, the disjointed phone call, and the awkward greeting at the door. The plants' fading hue sinks into my gut, consumed by rising anger.

"I feel terrible," Chelsea says. "I couldn't tell you on the phone. I wanted to explain in person."

Her eyes fill with tears, and I catch a glint of reflection from Allen's eyes. I feel like a pawn, captured and discarded.

"This is my fault," Allen says. "I hitched a ride at the last minute. Connecting with some colleagues on campus."

Clenching my fists, I find it easier to blame Allen. "First Mona and now Chelsea," I sputter. "Next time I find a girlfriend, I'll let you know."

"It's not like that," Allen replies in a muffled voice. "Mona broke it off."

"No, it's my fault," Chelsea interjects. "I should have told you on the phone. My mistake."

I stride to the kitchen, unsure what I'll do there, just get away. I grip the aluminum table with both hands and take several deep breaths, but the extra oxygen doesn't calm my mood.

When I return to the living room Allen shies away from my scowl, and Chelsea holds her hands out in appeal. "We both love you," she pleads. "We want you in our lives."

"Do you know how hollow that sounds?" I retrieve my old khaki jacket from the closet, checking for my keys.

"Where are you going?" Chelsea asks, alarmed. "You live here."

"This is your place," I grimace. "Always was."

"We should leave," Allen says. "We're so sorry."

"Yeah, one of your cycles of life." I push him away from the door and catch Chelsea's eye. "I quit. Find someone else to manage your apartments."

Retreating down the steps, I duck into my old Ford and clutch the steering wheel. The humming streetlights cast jagged shadows of elm and maple across the windshield. When the inside glass fogs, I know it's time to move, while I can still see. The car points downhill and I follow it toward the decaying downtown, over the steel Exchange Street Bridge, with the gray river dabbed by broken streaks of moonlight. I don't stop until the Ford brakes in a small parking lot behind My Mother's Place on Court Street.

Dirty windows and an uneven floor scraped by decades of hard-soled shoes are about what I expect from the dive bar. Dim light and thick smoky air scrape my eyes, but I feel oddly at home, a universe removed from Chelsea and Allen. They would never go to a place like this. Now I'm a certified townie, as they often joke. Not here for college, not anymore, just here to work and drink.

As my sight adjusts, I scan the shadows until I see her carrying a tray with two empty glasses. The bar snipe from Pearl's. She looks even better here, as if she gains power from her family joint, the pale lights accenting her auburn curls and moist lips. I take a table across from the bartender, waiting for her to find me.

She cocks her hips and reads my thirst, offering a glass of Genesee Ale in a soft voice. The only draft they serve. By my fourth round I ask her name.

"Debby," she whispers, batting her lazy eyes and looking toward the bar, as if checking for her boyfriend. "Are you okay?"

"Of course, I am. Better now."

She blows a wayward curl away from her mouth as she exchanges glasses between my table and her tray. "You look like a guy who drinks because he wants to drink. Not for fun."

"I'm having fun."

She gives me a downward glance like she knows what I really want and sways back to the bar to replenish her load.

The street door bangs open and her boyfriend stumbles toward the bar. He appears less trashed than he did at Pearl's, and Debby slides him a beer. I decide it's time to leave.

I can't go back to my apartment, really Chelsea's, not tonight. I could find Renee's place where she lives with Anton. He would love to see me. I could find a motel room, but I forgot to cash my paycheck. They'll want cash this late.

I drive out to Otsiningo Park where I tried to eat a speidi on Chelsea's last day in Binghamton. The unchewable cubes of marinated lamb resonate now with the scene at my apartment earlier this evening. The park is deserted, lit by a few streetlamps among the acres of ragged grass and struggling saplings. I squeeze the Ford between a dumpster and a brick bathroom, recalling it has running water to wash my face in the morning, if I can avoid the bored police patrols.

When I shut off the car my mind races. I should have thrown Allen and Chelsea out of the apartment. I should have hugged them. I should have stayed longer and listened. I was never good at listening to excuses. The frigid cold creeps through the rusted floorboards and up my legs. Stomping my feet for circulation, I restart the car, and its ancient heater spits damp air. I let them off too easily. They deserve worse.

First as a spark and then a rising flame, my anger blows more warmth than the engine. Before I realize my intent, I jam the transmission into drive and wind out of the empty parking lot, turning toward the apartment.

I'll tell them this is my place. And if they don't leave, then what? If it were anyone else in the world besides Chelsea and Allen, I'd throw them out the door. No time to dress. Let them scatter in the cold like rabbits, sleep in a pile of rotting leaves. The more I fume, Allen's face merges with the ugly sneer of Debby's boyfriend, and I wish I could escape to her, however unlikely.

At the front door of the apartment, I pause to still my nerves. My feet ache with cold and my hands quiver for action. Turning the key and pushing my way in, I find the rooms dark and silent. I search for signs of their presence or a note of apology. I creep like an intruder, a thief in the museum. My bed appears untouched, their coats gone.

By the time I hear a knock in the early morning my anger has evaporated to fatigue, but I still dread the encounter. It won't take much to push me back over the edge. My anger hovers beneath my chest.

Chelsea stands in a splash of bright fluorescent light from the hallway. "Are you alright?"

Allen stands behind her, cupping his hand above his eyes to shade the beam like he's watching me from far away.

"Never better."

"Thank God," Chelsea says. "You scared me with the way you left." She lightly grips my arm, but her fingers sink deeper than I expect. I want to say something, one last appeal, though this is not the place, not with Allen hovering nearby.

"God, whoever she is." Allen smiles nervously, always ready with an irreverent joke.

I cough to clear my throat, still staring at Chelsea, straining to keep my voice steady. "No need to worry. You okay?"

"This is crazy," Chelsea shakes her head and steps back. I can tell she smells my morning beer breath, a whiff of townie culture. "I handled this so poorly."

I glance between her and Allen, seeing the concern weighing on their faces. I can't be angry with them. Nor will I ask them in.

Chelsea says, "We figured you were working today, so we came early."

"Yeah, my holy forklift." I force a grin, echoing Chelsea's description when she tried to convince me to give up my dairy job and follow her to New York in August.

"Are you still quitting?" Chelsea asks in a whisper. She doesn't mean the forklift.

"I'm getting another place."

She watches my eyes, expecting more.

"How about I give notice?"

Chelsea nods and I detect a measure of relief in her expression, which tells me more than her arrival with Allen. She should know I would never leave her hanging without anyone to manage her apartments. "I'll start looking," she says.

Voice dropping to a whisper, Allen concludes, "Another acolyte to maintain the shrine." His joke falls flat though it carries a hint of empathy. I doubt our friendship will survive.

Chelsea raises her chin toward me, but no words emerge. Nothing further from either of us. Despite its abrupt and recent ending, our relationship already begins fading into memory, an artifact locked in a case.

Farewells flow like a stage play. I watch them clomp and tap down the stairs. Chelsea wears high-heeled boots; she's always precisely dressed. I need a shower and a fresh pot of coffee. On my way to the dairy, I'll pick up a copy of the Sun-Bulletin with its columns of apartment ads. Time to move out of the museum. Maybe I'll find a place closer to Mother's.

CIRCUS

JOINING THE CIRCUS

Debby wants to join the circus. She tells me in a dreamy way, lying on her side facing me, her eyes closed and a wet trail of drool on the corner of her mouth. She looks angelic, but I know she's drunk, talking impossible futures like drunks always do.

"The strong man has huge tattoos," she says, "and a shiny bald head."

"Like a bowling ball," I reply. "With tiny round eyes and a round mouth." I point my thumb and fingers at her to show how I'd grip his head and roll it for a strike. I lose my balance and lurch sideways, nearly falling off the bed.

Debby laughs and props herself up on her elbow to fire a cigarette. "He can get me a job selling concessions or feeding the animals. Just the tame ones I told him, but he says I wouldn't have to work if I didn't want to." She exhales through her nose. "I want to learn the trapeze. Or ride the horses." She tosses back her auburn hair like a shampoo model.

"You're pretty enough." I imagine her with pancake makeup under bright lights. "Why do you want to leave Binghamton?"

At that, we both laugh until we end up coughing. Anyone who stays in Binghamton is either looney or drunk. Bad jobs and worse weather. Outside the rain is blowing and beating an irregular rhythm above our heads, accenting our conversation like it does everything here. Now that I think about it, I expected the rain to start when Debby and I made love no matter how drunk we were. The dampness gives us an excuse to cuddle closer.

As she drifts off to sleep, she says, "I'm glad I got to know you tonight, Curt. You're a real dreamer. Wanting to learn computers." She nuzzles my chest while I stroke her curls. "You're so tough looking."

"I'm not that tough," I reply as she falls asleep, her breathing deep and regular. I remember how I caught her eye across the dance floor at Pearl's. She was slow dancing with her boyfriend, holding him up because he could hardly stand by himself, and she gave me one of those pleading looks, as if to say, "Get me away from this loser." After the house band took a break, he staggered out the door with a couple of other drunks. I waited until the music started again to ask her to dance.

Before long she said, "My boyfriend will kill us both if he comes back and sees me dancing with you." I laughed because he must have been passed out by then, but I read her fear. I walked her out to my car, and we ended up at my place.

Watching her sleep, I trace the line of her backbone with my hand. She quivers, as if she feels a mosquito, and starts to snore. She has a hard life. I can see it in the crow's feet around her eyes, though she looks younger when she's asleep. I smile at the thought of Debby with her wild, curly hair riding a white stallion as I lead him prancing around the ring. She looks great, standing up there on his bare back, and her dark eyes tell me she thinks the same of me. I hear the crowd cheering us on.

The next day I go down to the Park Diner where Debby works lunches on weekends, planning to ask her out to dinner. Just after she brings me a burger with onion rings her boyfriend swings into the dining room looking for her. He's in the same shape he was last night. When he sees her go into the kitchen he screams, "Debby, you whore, come back here!" He chases her into the back where he yells at her. Everyone stops eating and stares at the stainless-steel door. I stand up to help, thinking she's catching it because of me. She comes striding out of the kitchen with a tray of food like nothing happened. He stays in the back, still cussing though not as loudly. She sees me standing by my booth and walks over. "Sit down," she whispers.

"Maybe I should talk to him."

"You can help me by staying out of it."

She rushes away to deliver her orders and laughs for the benefit of the customers. She circles back to my booth. "My brother Daryl is back there," she confides. "He's the cook. The manager asked him to sub today."

"He has no right to talk to you like that."

"Mark doesn't know what he's saying. He's drunk," she explains. "But I'm sick of it. This is the last time he'll ever do this to me. My brother will see to that."

"My fault," I admit, though I don't feel sorry about it.

"It's not you." She glances toward the kitchen. "He wants me to marry him."

I stare at her in disbelief.

She regrips her tray. "I have to go. I'll get fired if anything else happens."

"I was going to ask you out to dinner," I smile. "Some place nice like Morey's."

"Thanks, I don't feel very hungry." She lowers her voice so I can barely hear her. "Call me later."

That night I pick her up at her brother's apartment where she rents a room, and we go back to my place with a couple of six packs. I repeat my desire to buy her dinner, but she won't go out because of Mark.

I tell her I want to join the circus. "Let's run away together," I suggest grandly. We both chuckle as I get up to retrieve more beer from the kitchen.

"The circus left town already," she informs me when I get back. "The strong man gave me the address for their winter quarters down in Orlando. They go there in October after their tour."

"The bowling tour?"

She ignores my joke. "I have no desire to visit Florida unless I'm drunker than I am now. My brother and me want to start a catering business at My Mother's Place. Daryl's a great cook, and I could serve for parties."

At the mention of her family's dive bar, I joke about how Mark guzzles the profits. She waves me off. "You could join us. You could do the books."

"And Mark wouldn't mind if I snuggled you in the back."

"None of that, now," she says seriously, sounding like we're already working together. "You said you wanted to learn computers."

I take a deep swallow. "Maybe I'll start computer school at night. I'm tired of driving a forklift. My boss wants to keep all the dairy records on the computer, but he ignored my offer to help. Old Crowley the owner loves him."

"Yeah, I heard you last night. You're such a dreamer," she says, running her hands behind my ears and pulling my face down for a kiss. Just talking about the dairy makes me tense.

"Where's Mark tonight?" I ask in a whisper, as if he might be listening.

"He's out drinking at Mother's. My brother's working so he'll get free beers even if I'm off." She stares at me. "Serves him right I'm here." She drains her beer and adds, "He's a drunk. The Devil's got him, but he doesn't believe it. Besides, he's on parole. I don't know why I put up with him."

I shake my head, swearing the Devil will never get me. We crack another round before falling asleep but talking about Mark broke our mood. I lie there thinking she might change boyfriends if I press her. Right now, I'm her safety valve. She must know I'd treat her better.

The next day is Monday. I don't feel like going to work, so I go out for a walk, slogging through the dark rain. I end up at Mother's, looking for Debby. She must have the day off. I stay for a few beers, even though it's early and the only other person in the bar is a one-legged guy named Artie, who hits me up for a couple of rounds. He says the beer drains into his missing leg. He can drink a gallon of beer without taking a piss.

Artie says I should come back tomorrow night because the waitress is a real looker. "She's like a daughter to me," he confides. "She always gives a guy a drink when nobody else cares if he lives or dies." I glance toward the door. The place is so dim I wonder if I'd recognize Debby if she walked into the bar right now, but I'd know she was there. I feel the imprint of her shoulder leaning against my chest.

Tuesday after work I see her at Mother's. With the sun shining through the windows for a change, the bar appears even dirtier than usual. Most of the men sitting on the cracked stools are career drinkers with yellow faces and broken red veins. Thin hands grip the beer glasses like life ropes and sharp elbows lean on the bar for support. "You could work in a better place than this," I say to her.

She flips her hair, and her smile fades into a grimace. "The manager at the Park Diner fired me and my brother. My uncle owns this place." She looks away and adds, "No one can fire us here."

"Your brother was just trying to break it up."

"The manager's an asshole. He called in a complaint against Mark, and the cops picked him up." Her eyes dart around the dreary bar, checking the tables. "Daryl and I have worked here since high school. We get a good dinner crowd, great burgers. Someday we'll fix it up like Pearl's."

"Then we could dance," I reply.

"Mark wouldn't dare come in here after me. There's people here who'd kill him if he did." I look up at the bar and I believe her. Daryl and the night bartender are both built like sacks of cement. Even Artie takes particular interest in our conversation though he can't hear us. She follows my line of sight. "You should see Artie dance on one leg. He's a real dreamer. Like you."

That night at my apartment I almost tell her I love her, and she should forget about Mark.

She seems distant and moody. As if reading my thoughts, she says, "Mark might have gotten out of county jail today. I don't want to be home if he comes looking for me. I should have called him. I better call him tomorrow morning."

I suppress a burp. All the free beers she brought me at Mother's. "I wonder where the circus is playing tonight," I reply, wanting her to think about something other than Mark.

"Not Binghamton," she answers, yawning.

"Wonder if they have record keepers in the circus. I was good at math, one of the best in my class."

"I was never good at math," she says.

"I want a better life."

"I know you do." She turns away and curls up her legs the way she likes to sleep.

"I think I'll go to computer school," I continue. "I'm tired of driving a forklift."

When she doesn't answer, I tap her shoulder. "Debby, you awake?"

"Yeah, the manager keeps all the records on his computer."

"That's not what I said."

"Sorry, Curt, I'm really tired."

In the morning we oversleep and by the time I drop her off, I'm late for work. My boss Sherman meets me at the door, his nose wrinkling under my breath. He gives me three days without pay and a written warning. I tell him to keep his warning and he fires me on the spot. Now I can go to computer school like I planned, but I spend the rest of the day sleeping off the Genesee Ale.

That night Debby says she doesn't feel right about making love while Mark is stuck in jail. They sent him back to state prison to finish his sentence for drunken driving.

"Debby, he's such a loser."

"You don't understand," she says into her pillow, "I knew Mark before he was a drunk."

"He's worse than a drunk," I reply, raising my voice.

"He isn't drinking now. Things will be better when he gets out." She faces away, like she's afraid to look at me.

"I need you, too."

Her voice drops to a whisper, further muffled by the pillow. "You're such a dreamer." She takes a deep breath and passes out. I wonder if she's just pretending to sleep.

Pushing myself out of bed, I head back to the kitchen. The more I think about her loyalty to Mark, the less it surprises me. She thinks better of him the farther he is away when she's not dealing with his eruptions.

I pop another beer by the light of my refrigerator and lean against the linoleum counter. I wonder why I care so much about her anyway. At first it was her alluring demeanor and the danger of Mark catching us. A way to erase Chelsea's lingering shadows, an adventure. Now I find myself unwilling to let the moment end. My eyes crave her lazy stare.

I decide not to press her too hard and let time take its course, but a few nights later I figure I gave her time enough. I stop in to see her at Mother's, and she brings me a beer on the house. I've become one of the regulars, still celebrating my freedom from the dairy. Artie wants to join the circus with me and start our own sideshow. Late at night he shows off the stump of his leg for beers, especially the scar on the end that looks like a tied sausage. He thinks we could make real money in the circus. He says I can sell the tickets because I'm good with numbers, as long as he gets to be the star of the show. I tell him how I'm going to start computer school, though I haven't enrolled yet. While we discuss our plans, beer after beer, I watch Debby pass between tables. She avoids my eyes when she brings me a fresh draft.

When I can't stand her distance any longer, I follow her back into the kitchen where she takes a deep drink out of a beer glass she keeps by the sink. When she puts it down, I whisper, "Debby, let's get out of Binghamton. Tonight."

"You know I can't." She starts to walk away. "I have my own life here."

"Listen to me. I love you," I insist, leaning against the walk-in cooler.

"You're just drunk."

"I'm not that drunk. We can get away from here, start a new life."

"You're such a dreamer."

"We can get married. Join the circus, anything. Go to Florida."

"Stop it, Curt. You're not supposed to be back here." She furrows her eyebrows. "I talk a lot of shit when I'm drunk. Forget about it."

"You're sleeping with someone else, aren't you?"

Debby freezes and flashes with fear like I might hit her. I realize I'm yelling. Her brother's face appears over her shoulder, shiny with oil from the deep fryer. He knows I can take him when I'm sober, so he doesn't stand too close. I feel woozy and I grab the handle of the cooler to steady myself. Debby watches me warily, her expression reminding me of that Saturday afternoon at the Park Diner. The way she looked at Mark.

Her brother reaches out for me, but she pushes his hand away. "I know you don't mean any harm," she says softly. "You're just drunk." She takes a tiny step backward.

Raising my foggy head, I force a smile, but no more words emerge.

Debby nods toward her brother and says, "He's all right now," and they leave me slumping against the cooler like an empty keg.

In a few minutes I pick myself up and return to my table. Debby walks over and slides me a draft beer on her way to check on her other customers, just like nothing happened. My throat feels sore, and my hands shake. I couldn't lift the glass if I wanted to.

"Mind if I take a sip?" Artie says. "My leg feels empty tonight." I didn't notice him approach. He grabs the beer and whispers, "You look like the Devil's got you."

"You don't know what you're talking about," I reply.

He gives me a funny look. "I know a drunk when I see one." He raises his voice so the winos at the bar can hear him. They must have heard me yelling at Debby in the kitchen. I should have left through the back door. He takes a swig from the beer glass and draws courage from his buddies. "You and me might be friends, but if you ever talk to Debby like that again, you'll regret it. You mark me now."

I swipe away the finger he's waving at me, and I grip the chair like I intend to stand up. He hops away to the safety of the bar, the beer sloshing out of his glass, my glass.

Debby appears at my table. "I thought we might have to call the cops for a minute there." She grins as if she gave me a compliment. When I fail to reply, she adds, "I should be mad, but I know you're just drunk."

"I know what I'm doing. What I did."

She glances down at my left hand, and I realize how tightly I'm clutching the chair, like I might pick it up and throw it. I let go and say, "I meant what I said."

"You said a lot of things."

"I said I love you."

She says, "You're such a dreamer."

"I want a better life."

"I know you do."

I try to stand up and she offers her arm. I lean on her more heavily than I intend, and we nearly fall over. She laughs and pats me on the hand. Now everyone in Mother's Place is watching us, not just the drunks at the bar.

I straighten up and release her arm, swaying back against the chair. I manage to keep my balance. Our eyes meet briefly, reminding me of how we locked eyes across the dance floor at Pearl's, her look now oddly distant. "Be careful walking home," she says automatically. With a quick smile she adds, "Good luck in the circus." Her voice fades as I tune my ears to the rain falling heavily outside and pelting the filmy windows.

I should say something, thank her for helping me at least, but I'm afraid of what I might say. Glancing toward the floor, I tap her shoulder lightly and head for the door one step at a time, hoping the rain will sober me up. I only have few blocks to walk home but it seems far enough.

SHIFTER

Renee shows up at the front door of my apartment the week after I get fired from Crowley Dairy for drinking. Her blue Falcon with its daisy decals chugs at the curb, valves clanging. Relieved she won't expect an invitation into my dirty living room, I step out on the porch, and we share a quick hug.

She scans my three-day beard with her clear blue eyes, long face tipped to one side, framed by soft blonde hair. "Everyone's worried about you, Curt."

I laugh, throwing back my shoulders and puffing out my chest. "You can tell the crew I look great."

She glances back at her car and smiles. "Maybe you'd like to go to Argo's for dinner tonight. Friday night fish and chips." The corners of her lips quiver. I smell a hint of happy hour beer, but maybe I'm catching a back draft of my own breath.

I lean against the door frame. I'm in no shape to go anywhere tonight, not even with Renee.

"I can catch you up on the news from Crowley's," she offers. We often meet for breaks during our shift. She works the lines, milk one day, ice cream the next, and when the pallets are filled, I spear them with my forklift and load the trucks.

"How about I pick you up at your mom's house tomorrow instead? We can drive up to Ithaca."

She checks the curb. "I love Ithaca." She stretches forward, raising her eyebrows and whispering in my ear, "Sherman and Julie are having an affair."

I grin and shake my head. "Hippos in heat."

She bursts into laughter, clapping her hands and twirling on the worn planks. Her cheeks glow pink when she sways to a stop. "That's not very nice," she says, her grin lingering.

"Sorry," I reply. I feel my own face flush but I'm not that sorry.

"Do you know the way to my mom's?"

"Owego, right?" Renee left her boyfriend Anton and moved back to her mom's place a few days before my drunken romance with Debby got me fired. From what I heard, Anton's a jerk. He thinks he's a celebrity because his family owns a trucking company and his brother's a cop.

Renee reaches into her shoulder purse and rips a deposit slip out of her checkbook, writing the address with a felt tip pen. "Just off Main Street." She fakes a bow and hands it to me.

"See you at six," I reply.

The next evening her mom answers the door wearing a flowered apron and a warm smile. When she asks us to stay for dinner, Renee says we have other plans.

When she closes my passenger door Renee whispers, "She likes you better than Anton."

I grin as I shift into drive but the transmission whines like an idling jet, the car standing still. I try second and the old Ford Galaxie strains into motion.

Renee smiles and raises her eyebrows. "Maybe we should take my car."

"Your engine's about to explode."

"I love my car." Her face droops.

"I love the decals." I turn sharply onto the highway and press the gas. "Maybe if we took your transmission and my engine."

She shoots me a sideways glance. "We'd be late for dinner."

"Worse things have happened."

The heavy Ford rumbles up Highway 96 and I avoid stopping. We fly through Ithaca and skirt Cayuga Lake to catch the sunset before heading back to town. After splitting a pizza for dinner at Rizollo's, we order an extra pitcher of beer. We talk about Debby and Anton long enough to bury them, I hope.

Renee tilts her head and taps my elbow to change the subject. "They already fired the guy they brought in to drive your forklift. He missed a pallet and speared about a dozen cases of milk. Then he jumped up and threw a wrench through the wall, screaming and blaming the forklift."

"Maybe there's hope for me."

"Sherman knows he made a mistake."

"He's made a few."

She grins, shaking her head and glancing out the restaurant window. Neon signs and headlights draw fuzzy scrawls in the heavy mist. "My mom asked me where you go to church." She waves her hand. "I said it's none of her business."

"Sounds like my mother." I've stayed away from my family up in Syracuse until I get my life straight. "Anton goes to your church, right?"

"Good Catholic boy, my dad thinks he's a great catch, but my mom doesn't like him."

"What's not to like?"

Renee laughs and leans back, tipping her chair and catching it just in time. We decide to drive back to Owego while we still can, leaving the restaurant arm in arm. I feel better than I have since I lost my job.

I coax the Galaxie into gear after a few tries. The tires spin on the wet asphalt when I swing out and head toward a shortcut back to the highway. Renee tells me Anton is not that bad as I twist through the neighborhood of brick houses and thick trees, straining to read the street signs.

Soon I'm lost. After a left turn up a hill the street glows with Greek houses on either side, the fraternity row by Cornell lit up for Saturday night parties. A U-Turn is my best chance of finding my way. The old Ford can't make the tight arc, so I back up downhill in a three-point turn. My headlights frame a sign for Sigma Xi, barely visible in the mist, and we hear Elton John wafting over laughter and high voices.

I notch the shifter into drive but the transmission whines, failing to engage. The car starts rolling backward. I quickly try second with no effect. I slam on the brakes. The tires skid and we keep sliding. With a loud crunch we hit the corner bumper of an old green Chevy parked on the street behind us.

I test each gear one by one. More lights flare and the brothers pour onto the lawn.

Renee shrieks.

"Hey, you!" a voice screams.

I finally urge the Ford into second. We inch forward as someone slaps the trunk lid. A stone ricochets off the rear window. We gain speed and a crowd chases us up the hill. I spin around the first right, back the way we came, then a quick left, stomping the pedal as the road levels off. We whip past several cross streets, rising up the crown and lifting off before crashing down and rocking back in our seats.

After another turn, I slow to look around. Most of the houses on this block are dark. I pick one with tall bushes lining the driveway. I turn in and shut off the lights and engine.

My hands shake. I hear yells and screeching tires. They're looking for us. A car drives slowly up our street. As it passes, I identify the green Chevy I hit. Renee sees it too. We slump in our seats. The Chevy moves on.

Taking a deep breath, I turn toward Renee's rigid profile. "You think we should go back?"

"You hit the guy's car."

"Just the bumper. Might not be any damage."

"You have insurance." She turns toward me, a pale beam of streetlight falling across her face.

"Had." I wave my empty palms.

She sinks back in her seat. "We left the scene and we've been drinking."

"They wouldn't call the cops. They'd just beat the shit out of us. Me anyway." I jerk my chin back and forth from imaginary punches and force a laugh.

Renee draws a thin smile. She sits up and forms a lion face more alluring than ferocious in the dim light. "I'll take one or two myself."

I study the street. "Don't worry, I'm not going back."

We wait long enough for the frat boys to return to their kegs before creeping down the driveway. Reverse works okay and it takes a few tries to roll forward.

The next turn feels familiar, and we soon hit the route back to Owego. The ride is quiet with our mood dampened by the accident. I find Renee's hand on the seat between us, but her loose grip feels formal.

I stay in gear when we pull up to her mother's house. Renee drags my head over for a kiss, her lips soft and yielding. I wrap my arms around her shoulders, strands of hair flowing through my fingers.

"I'm glad we escaped," she whispers, her breath warming my cheek.

I comb her hair back. "We'll do better next time."

She plants a sisterly kiss on my forehead and pats my hand. Her eyes dart away as she slides out the door and jogs up her parent's steps. She waves without turning around. As I watch her step inside, I realize she's going back to Anton. I must have misread her message in the first place.

I rest my forehead on the cold steering wheel, vibrating with the engine, straining against the brakes. I ease the car forward and crawl up the block with one more glimpse at her mom's porch light. Back on the highway the approaching headlights sting my eyes, and my foot slams the accelerator, oblivious to the persistent rain.

In the morning I find a small dent in the right rear panel of my Ford from the wing of the Chevy's steel bumper. The new wound doesn't mar the Galaxie's tarnished beauty, but its days are numbered unless the transmission suddenly springs back to life. The size of the dent confirms my guess the frat boy's Chevy sustained nothing more than a scratch in the chrome if that.

Upstairs I sip a beer and clean my apartment, filling two bags with Genesee cans. I'll have to dry out a few days before I return to the dairy and talk to Sherman about my job.

ARTIE'S DODGE

I scramble to answer the pounding on my front door, surprised to have a late afternoon visitor and even more surprised to see Artie leaning on his crutch and grinning with his remaining teeth. "Hi there, Curt," he says.

I smile back, not sure what he wants. Artie always has an angle. He pushes into my apartment, and I notice he has shaved for a change. I smell the Aqua Velva.

"What're you doing?" he asks, staring at the open booklet on my chair. He spies my open beer can and winks at me before helping himself to a swallow.

I shake my head, hoping he remembered to spit out his plug and brush his teeth. Artie's a master at coaxing free beers from his friends and acquaintances at My Mother's Place, though he's easily offended if anyone calls him on it. He pays for a round now and then just to keep his honor.

When he leans over my notepad for a closer look, I tell him, "I'm studying my computer course. I got it in the mail today."

"I thought you were taking a course at Broome Tech."

"Can't afford it."

"Do you have a computer?"

"I can use one at the Binghamton library."

Artie snorts like he doesn't believe they have computers at the library. Unless they moved the library into the back room of Mother's he would never know for sure. The past few days I've been staying away from the bar myself, hoping to dry out before trying to get my job back at the dairy.

"You need to get out of here," he says with a wave of his free hand. "It's not good to stay inside all the time."

"I told you I'm studying. I can't study at Mother's."

"I don't mean go to Mother's," he says. He looks at me seriously. "You need to get over Debby."

"I don't care about Debby."

"Yeah, and I can kick a football fifty yards." He glances down at his right pant leg pinned up under his thigh stump the way he does when he says the beer drains into his missing leg. "You got fired because of her and you ain't been the same since she went back to her boyfriend. Now you're sitting here drinking by yourself. You won't go to Mother's because she works there, and you don't have a car to go anywhere else. It ain't healthy drinking by yourself."

"I was doing just fine before you came in and told me how bad I feel." I force a laugh and retreat to the kitchen for a fresh can of Genesee. He's right about Debby. In a way, she's my missing leg. The beer drains into my memory of her, the place where she used to be.

"You never should have sold your car," Artie says when I return to the living room.

"I got fifty bucks from the wrecker. Better than paying for a new transmission."

"How are you going to get a job without a car?"

"I can take a bus or a taxi."

"Buses don't go everywhere, and taxis are expensive. And where's your fifty bucks? You blew most of it in Ithaca with what's her name."

"Renee. You said I should forget about Debby."

"Not with a wino like her. You'd been better off spending the money on me. At least I'm still here."

As long as I have beer in the refrigerator, I'm thinking.

"Sometimes I need a car to go places," he continues. "I might need to go up to the vet's hospital in Oxford."

"Are you complaining because I sold my car and you want me to drive you some place?" I ask with a grin.

He chugs the dregs of his beer, formerly my beer, and says, "No, I just think we should go out looking for a car."

"You crazy? I don't have money to buy a car."

"Maybe I want to buy a car."

Smiling and shaking my head, I refrain from stating the obvious fact that his missing right leg would make driving difficult. That's only part of the problem. I doubt if he has a driver's license, and I doubt if he has the money. I know he receives disability checks, but I figure most of that money drains into his leg. As he stands up to leave and tucks his crutch under his armpit, I say, "I bet you're planning to take Renee to Ithaca yourself, you old fox."

"Better me swilling beer with Renee than you," he counters.

Ignoring the steady drizzle, he leads me several blocks down Chenango Street to a used car dealer. He's complaining about his thirst by the time we get there. The car lot is one I have passed by and ignored for years, so small that the dozen or so cars might have been parked by downtown shoppers or residents of the nearby brick buildings, all blackened with decades of soot. Only the tattered plastic flags strung between two telephone poles mark it as a place of business. The owner's sign has long since fallen, and it leans against a wall.

We approach a man sitting in a huge green Buick near the back of the yard. He shuffles a stack of paper and when he rolls down the fogged window, I realize they are betting slips. He welcomes us with a big smile.

Artie already has his eyes on a car. Leaning on the Buick he points his crutch at a gray Dodge Dart. "Six hundred dollars," the salesman tells us. "Great car, low mileage for its age. Came up from Florida. Check out the great body." He holds a huge hand out the window for us to shake. "My name's Fred."

Artie shifts his crutch to his left hand as he leans down to return the greeting. "Freddy," he smiles. "I didn't know you sold cars. We see you every Wednesday night at Mother's during football season."

"Yup, that's me." He looks different in daylight, much heavier, with deep lines in his sagging face. He grunts as he pulls himself out of the Buick, leaving the betting slips on top of the cracked dashboard.

He follows us over to the Dodge, and I take a quick walk around the car. I can't find any deep rust or body putty but most of the paint has peeled off the hood and roof. Even the primer is missing in spots. "Must be over thirty years old," I say.

Freddy waves his hand back and forth like he's declining a beer. "Nah, it's a '75. They made solid cars back then. More steel."

Artie stands aside and watches me take another lap around the car. "Look underneath it," he says. "Check for oil and check the tires."

Now I understand why Artie brought me along, so I can crawl under the car. I can't see any oil on the pan or the gravel underneath. "The tires should make it through the winter." I grin. "If you don't take too many trips to Ithaca."

"Let's go for a spin," Artie says, looking at Freddy, who glances down at Artie's rolled-up pant leg. Artie nods toward me and I pull out my driver's license.

The Dart starts well enough, and we wheeze out of the lot, rocking on the sprung suspension and riding low as a tank. I can feel the uneven surface of the street through the floorboard. I avoid taking the car on the freeway, but it runs well enough.

When we get back to the dealer, Artie tells Freddy that the car is junk, hardly worth three hundred, and I enumerate its dents and stains. Finally, Freddy says, "Five hundred and

I'll throw in the tax and registration." He reaches into his jacket and pulls out a cigar. He places the tip between his lips and rolls it back and forth with his tongue.

Artie eyes him for a second and glances back at the car. I smile, still wondering if he's serious, but Artie leans against the door frame and pulls a roll of bills out of his back pocket. He peels off five one-hundred dollar bills and snaps the blue rubber band around his remaining money. He shoves the roll back into his jeans where it raises a shiny bulge I hadn't noticed before.

Freddy waves us back to the Buick where we crawl inside and Artie signs the paperwork, which consists of Freddy's loopy hand filling in the blanks on a Xerox copy about as faded as the paint on the car.

"Home, James," Artie croons when the business is finished. He slides into the passenger seat of the Dodge and nods his head with satisfaction, glancing over at me as I drive the few blocks to his apartment. When I turn down State Street, I smile and say to him, "Now what are you going to do with this car? Maybe you should move out of your apartment and sleep in it."

"Why do you say that?" he asks, suddenly offended. "I ain't no street person."

"Sorry, I was kidding." He often looks like he slept on the street but after seeing his roll of bills I wonder how much of it is an act, like the way he shows off his stump for free beers at Mother's.

"Why are you stopping here?" he asks when I pull up in front of his apartment.

"I thought you wanted to go home. Would you rather go for a ride in your new car? Or show it off at Mother's?"

"I don't want to go for a ride. Not today." he replies. "Let's just take it back to your place."

When we arrive at my building, I pull into my parking space and offer to pop him a beer, which he gladly accepts. I figure that's why he wanted to come back to my place. He flashes a wide smile with his bent and missing teeth, reminding me of a Jack-o'-lantern, the way he looks when Debby agrees to dance with him or when someone springs for a pitcher of beer.

After I lock the car, I hand him the keys, and he pushes them back at me.

"You can keep the keys," he says. "I figure it's okay to leave it in your parking space since you don't have a car. Good to keep it off the street."

"Sure, it's okay," I reply, wondering if he is trying to con me somehow. Artie always has an angle.

"Just remember it's my car," he says with a wink, and I realize what he's getting at.

"You mean I can use it?" I ask, betraying my surprise.

"If you're careful."

He gives me that wide grin again. I wonder if I should decline his offer, not wanting to owe him, though he's right about my needing a car. I can drive to job interviews or even a computer class. When I reach out to shake his hand and thank him for the favor, he cuts me off.

"Shut up," he says.

With that we head upstairs to finish my six-pack of Genny.

CELEBRATION

I shuffle down State Street in the late morning, my headache pounding with each step. Artie hops out of his apartment doorway as I pass. He mumbles a greeting; something's bothering him.

We cross the Washington Street Bridge, though it's out of our way. The gray planks laid across the grates make it easier for Artie's crutch, especially in the light rain.

He stuck by my stool last night at My Mother's Place when I bought a few pitchers to celebrate getting my job back at Crowley Dairy. Now he expects me to buy his coffee. By the time I start work on Monday I'll be dried out and freshly showered. I can hardly afford the coffee and cinnamon roll at the Park Diner but I'm still celebrating.

The wide windows in the dining room frame a scenic view of the dam and pull the customers' eyes away from the decaying bridge and the garbage on the riverbank. I steal a glimpse outside as we head back to the red vinyl booths behind the counter, where the tourists seldom sit.

Mary slides two stoneware mugs of coffee and a pastry plate across the Formica table without saying a word. She nods at Artie, ignoring me. The old waitress never liked me. She never liked Debby either. She continued her silence toward me even after Debby left her weekend job at the diner.

I watch the half and half swirl in my cup. My boss Sherman fired me from the dairy last month after I spent a week drinking with Debby and showed up drunk if I showed up at all. Once her boyfriend got out of jail, I ended up with no Debby and no job. Sherman hopes I learned my lesson.

"Wake up, Curt." Artie says, avoiding my eyes when I turn toward him. We often meet on Thursday mornings to talk about Wednesday's betting night when Freddy comes by Mother's to pay off winners from last week's NFL games and take bets for next week.

"Debby picked the Jets again." I recall.

"She got half the bar to pick the Jets."

"Freddy should pay her a commission."

"He gives her plenty of tips."

"Your breath is terrible." I wave my hand. The stench of his chewing tobacco and stale beer is especially ripe this morning, accented by my hangover.

Artie helps himself to a piece of my cinnamon roll to sweeten his breath. "You threw around a lot of money last night."

"Just a couple pitchers."

"They ain't paid you yet."

"They gave me back my retirement deduction." I hadn't expected the check, but it should last me until payday. "Found money."

Artie shakes his head like he doesn't believe me. He shifts in his seat. "What if someone found money on the floor? No one would know whose money it was." He stares at me.

"You lost me."

"You're the only one who knows I sometimes carry a roll of bills."

I remember him pulling out the roll of hundreds when he paid cash for his used Dodge a few weeks ago. "You had your roll last night?"

"I just cashed my disability check and paid my rent." He studies the raindrops beading on the window. "What if it fell on the floor and someone stepped on it? No one would know the bills were mine."

I feel my headache rise. "I didn't find any money."

"You know I trust you," he replies, though I'm not sure he still does. Loaning me his car was part of the reason I could ask for my job back.

"Maybe somebody will find it."

"I know what I'd do if I found some cash and I didn't know whose it was."

We both stare into our cups. I decide to go home and nurse my headache. We chug our dregs of coffee and head for the cash register.

Fishing my money out of my pocket, I look at it twice. I give Mary a twenty, but I know I had a ten. Now all I have are two more twenties and a few ones. I see a ten lying on the back of the counter next to Mary's tip jar. Last night after Mother's closed, I braved the rain for a snack at the diner. The ten must have fallen out of my pocket, and she picked it up. Nowhere else I could have lost it.

"That's my ten."

"No it's not," Mary replies.

"I dropped it last night."

She shakes her head and laughs tightly. "You're just saying that."

"I'm sure it's my ten," I say, raising my voice.

Artie chimes in, "No one can say whose cash it is unless they're the one holding it." He pushes out the door.

Mary draws a stern face and shoves my change across the counter. I stare at the money for a long moment as my headache threatens to pop out my ears.

"Damn," I yell, slamming the counter with my open hand. The coins fly up and rattle across the floor. Everyone stops eating and watches me kneel on the dirty linoleum to pick up my change. I stand and glare at the rubberneckers until they all turn away, and I slowly step outside.

The damp air cools my anger but not my headache. Artie is gone. He can hobble on his one leg fast enough when he wants to get away. I still can't believe he thinks I found his money. Our friendship should be closer than that.

Taking the Exchange Street Bridge, I cross Court Street and head up Chenango Street toward my apartment. Pausing, I turn around and walk the two blocks up Court to Mother's instead. Although I should save my remaining cash, the lunch crowd will soon file in, and I might lose my headache in company.

Mike the bartender slides me a Genesee draft as soon as I claim a stool. He has Popeye forearms with a large red heart tattoo pierced with a blue arrow and "Mother" written on a scroll. He says it has nothing to do with his job. I wave him over and ask for an Alka-Seltzer and a glass of water. A quick pout appears as he recalls the night before, and a grin cracks his thick beard. I'll save the beer for later.

I watch CNN on the bar TV as the place fills up with state office workers and lawyers from the Binghamton courthouse, men in polyester suits and permanent-press shirts and ties except for a few women in dark skirts and polyester blouses. Bored of listening to Ronald Reagan, I scan the room behind me.

"The best jobs always go to people from downstate, especially the government jobs," Carl, one of the Mother regulars, says in a deep voice. "That way our officials have no stake in our problems." He sits a few stools down the bar and winks under his white eyebrows and tweed fedora.

I stare into my empty Alka-Seltzer glass and wonder if I'm ready for the beer. "Artie says he lost some money last night."

"We all lose money on Wednesday nights," Carl replies.

"Fell out of his pocket."

Mike overhears us and shrugs his shoulders.

"Debby would know if anyone found it." His face reddening, Carl clears his throat and reaches for his after-lunch cigarette. "More likely it found one of the lawyers." He steals a glimpse toward the kitchen and I'm already striding in that direction.

Pushing open the aluminum paneled door, I call "Debby," louder than I intend. I forgot my headache and my residual anger from the Park Diner for a minute. Now it comes roaring back. She gazes up from the salad cart, squinting from the shock of my interruption.

Her brother Daryl rushes over and stands in my face, holding the long fork he uses to stir the fry baskets. A former football player, he always protects her. When it's not about Debby he's my friend, but he glares at me with his wide eyes, face shiny with oil. "Curt, you know you're not supposed to be back here."

I hold up my hands in surrender. Debby slides over and says, "You know better." Her familiar cologne makes me dizzy, and I reach for the stainless-steel table to steady myself. One side of my brain reminds me I'm over her, but as I stare down at her questioning brown eyes and her auburn curls, I know I'm still living the hangover of our romance. I study her smooth round face with its hint of freckles, hardly visible through the extra makeup she wears when she's been drinking.

After a deep breath, I ask, "Did you find a roll of money last night?"

She shrugs her shoulders. "Sometimes I find change. I consider it a tip."

"You'd remember a roll of hundreds in a blue rubber band."

Daryl reaches over to pull a basket of shrimp out of the fryer and dumps it on a plate.

"Who says I did?" She turns away and goes back to making her salad.

My patience begins to fray. "Did you?"

Daryl casts me a cautioning look.

"What if I did? Are you trying to say it's your money?" She grimaces.

"What if I said it was Artie's money?"

Her eyes soften. No one wants to hurt Artie. She squeezes her brow. "He doesn't have that kind of money."

"Where is it?"

"Never said I had it."

I glance at Daryl and grab the steel table with both hands to calm myself. I lean down and see my distorted reflection hatched with lines scraped by years of dull knives. Debby passes behind me with a tray for the dining room and I follow her scent out the swinging door.

Daryl frowns as I stand and clench my fists to get some circulation.

"Talk to Freddy," he says.

I find Freddy in his office, the pale green '65 Buick Riviera in the back of his used car lot. He starts it up when he needs heat; the old tank never moves. He sells one or two cars a year, but his real business is running bets. As the steady drizzle turns to rain, he waves me over to the passenger door.

A cloud of cigar smoke with an odd chocolate smell wafts from the door. I slide into the seat and roll down the window. I cough and Freddy chuckles. He holds the cigar stub above the steering wheel and fires it up with a silver lighter. Damp from chewing, the butt finally begins to smolder. Freddy raises it to his lips just as it goes out.

"Maybe you should close the window," he says.

"I won't be long."

Piles of betting slips line the faded vinyl dashboard and Freddy holds a cloth deposit bag from New York Bank on his lap. The old bag hasn't seen the inside of a bank for years.

"Did you take a big bet at Mother's last night?"

"I took a lot of bets." He squints at me and chews his cigar stub. He wants to blow me off, but he owes me. I covered for him last week when he was too sick to make his rounds. He threw me a nice tip.

"Roll of hundreds in a blue rubber band."

He laughs and the seat quivers. "You still hot for Debby?"

"It wasn't her money."

"How do I know that?" His voice is muffled by the stub in his teeth. He waves a hand at me. "She was too drunk to count it." He swallows a breath and peers across the center console. "Was it your money?"

"You know I don't bet since I lost my job."

He shakes his head. "It's too late."

I nod toward the dash. "You'd take a bet now, wouldn't you?"

"That's different. You want me to give back her money and you know I can't do that."

"Maybe she picked a winner."

He explodes with laughter, sounding as if the old Buick started up. He shifts his bulk forward with a grunt, the cigar stub stuck to his lips. He scans the piles of slips and sways toward my side. I catch the swamp aroma of his cigar. It smells worse unlit.

I lean away and smile. "She bet on the Jets."

"And the Bills," he chuckles as he retrieves her slip.

I take the sheet with Debby's signature squeezed into the small box at the bottom. The week's games are listed with their spreads, and the odds are printed next to the signature box and the bet. She circled four teams, ten to one odds if they all beat the spread.

"She loves Joe Namath." I shake my head.

"He's long gone." Freddy sees me checking the total. "Her roll looks bigger than it is; a hundred on the outside. The rest twenties and mostly ones."

"186 dollars." I read off the slip.

Freddy takes it from me and flops back in his bucket seat, rocking the Buick's suspension. He reaches for his lighter.

"You haven't turned it in yet."

"Curt, you know the boys in Scranton would break my knees if I shorted them." He flicks his lighter.

"How would they know?"

He manages to laugh while sucking on the butt. "They always know."

"What if I bought the bet?"

He leans forward and drops the stub in the overflowing ashtray. "What do you mean?"

"If her bet loses, how much is your cut?"

Eying the sun visor he says, "Twenty-five percent."

He's high balling me. "What if she wins?"

He laughs again.

"The Jets beat the spread two weeks ago."

"Would you bet the Jets?" Freddy picks up the cigar butt, wheezing to catch his breath.

"How about I give you twenty and you give me back the roll and the slip?"

"You want me to bet my knees for twenty bucks?" He checks his watch. He's thinking about his pickup time.

"Forty." I flick my wrist. "That's all I can do." It will leave me with thirteen dollars until payday.

Freddy chews his cigar for a long moment. He unzips the bank bag, pulls out his tally sheet and draws a line with a flourish of his felt tip pen. He hands me the roll with the hundred still visible under the blue rubber band. He whips Debby's slip off his dash and pushes it into my chest. "I might need you to help me again." He looks me in the eye.

"I might need the money."

"Count it." He always tells people to count their money, though I know I can trust him. Holding all that cash gives me a slight surge of power as I shove the roll in my pocket and reach for the door handle.

I walk quickly toward Artie's apartment, turning up my collar to the steady rain, but I recall his attitude at breakfast and head for Mother's instead.

"You're soaked," Debby says when I push my way into the kitchen.

I wave Daryl over before giving Debby the roll of bills and her betting slip. "That was going to be our stake to buy Mother's," she says, giving me a sad look.

Icy water rolls down the back of my neck. "Jets and Bills?"

Her brother breaks into a smile.

"Give the roll back to Artie." I tell her, hoping Daryl will make sure it happens. "You'll still buy this place."

"Always the dreamer," she says.

Back at the bar, Mike jokes it was the first time I ever left a beer sitting on the bar as he slides me a fresh Genesee. He waves his hand to signal it's free. My headache has begun to fade, and the lunch crowd has thinned out.

Soon Artie comes in looking for discounted leftovers like he always does. He passes behind me and sits farther down the bar. I pretend to watch Reagan on TV.

Debby comes out to clear a table and waves Artie to the back. He hops to the kitchen and pushes open the door with the top of his crutch.

Within seconds he bursts out and twists in a jig on his remaining leg, a show he does for free beers some nights. He raises his crutch above his head and twirls it like a baton. He bows and waves his old Mets baseball cap, though he doesn't circulate for tips as he usually does. Instead he heads for the stool next to me.

"Debby found my money," he whispers. "I'd buy you a beer, but you already have one."

THE VISITOR

I haven't seen Renee since our trip to Ithaca while I was off work and she was off Anton, except for the night she left me a paper plate of oatmeal cookies that complimented my Genesee Ale sandwich for dinner.

The day I start back at the dairy, Renee and I meet for our morning coffee break like we did before I got fired. Both of our cars ended up in the salvage yard. I hardly miss my old Ford Galaxie, but she mourns her blue Falcon with its daisy decals.

"Curt, can you give me a ride home?" she asks when she finishes her Styrofoam cup of machine brewed coffee.

"How did you know Artie loaned me his car?"

"Small town," she laughs. "Actually I didn't know."

"What about Anton?"

She raises her eyebrows. "He's like family. We grew up together." Her words sound rehearsed, like she's repeated them to everyone else, explaining why she went back with Anton.

"I mean, won't he pick you up?" I already heard the rumor.

"He wants me to take a taxi in case he has to work late."

"Sure, assuming the Dodge can make it up Mill Street."

After our shift she directs me to the newest and largest house on a narrow side street. I turn into the driveway and smell fresh paint and a mowed lawn wide enough for golf, exuding the wealth of Anton's family and their trucking company. Strings of colored lights reflect off a swimming pool in the backyard. Renee jumps out of the car and waves as she runs up the slate walkway.

Anton waits under the front door lamp. He doesn't wave. I never met him, but I know him and his brother around town. His older brother Karl is the friendly one, even if he's a cop.

A week later I wake up to find the side mirrors smashed on Artie's Dart in the gravel parking lot below my apartment. Driving the car might not be safe. I have no other way to get to work, no spare money for a taxi, and I tell Renee in case she wants to call a cab for her ride home. She says the missing mirrors don't bother her.

Luckily, Sherman's brother owns a body shop.

"It was probably teenagers on a romp," my boss says. "Should only cost a few bucks."

"My landlord's too cheap to replace the security light."

Sherman shrugs, scanning my eyes and clearing his throat. He's checking to see if I'm staying sober like I promised. I expect him to turn away since his interactions with the crew are typically short, order and response, as he circulates the dairy floor solving the crisis of the day. I unconsciously straighten my shoulders.

He asks, "Do you still want to help with the manifest?"

"Sure," I reply, though I had asked to work on the computer.

"You can start by checking the manifest against the bills of lading." He tilts his head toward the table piled with paperwork and the row of clipboards hanging from nails in the wallboard. "Do it after your shift."

Sherman's already walking away when I nod my assent.

Fixing the car gets more expensive when I wake up to a crash and a crunch on Monday night. In my robe and slippers, I run out into the chill air. Hearing me, a figure flees the lot, picking up his pace. I chase him, yelling for him to stop as he passes under a streetlight carrying a toy baseball bat. The hood of his sweatshirt falls back as he turns around and the yellow beam glints against his face. He doesn't look like a teenager. He takes off into the shadows and I'm too cold to chase him further.

Red shards from the left tail light litter the muddy gravel. At work Sherman says his brother can use a few more bucks as he stares into my eyes again. He praises me for my diligence in reviewing the manifests, but I wonder if he believes my vandalism story.

That evening I check with the lady next door whom I've never met. A sneering wooden owl greets me from her porch beam, its round eyes flashing annoyance like the face answering the door. She reports two young boys savaged her rose bed, could have been a rabbit, though she should have called the cops. Calling the cops never appeals to me. My lanky frame, dark hair, and mustache match too many open warrants.

Instead, I move my bed under the window overlooking the parking lot. The streetlight at the corner glares like a beacon, but I try to sleep with the shades up. No one shows. In the morning Sherman accuses me of a hangover but I claim I have a cold. I can't keep this up for long.

Two nights later I'm lying awake when I hear the crunch of gravel. Already dressed, I jump to my feet and sprint outside. Shining my flashlight toward the back of the Dodge, I spy the same hooded sweatshirt with gloved hands holding a cinder block, ready to crash it on the trunk. He stands rigid as if waiting for me. When I rush him, he throws down the block and swings his arm, catching me off guard and swatting the flashlight out of my grip.

He drops into a crouch with arms at his side, reaching toward me like a linebacker. I hunch over and bend my knees, raising my fists to protect my face in a boxing stance. I take a deep breath. The air no longer feels cold on my face and my focus narrows on the hooded figure, his face hidden in the dim light.

He charges me, his hands low, lunging, but leaving his head unprotected. I slug him with my left fist, careful to keep my balance as I step away. He backs off, shuffles and dashes forward. I jab him again, avoiding his grasp. He feints to the right and darts to the left. I hit him hard with my right hand, catching his jaw. He jerks to a stop.

I feel the rear fender at the back of my thigh as he poses for another rush. I'm cornered, not good. He jumps at me and grabs my sweatshirt, dragging me downward. His weight pulls me sideways and I reflexively spin around and jam his hand away. He flies backward, his butt crunching against steel. He rolls to his feet and stands, favoring his right leg and quickly pulling the hood down over his brow.

We square off again, but he starts backing away and I let him. When he gets about halfway across the lot he swings around and squares his shoulders, fighting not to limp as he strides toward Chenango Street.

Back inside I steady my nerves with a few sips of Genesee. It's just past midnight though I should get enough sleep to convince Sherman of my good health.

The next morning when I pick up Renee, I tell her about my latest midnight encounter, spinning it like a joke. "Someone wants me fired. They're doing it for the forklift."

"Don't park the forklift at your apartment."

"Could be Debby's boyfriend, except this guy was sober."

"Why should Debby's boyfriend care? He already has her." She laughs and pokes my shoulder. "Good thing for you."

I pause as a school bus strains to make a left turn on the narrow street. With a short laugh I ask, "Did Anton run out of Slim Jim's last night and drive down to the 7-11?"

She evades my question, staring into the gray dawn.

"Anton thinks he can do anything because his big brother's a cop," I grin. "If he's mad at me for taking you to Ithaca and giving you rides, you could be next."

"Just some teenage vandal like Sherman said." She adjusts her dairy hairnet. "Besides Anton would never touch me. I have four brothers, remember. Sometimes a Catholic family is a good thing."

"He should buy you a car."

Renee cracks a smile. "I'm trying."

When I drop her off that evening, she says, "I hope you find the vandal."

"Thanks, my car has a few lights left."

As I climb the stairs to my apartment with my six-pack and a six-inch sub, a patrol car pulls up in front of the building. I ignore it and step inside, but a knock catches me before I reach the kitchen.

Swinging open the front door I face the guy I saw with Anton a couple of times. Now Anton's brother Karl wears a blue uniform and a scowl. One hand rests on his revolver and the other on a can of pepper spray clipped to his black leather belt.

"I hear you attacked someone last night," he says in a stern voice. "You're lucky he hasn't filled out a complaint."

I scan the creases on the cop's pudgy face, a cop without a written complaint. "Your brother's a shit."

He jerks back as if I pushed him. "I never said anything about my brother."

I let him fume for a second.

He raises his chin and squints. "I should run you in."

"Did he tell you what he did?" I nod toward the parking lot. "He smashed two mirrors and a tail light on my car."

"You're lying.

"I saw him." I raise my voice. "Do you want me to fill out a complaint?"

"If you're telling the truth, you could." Karl flashes a tight grin.

"I have a witness, one of my neighbors." No one said they saw Anton or anyone else, but someone might have. "You want to arrest your little brother?"

He looks me up and down like I'm standing in a lineup. One glance at his pager and back at me. I suddenly feel sorry for him, caught between Anton and his duty, if it was Anton. I don't feel too sorry.

"This isn't over." He turns and strides away.

During coffee break on Monday morning Renee dances up and announces that Anton bought her a car, a used Chevelle.

"Blue?" I smile.

"How'd you guess?" She pulls off her hairnet, swinging her blond hair.

"And you bought daisy decals."

She laughs. "We had to drive all the way to Syracuse!"

I slide a quarter into the coffee machine and wait for my Styrofoam cup to fill. When I set it down on the aluminum table, Renee says, "Anton says he's sorry."

I shrug my shoulders, doubting Anton's remorse.

"He's sorry for not buying me a car sooner.

VAMPIRE

MESSAGE FROM THE VAMPIRE

A loud ring shatters my sleep, growing louder with each cycle like a police car racing up the street. I stagger to the living room, kicking a beer can out of my way. The wall clock reads 12:35. I snatch the telephone and hear a woman cry, bubbling over with short breaths between sobs, drowning her words.

I expect a different call waking me up. Julie, my mentor in accounting, warned me that if I screw up my punch card input, I might get a call from the vampire, the computer operator who runs the accounting jobs overnight.

My keypunch skills are suspect, but not enough to make a vampire cry. I wait for the sobs to shorten, the breaths deepen. "Curt here."

"I'm so sorry," the woman says hoarsely before rising in another crescendo.

I try to identify her voice.

"Gloria," she spurts out before I ask. "Bill's wife."

It takes me a few seconds to match the name with Sherman. No one calls him Bill at work, though I remember her calling him Bill when he invited me home to dinner last week to celebrate my new assignment.

"I'm so sorry to call you. Maybe he'll listen to you." She swallows back her tears. "He thinks a lot of you."

"What's wrong?" I ask, suspecting the answer. Sherman's affair with Julie has been the headline of dairy gossip for weeks. This morning in the break room my friend Renee leaned across the steel table, her white apron smeared with ice cream, smelling like a carton of Neapolitan, whispering that Sherman and Julie were spied holding hands at K-Mart.

"He hasn't come home yet." Gloria's sniffles leak between words.

The sheer bulk of the passion between my boss and Julie has been an easy source of jokes, like my telling Renee this morning that their combined quarter ton was heavier than the daily run of ice cream, our laughter now hollow echoes. "I don't know where he is."

"Everyone knows where he is," Gloria counters, her tone turning to anger. "Do you remember Marshall?"

A curly towhead, Sherman's young son took a liking to me, his new toy.

"He waited by the door all night with his tomato basket, waiting for his daddy to take him outside to pick his tomatoes."

"He's proud of his tomatoes."

THE BRIDGE ON BEER RIVER

"I'm so sorry I called you. I hardly know you." She resumes crying. "Why would he want to break up our marriage and leave his two kids?"

I shake my head, unsure what to say.

"I'm taking the kids back to Washington."

I feel the weight of Sherman's affair pulling me down.

"Will you talk to him and remind him we love him? Marshall and Sheila love him." She takes a deep breath. "I love him more than anything. I don't know who else to call."

"Gloria, I feel horrible. But I don't see how I can change anything."

"He respects you. He would listen to you." She takes a deep breath. "He would respect you for talking to him."

No, he might fire me for good. My employment is fragile. Less than two months after he fired me for drinking, he hired me back. Then he gave me a chance to learn computer skills by recording shipments after my shift, provided I stay out of trouble.

Gloria treats my silence as a maybe. "Please, Curt. I trust you."

I pull the receiver away from my head, feeling the blood rush back to my ear. I hold it sideways in front of my face like the jaw of a trap before turning it over to my other ear and whispering, "I can't promise anything."

"Just talk to him. Thank you."

When I drop the phone in its cradle, I know I should go back to bed, but I head to the kitchen. I slide a can of Genesee out of the refrigerator and pop the top, throwing back a long swallow and thumping the door closed.

The phone rings again. Why would Gloria call me back?

"Did I wake you up?" asks another female voice. I hear the whir of machinery and air-conditioning.

"I'm already awake."

"Me, too. It's Angie the computer operator."

"Hi Angie," I say uncertainly. This is the call Julie warned me about.

"Your input job failed, and I fixed it. I want to show you what I did."

"I followed the manual."

"We all make mistakes. I get in around six."

"I start at seven."

"Six p. m." She says emphatically.

"Sure, anything for the dairy."

"What a trooper," she says with feigned enthusiasm. "Time to run the backup!"

Hanging up the phone, I chug my beer and head back to bed. I have a big day tomorrow. First I tell my boss to stop boning Julie, and then I go down to the morgue and meet the vampire.

We're behind schedule the next morning when Sherman and I watch a truck pull away from the loading dock and another back in. I jump off my forklift to stretch my legs. An Army Ranger during the Vietnam War, Sherman's weight has doubled since he plied the jungle, but he seldom talks about those days.

"Damn Teamsters," he grimaces. "If Reagan wants to break a union, he should break the Teamsters."

"He could try." The drivers took their normal break even though the shipments were ready to load. Now we'll be working late.

Sherman can tell I have something more to say. He furrows his brow.

"It's really none of my business…" I begin.

"You're right. It's none of your business." He drawls in a low gravelly tone just louder than a whisper. When he's angry his face glows deep red, almost purple. He's not that angry yet, but a red bruise blossoms on his cheek.

I shrug my shoulders.

He frowns. "Gloria asked you to talk to me, right? Sorry she dragged you into it."

I don't say anything.

Sherman lays his big hand on my shoulder and says, "I dug the tunnel and I have to dig my way out."

I dip my shoulder and slide away, nodding my head as I climb back onto my forklift.

By the time the last truck belches its cloud of exhaust and pulls away, my legs are numb and my butt aches from my long day of sitting in the forklift cockpit. I have just enough time for a 25-cent cup of machine coffee and a Snickers bar before heading down to the air-conditioned computer room known as the morgue.

When I push through the air-locked door, I see the back of a small woman sitting at a terminal on a wooden table lined with a keypunch machine, a card sorter, a tray of punch cards and an overflowing ashtray, all littered with cardboard chads. Next to the table rises a blue cabinet with white block letters identifying the PDP-11 main frame.

As I step up to the raised floor, Angie leans forward and her worn black jeans tighten around her cheeks, pushed up by the cushion of her stool. She spins to face me, resting her elbows on her knees, and she eyes me with a tilt of her head. I try not to stare at the cleavage framed by her wide necked black tee shirt, but she catches my glance. She grins and looks away as she sits up straight.

"You must be Curt," she says in an official tone as she purses her blackened lips. "Your mustache is famous."

Feeling suddenly warm despite the frigid air, I take her extended hand for a quick shake before she pulls it away.

"And you're Angie."

"Bingo."

She pats the stool next to her. I roll it out from the table and sit down.

"Your job failed to run last night." She points at her monitor. "You see this percent sign?"

I lean toward the screen and make out the white symbol on the black screen above the pulsing input marker. I follow her finger, breathing her earthy perfume. She twists toward me to make sure I'm listening and her long black hair brushes my shoulders.

She waves her hand, black fingernail polish gleaming in the diffused light. "You need a card with a percent sign just after the header card."

"I didn't see that in the manual."

"Not there. We got an update this week and the idiot who wrote the program added an enhancement," she sneers.

I shake my head as she sighs and reaches for her pack of cigarettes. "Took me a while to figure it out."

Sliding her ashtray closer, I push my stool back to give her room to light her Newport. She blows out a cloud of menthol smoke, and says, "I could hack the executable, but it's easier to fix the inputs until they send us an update."

She leans back as a wisp of smoke rises toward the ceiling vent. "Maybe I could run the backup," she muses. "Nah."

"Percent card, it is," I reply.

"Until I tell you different." She points at my face with her cigarette. "Are you on mail and messaging?"

"I just got a terminal."

She stares at me and raises her eyebrows.

The trucks are late again the next morning. After missing lunch and working through the afternoon shift, I bring the manifest copies upstairs to enter the data on punch cards when one of the two keypunch machines frees up. While I wait I sit down at my terminal and log into the system and mail, hoping to exercise the new commands I learned from the PDP manual last night. I see the reassuring entries from the last run:

```
sys: ShipJob running
sys: ShipJob finished
**ShipJob SUCCESSFUL**
```

In a moment, another message appears:

```
vmpire: hey?
```

I'm about to type a response when I hear the click-flap of Julie's high heels behind me. Renee says Julie has worn high heels so much she can't wear any other shoes. Several years older than me, Julie is a large woman about my height in her heels and conspicuously voluptuous. She typically wears tight polyester blouses and even tighter slacks, the elastic band of her panties gradually sliding down to divide the top and bottom of her full butt as she walks with a rhythm of sways and jiggles. She winks as I face her.

"I hear you were summoned by the vampire," she whispers. holding up her hands and extending her long red fingernails like claws.

"My job failed."

"I answered my subpoena earlier." She throws back her shoulders and shakes, recalling the frigid memory of the computer room, straining the buttons on her blouse. She glances toward the two older women typing at the keypunch machines. "Now we all know about the percent sign."

Julie taught me how to use the keypunch machine and the card sorter even though she hates them. The smartest person at Crowley, she's the queen of the order books and ledgers, just as Angie's the queen of the morgue. Old Crowley never makes a financial decision without asking Julie's advice. She spins sums like a calculator, adding up columns of numbers in her head faster than anyone can type them. She says the punch cards slow her down.

"She wants me to learn mail." I reply.

"So she doesn't have to pick up a phone and call you." Julie shakes her head. "You know she came here with Sherman. They were a package deal along with the PDP-11 because Old Crowley wants to automate the dairy."

"Great for me." Julie knows I want to catch the computer wave.

"We will be much more efficient when we have all our production data on the computer," she says in a hollow tone, mimicking Crowley and nodding like a bobblehead.

Her eyes suddenly dim. She stares at me and whispers, "Someone said Sherman looked angry yesterday when you talked to him on the dock."

"The drivers took a break when he wanted to load the trucks." I leave out the detail she's fishing for.

"Teamsters," she hisses, gazing into my eyes. She spins on her pointed heels and sways back to her desk where she pulls a thick order book from her shelf and drops it on the steel surface with a loud thud.

Turning back to my terminal I type:

msg vmpire

hey

vmpire: can you give me a ride tomorrow? my car's going to the shop

msg vmpire

what time?

vmpire: working first shift

msg vmpire

6:30?

vmpire: go ahead, kill me

The next morning when I pick up Angie she's dressed in her black uniform, and I notice the deep red lipstick as soon as she climbs in.

She catches my double take and smiles. "Gotta keep everyone off balance. My plan for world domination."

"I'd like to hear more about your plan," I laugh. The color looks good on her, a contrast to her usual pallor.

On my way to the breakroom in the afternoon, I swing downstairs and drop my bundle of punch cards in the mailbox by the door of the morgue. I haven't seen Julie or Sherman all day.

"Maybe they have a date," Renee whispers over the steam of our Styrofoam cups.

"An extra-large sale at K-Mart?"

Renee brushes a cookie crumb off her white apron. "Word is that something's wrong." She raises her eyebrows. "Maybe they're trying to patch it up."

I drain my coffee, smirking from the bitter metallic taste but the coffee gets me through the afternoon.

When I pull up to Angie's apartment to drop her off, she surprises me by asking me in.

Sweeping ahead of me she unlocks the door and lights a square black candle on a dark-stained coffee table. A thick joint rests on a translucent glass ashtray.

"Do you like lasagna?" she asks, shaking out the wooden match. "I bet you didn't know I was Italian."

"Pasta's the only thing I can cook. Never attempted lasagna."

She stares at me with the stoic expression she uses when explaining the computer system. "You can stay?"

"My beer will go flat at Mother's."

She shivers and cracks a smile. "I can't believe you go to that dive." She switches on her stereo, raising a stack of records to the top of the spindle. After a click and a flop, The Doors "Strange Days" erupts from two floor speakers.

She retrieves the glass ashtray and leads me into the kitchen.

I forget about my lonely draft and everything else as the warm scent of oregano and garlic fill my senses. After dinner Angie rolls another number on a Black Sabbath album cover, her head bobbing to the beat. Her dark hair waves in the gentle drift of the ceiling fan, gaining body in the candlelight, as if she might levitate at any moment. She sits with her legs crossed and holds up the joint like a talisman.

The deep rhythm from the stereo vibrates up through my soles. I lean my chin on my hand as the flame of her farmer match frames her face.

"Why don't you have a girlfriend?" She exhales and passes the joint, our touch lingering for an extra second.

"My girlfriend's waiting in a glass at Mother's."

"I don't believe that."

"Long story." I take a deep hit.

"I've heard the Crowley version." She tilts her head and hooks a strand of hair over her ear. "I want to hear your story."

Leaning toward her, I touch her free hand and she drops the smoldering weed in the ashtray. Her dark red lipstick tastes oddly sweet as we kiss. She pulls away and runs her tongue over my mustache. We stand and embrace, kneading our flesh as we fall toward the bedroom.

The scent of our eager sex fills the air like dew, damp on the black sheets when we finally roll apart. I lie back and stare at the images flickering on her ceiling as Angie fires up a long wooden match over the candle. She inhales her Newport and squirms back onto her pillow.

"I don't want a boyfriend."

I laugh. I recall how Debby staggered back to her boyfriend after our drunken one-week romance and Renee never broke the yoyo string tied to her boyfriend Anton.

Angie elbows me in the ribs. "I'm serious."

"You're safe with me."

She laughs. "Maybe I should say I'm not serious."

I turn to face her. "You're serious about the PDP-11."

"Too cold, even for me." She leers.

"But you came to Crowley with the computer." I raise my eyebrows, accusing her of an illicit affair with the blue machine.

"Sherman brought the relic from Universal Instruments, and he made me queen of the night shift." She looks up at the ceiling tiles. "When I finish the MRP project we'll only be ten years behind the times. We should have a VAX station and PCs."

"I'm one of the relics."

"You're easy. Julie freaks out whenever I tell her anything. I wish Sherman would calm her down." She shakes her head and looks into my eyes. "I'm glad I don't work with them as much as you do."

I shrug as she snubs out her cigarette and secures the roach in a brass clip, its leather lace strung with black beads. She lights the roach over the ashtray and pulls it back for a hit.

"Let me tell you something about Sherman." She leans across me, her breasts brushing my chest, and hands me the clip. "He always goes back to his wife. It doesn't matter what you said."

The smoke curls away as the roach burns out. She lifts it from my fingers and drops it in the ashtray. The black sheet slides down her shoulder, revealing the point of her nipple, and my pulse quickens. Angie tucks the sheet under her chin and sits up. She shakes her head and smooths her hair behind her ears. She checks her alarm clock and says in a serious tone, "We need to get to work."

I sit up, startled. "I'm in no shape to drive."

Angie laughs and pushes me back down. "I mean it's time to run the backup."

The next morning, I meet Renee for our morning break. Just as we sit down to enjoy our Styrofoam cups of machine brewed coffee, aluminum chairs scraping on the worn linoleum, Julie rushes in crying. She evades our eyes and slides a quarter into the shiny brown coffee machine. Her hands shake as she lights a cigarette and sits at the other end of the breakroom.

"I didn't know she smokes," Renee whispers.

I stare into my cup as Renee goes to the refrigerator for a carton of milk, one of our few company benefits.

"When can I drive your Chevelle?" I ask as she slides back into her chair. I study her clear blue eyes.

"When Anton dies." Renee forces a laugh. "He'd kill me otherwise."

Her boyfriend and I are not the best of friends. Hearing me, Julie stands and flashes a cold stare before spinning on her high heels and clomping out the door, her panty line riding lower than usual.

"Maybe we should just fire up the Chevelle and leave."

Renee shakes her head, swinging her blonde hair. "It's not your fault."

"She thinks so."

"Sherman told her you had nothing to do with it."

The hot coffee burns my tongue. I blow into the Styrofoam cup.

"Don't worry about her," Renee whispers, leaning toward me. "Her husband and kids want her back."

"They don't have to work with her."

I take a deep breath, the air searing my burned mouth. Today is payday and the bartender will be lining up my first pitcher and a fresh glass at Mother's. Always good to have a backup.

SACK THE QUARTERBACK

"We're getting married!"

I spin around on my bar stool perched between Artie and Carl in My Mother's Place. Debby beams at me, holding the arm of a guy I've never seen before.

"I thought tonight was your night off," Artie says to her with a confused look.

"Congratulations," I say, nudging Artie as I extend my hand toward Debby's fiancé.

"Joe, these are my friends Artie, Curt, and Carl," Debby rises on her toes and shakes her auburn curls out of her soft brown eyes.

Joe is about my height but heavier. His unkempt dark hair frames a rugged, sagging face, blue eyes, and a dimpled jaw with a loose grin. He looks familiar. When he dips his head and says hello, I make the connection. He looks like Joe Namath, the football star. Artie sees it too.

Joe tightens his grip, squeezing my hand until it hurts. I return his grin and clench my fist until his eyes glaze with pain and he lets go.

Debby doesn't notice our contest. "We met last night at Pearl's. We were pretty drunk, but we were still engaged when we woke up this morning!" She gazes toward me though she focuses farther away, raising my suspicions. During our brief romance I learned there were two Debby's: the six-pack Debby out for adventure, and the Monday morning Debby who wonders how her latest romance is helping her plans.

"Congratulations," Artie and Carl stammer.

Joe nods his head. I don't like him, but I tell myself it's not because he squeezed my hand or because he met Debby at Pearl's like I did, dancing on peanut shells and holding her tight body through the slow dances to close out the night. He studies Artie and Carl and avoids my stare. Maybe she told him about our drunken fling.

Debby pivots toward the door. "We're going out to dinner to celebrate."

We watch them leave with their gray silhouettes framed in the dirty window as they pass by on the sidewalk.

"Our Debby's going to marry Joe Namath," Artie shakes his head and smiles. "She always had a soft spot for him."

Carl chuckles. "Joltin' Joe."

"Broadway Joe." I laugh.

"Same difference." Carl flicks his lighter over his pipe. "Those athletes are all mutants anyway."

Sunday night I'm back at Mother's with Artie and Carl, waiting for Hee Haw on the bar TV. Joe sits at a side table where Debby can drop him free beers and winks. Her shift hasn't started yet.

Artie elbows me. "You should buy a TV."

"You just want to come over and drink my beer."

"You have a phone now."

"That's for work, in case my reports crash."

Artie winks. He knows I'm trying to learn computer skills, so I don't spend the rest of my life driving a forklift at Crowley Dairy. But Artie doesn't believe in computers.

Carl clears his throat, staring at the old RCA hanging from the sooty ceiling. President Reagan's sincere image flickers in and out. Carl holds his hands one on top of the other and claps them like a duck beak. "Ronald Reagan is an ideologue without any ideas."

Artie twists his head as the bar door opens from the sidewalk. "I didn't know Mark was out of jail."

"Trouble," Carl mumbles.

We watch Mark, another of Debby's old boyfriends, stride toward Joe's table with a tall, dark-haired woman. She walks with perfect posture, head erect like a model, with red lipstick and short hair done in curls. She pulls her full-length black fur coat tight around her.

Mike the bartender drops his towel and sidles over to me. He raises his head and tips his chin. I follow him to Joe's table. Scrambling like a fighter jet, Debby races out of the kitchen and slides into a chair next to Joe. Mark and the woman look down at Joe for a long second.

"Hi, honey," the woman says. She slaps Joe in the face. Her coat falls open, her hands resting on the hem of a pink sweater circling her thin hips. "I was wondering when you were coming home." She doubles her fists, keeping her stern face pointed at Joe. Her practiced act recalls a forties movie, her eyes glazed with pain and anger.

Joe flinches and gazes at Mark, who smiles.

"I was planning to call you, dear," Joe grins.

Mark roars with laughter, his voice exploding in the silent room. I've seldom seen him sober before. He appears larger when he's not crumpled over a beer glass, and his fleshy cheeks stretch over his wide jaws.

The woman's face glows red. She takes several deep breaths and spins around. She raises her chin and walks slowly toward the door, her heels clicking. She waits for Mark to open it for her and steps out with Mark chuckling behind her. He pauses and blows a kiss to Debby as he pulls the door shut.

Debby frowns. "Who was that?"

"Some crazy woman I knew in Pittsburg." Joe's hand quivers as he reaches for his beer glass.

"We should call the cops." Debby snarls.

Joe shakes his head. "She belongs in an institution, not jail."

Debby rests her hand on his forearm and pecks him on the cheek. She's still wearing her jacket, wet from the drizzle outside. She glimpses back toward the kitchen and her brother Daryl hovering by the door, giving him a quick shake of her head.

Feeling like an eavesdropper, I tap Mike on the shoulder. Back at the bar he pours me a free beer for backing him up.

The beer turns into a pitcher as we watch Hee Haw actors dressed like corn stalks repeat jokes from Saturday morning cartoons while Carl describes the decline and fall of the American Empire. He writes a column for the Binghamton Sun-Bulletin. Artie says they print his mug shot black and white to disguise his permanent pink flush.

When the show ends, I slide my change across the bar and stand up.

Artie elbows me. "Watch this." He tips his forehead toward Carl.

Carl sways back on his stool, his eyes closed. He leans forward and sways back again. He reaches his hand up to his black horn-rimmed glasses, and in one motion he pulls the glasses away from his bushy white eyebrows as his forehead clomps down on the bar.

"He always takes off his glasses when he passes out," Artie chuckles.

I nudge Carl and raise him up, fixing his glasses on his drooping head. "I'll walk him home; it's on my way."

When we get to his apartment, Carl fishes out his key and turns the lock, muttering about Reaganomics.

I take a long way home, passing by Mark's building on Henry Street. His lights are on.

My one-week romance with Debby came when Mark was in jail, though I didn't know it at the time. Debby forgot me once he came home and then she dumped him a couple weeks later.

He swings open the door on my first knock. "My old friend Curt."

I lift the steel toe of my work boot up on the threshold to block the door in case he tries to slam it in my face. We were never friends. "Hey Mark, it's been a while."

He looks down at my foot and grimaces, waving me in. "I wanted to talk to you."

I tighten my lips and stare at him.

"You think I want to talk about Debby." He laughs. "You can't let her go, can you?"

"She made her choice."

He shakes his head, and his eyes lock mine. He flips his hand toward two old stuffed chairs. We sit down, still eyeing each other.

"What do you want?" I ask.

"You work with Freddy, right?"

"I helped him a couple times." When Freddy was sick, I collected his weekly football bets and paid off winners.

"I heard he runs the construction unions."

I crack a smile.

"Can you help me get a job? Talk to Freddy for me?"

Everyone thinks they can ask me for favors because I know Freddy. Usually they're looking for a loan or a betting tip. No one's ever asked me about a job before.

"I'm serious," Mark persists.

"Freddy would want something."

"Is that why you don't ask him for a job?" Mark scans the white tee shirt under my unbuttoned jean jacket. "You look like you could work construction."

"I got a job."

"The dairy doesn't pay much."

"I want to learn computers."

Mark snickers. "What does Freddy want?"

"He'll want you to work hard and not fuck up. Not make him look bad." I pause. "That's if he decides to help you."

"That sounds like your conditions."

"You asked me."

"So you'll talk to him?"

I catch Mark's eyes. "Maybe I'll see Freddy this week."

He grins.

"Who was the woman you brought to Mother's tonight?"

"Mary's hot, huh? She's rich, too." He shakes his head. "Sorry, she already drove back to Pittsburg."

"Is she married to Joe?"

Mark fumes. "How could Debby hook up with someone like him? I can understand a loser like you or me. But we wouldn't rip her off."

I study his dark expression. "What do you mean?"

"I met him in the joint. He's a pro." Mark shifts forward in his chair. "He told me about Mary. She was smarter than most and caught him draining her account before their wedding. She got him busted." He shakes his head. "The next thing I know he's taken a room above Swat Sullivan's. My fault for talking about Debby and her restaurant dreams."

"You could have told her."

"She'd never believe me." He squints. "Her brother won't even talk to me."

I stare at the scuffed wooden floor. "Aren't you worried about Joe?"

"I can take care of him," Mark sneers. "I thought about visiting him at Swat's but it's not worth my time. I'm on parole. More fun to pay him back like I did tonight." He stares at me. "I ain't worried about Debby either. She can take care of herself. But you still care about her."

"Maybe I never liked Joe Namath."

"Yeah, the Jets suck."

The next night I stop by Mother's for Monday Night Football. Carl remembers me taking him home and stands me a beer. Artie offers to drink it if I'm not thirsty enough.

Joe stops by our stools during half time, wearing a sheepish grin, avoiding my eyes. I wonder if he wants to apologize for Mary's outburst, but his thoughts are elsewhere. My stomach twists with his proximity like a whiff of rotten meat.

Debby saunters over with her tray. She nods toward me and winks at Joe. I stare into my beer to give them space. I glance back as Debby leans around Joe's shoulder and kisses him on his chin dimple.

She catches my eye and gives me a troubled look. Our brief romance is long over, but her brown eyes draw me like an SOS signal. I can tell she's deeply worried, and in her universe, money is usually the problem. She breaks the spell and sways off to a table.

Joe looks at me and shrugs. I drop a tip on the bar and head home.

The next day when I spear pallets with my forklift, I imagine them with chin dimples and lazy blue eyes. When I'm not sacking the quarterback, I wonder what I will say to Freddy. No one ever outsmarts him. He acts like a poor man, wearing a tattered gray jacket, straining to carry his large gut when he collects his bets on Wednesday nights, rasping as he inhales his cigars. Each step is a struggle. But I've seen him in his silk robe gliding across the pegged oak floor of his mansion on Front Street.

I stop my forklift and gaze at a pallet stacked with crates of sour cream. What would Freddy do about Joe Namath?

After my shift I head down to the computer room to drop my punch cards in the mailbox. The door opens with a gush of freezing air, and a small woman in black emerges. The vampire.

"I was about to message you." Angie squints up at me, tilting her head to the side, her black lipstick reflecting the fluorescent light of the hallway. The cold never bothers her. She wears a tight black tee shirt with a deep neckline stretched over her ample breasts.

"My shipping job ran okay last night," I stammer, trying not to stare at her cleavage.

She smiles. "You'd hear from me if it didn't."

We go out together sometimes, though she's made it clear she's not looking for a boyfriend. I keep my distance.

She says, "I'm taking the rest of the night off and I feel like dancing. Why don't you take me to Pearl's?"

I haven't been inside Pearl's since I met Debby there. The country western bar is a favorite of the college crowd. Scanning Angie's macabre outfit, I grin.

She makes a horse-riding motion, one hand on her hip and the other circling her head as she leers up at me. "I can transform into a country girl."

My cheeks grow warm. "You can go the way you are, keep them off balance."

She laughs. "You remembered."

"How can I forget your plan for world domination?" I nod my head. "I have to do something first."

I make one stop before pulling into the gravel parking lot behind Swat Sullivan's. The Irish bar is more of a dive than Mother's though it's a college hot spot. The students and professors like the dark wood and dim light for Guinness pints and poetry readings. Their map of downtown Binghamton has two destinations, Pearl's and Swat's.

I thought the second-floor rooms were abandoned until Mark told me Joe rented one. A black wooden staircase leads upstairs from the bar, but I take the rickety back stairway, stepping over the rotted planks.

I rap and rap louder. I'm about to give up when Joe cracks open the door.

He smirks at me and glances back into the room.

"I brought you an engagement gift." I lean on the door, but he holds it firm.

His chin drops into the loose grin that makes him look like the real Joe Namath. He takes a step back.

I push through the door. The dim aluminum lamp casts a yellow tint on the worn white bedspread. Dusty gray curtains block most of the late afternoon sunlight. The brown carpet is matted and pressed flat like compost. "Nice place. Do you pay by the hour?"

"Very funny, you should go on tour."

"I thought you were moving in with Debby."

"Why do you care?" His eyes shift to the side table by the bed. A shopping bag from Ritz Camera and a scattering of money lie next to the lamp. He recovers his grin. "You want her back."

THE BRIDGE ON BEER RIVER

"Everyone says that but me." I glare at him. "How do you know Mark?"

"You and Mark," he laughs. "Debby's exes."

"Yeah, she likes to pick up strays. Like you."

He stands up straight. "I've had enough. Get out of here."

"Don't you want your gift?"

"Mark and I used to work together."

"He told me about Mary."

"She's crazy. We dated twice and she's been trying to get money out of me ever since."

"What about Debby?"

He scowls. "That's none of your business."

"She never had much."

He sneers. "Debby brags about buying the bar with her brother and turning it into a restaurant." He shakes his head. "She had to borrow money from me to make the deposit on her apartment."

"Sure she did." Her worried SOS look hovers behind my eyes. "Did she loan you money?"

"I told you to get out of here," he fumes. "We're finished."

"Did she give you access to her bank account like Mary did?"

He steps back and doubles his fists, his face flaring red. His eyes dart toward the side table, but they avoid contact with me.

I walk over to the table, my soles slipping on the carpet. I throw an envelope next to the lamp. "Here's your engagement gift."

His eyes shift between the table and me, and back again.

I turn to face him. "It's a Greyhound ticket to Pittsburg."

"I ain't going nowhere."

"You should use it. Go see Mary."

He heaves with anger.

I keep my eye on him as my hand hovers over the envelope. "If you don't want it, I'll take it back. Maybe I'll go see Mary."

Joe sucks in a deep breath and stares at the cracked ceiling. He leans forward and snatches the envelope. "I'm through with this shit town anyway."

I pick up the Ritz bag. Inside are a brand-new Nikon camera and the receipt. I shift it to my left hand and take a twenty from the pile of money. "This should cover the ticket," I smile as I shove it in my pocket.

"The camera's a gift for Debby," he yells. "You can't just steal it."

"I'll give it to her and say it's from you." I head toward the door.

He blocks my path and spews, "Who the Hell do you think you are?"

"I'm Curt." I shove him away and reach for the door handle.

Joe grabs my shoulder from behind and I whip around, knocking his hand off. But he swings his right fist in a wide arc, catching my jaw hard. My head snaps back and I fall, bouncing off the end of the bed and landing on the floor, dazed.

I should have expected his sucker punch. I take a deep breath. The carpet smells worse than it looks. The scent of mildew and ammonia mask the sour odor of dried beer and puke. I want to stand up more than anything. I can't.

Joe leans over me, his triumphant grin burning through my fuzzy eyesight. If he were smart, he would kick me now and end it. Roll me into the hallway, shove me down the stairs. Instead he reaches for the Ritz Camera bag lying where it fell next to my right hand, cushioned by my thigh.

I clutch his wrist, focusing all my strength on that one spot. His arm stops cold, his hand grabbing air. I raise my head and tighten my fingers, my grip tempered by wrestling thousands of milk crates. I never dropped one. My head clears as I twist his wrist and use it to lever myself up. He takes a wild swing with his left hand. I lean back as his fist grazes my shoulder.

Still holding his wrist, I gather myself in a low stance. He starts another swing, leaving himself off balance. I pull him down and knee him in the stomach. He grunts and launches toward me. I lean back and hook the side of his head with my left fist as he caroms sideways off the wall.

He coughs and rolls to his side, shaking his head. I stare at him, waiting for him to stand up, breathing hard and

127

stretching my jaw where he caught me by surprise. He wipes the back of his hand on his mouth, sees a smear of blood, and drops his head down on the floor.

I wait while my pulse slows and watch Joe breathe. He simmers with anger but shows no sign of getting up. I hold his eyes as I walk toward the door, retrieving the shopping bag.

"You're an asshole, Curt," he says to my back.

I glance back. "You're just being nice." I slam the door and stride down the stairway, inhaling the fresh air.

Back home, the weak shower drains off my day of wrestling milk crates and quarterbacks. I stand in the water longer than usual, the hot steam soothing my jaw and shoulder. After Joe's room at Sullivan's, my sparse apartment feels like the Waldorf Astoria.

When I pick up Angie, I don't tell her about my errand. By her soapy scent I know she also washed off her day at the dairy. She replaced her black lipstick with deep red for our trip to Pearl's, but otherwise she retains her dark vampire appearance.

At the honky-tonk bar I stomp on peanut shells with my steel-soled work boots as Angie glides across the dance floor, shocking the college crowd with her steps and her deathly pallor. They give us plenty of space.

"I want to ride that horse." I point toward the full-sized plaster cast of a bronco bucking up from the top of the bar, the tips of its hooves inches from the hanging lights.

"You're too heavy." She pokes me in the arm.

"You want me to toss you up there?"

She laughs. "You know the legend?"

"That says the horse will fly away when a virgin graduates from the university?"

"No, the one that says a vampire doesn't need any help, especially from her prey."

"I never heard that one."

She leans into me. "I just made it up."

We leave Pearl's soon after, but we don't stop at Mother's. Angie won't go near the bar. She takes me back to her apartment where I'm a willing victim.

The next night is Wednesday, and I know I'll see Freddy picking up bets and paying off winners at Mother's. I take my stool between Artie and Carl. They don't notice the Ritz Camera bag when I set it down at my feet.

"You missed the action last night," Artie says.

"I had to work."

"Ha. I heard you were out hunting with the vampire." He smiles, a wad of tobacco bulging in his cheek. "Glad you're still alive."

"Not like Joe Namath." Carl peers at me over his horn-rimmed glasses. "Debby released him and now he's a free agent."

Artie chuckles into his beer glass. I turn away when he takes a swig without spitting out his plug. "She came in crying, and she said Joe left her. By the end of the night her story changed. Now she says she threw him out."

I shake my head. "She has to maintain her perfect record."

Artie gazes at me for a second. "She says he stole money from her."

"Those athletes always need cash," Carl grumbles. "That big contract and now he's broke."

Debby emerges from the kitchen. She doesn't look like a woman in mourning. Her eyes gleam in a distinct way when she's ready for a new boyfriend. I wave her over, hoping Angie's bite has given me immunity, though I shiver when she touches my shoulder.

I lift the shopping bag and hand it to her.

She smiles with surprise. "Thank you, but what do I want with a camera?"

"It's a gift from Joe. The receipt's in the bag."

"You can get your money back," Carl says in his professional tone. "Ritz is good about that. The Press buys all their camera equipment there."

She reads the amount, and her cheeks redden. "How did you get this?"

I study the bag, avoiding her glare.

Her face darkens into a scowl. "I don't want to know."

She takes the bag and strides back to the kitchen, the door gaping and swinging in her wake.

"You're welcome," I mumble in her direction.

Artie slaps me on the back.

MAKE IT HOME ALIVE

I never asked for Rich's help fixing my front door, but I'm getting it anyway. He pulls up in his red Ford pickup with a lumber rack and a toolbox in the bed. He waves as I wrestle the heavy door off its hinges and lean it against the chipped frame.

He first showed up at My Mother's Place a couple of weeks ago. He's good company at the bar, telling me how he built houses in Florida and Boston, more recently Elmira. Last night when we put away a pitcher of Genesee Ale, I mentioned my Saturday morning project, hoping to straighten the door before the upstate New York weather turns colder. Rich jumped in and said he'd stop by in the morning. I didn't believe his drunken promise, and he didn't believe I know how to hang a door.

"Where's the rub?" He asks, grinning under his thick red mustache with just the tips of his teeth marking the top of his mouth. Shorter than me but stocky and strong, he reminds me of Yosemite Sam. He steps up on the porch with a tray of chisels, screw drivers, a small saw, claw hammers, and a tape measure. He wears a Red Sox T-shirt frayed at the neck. He sets down his overflowing tray next to my cheap hammer and screwdriver.

I show him where the warped door catches the upper frame, requiring a stiffer kick each morning.

A small U-Haul box truck pulls up behind Rich's pickup. A guy in a yellow baseball cap and a camo T-shirt jumps out of the cab and jogs up the sidewalk. His young face is deeply tanned, and he squints as he reads the faded white address numerals on the black mailboxes between my door and the upstairs door. A girl's face with clear blue eyes and a wave of golden hair peers around his shoulder. She has a slight blemish below her left eye, partially covered in makeup--could be a bruise or a small birthmark.

The guy extends his hand to Rich. "We're your new upstairs neighbors. I'm Charles and this here's my wife, Donna." He speaks in a deep drawl and inflates his chest with pride. The black letters on his T-shirt read, "Smith and Wesson University."

Rich points at me while his eyes rest on Donna. "There's your new neighbor. Where y'all from?"

I smile at Rich's sudden southern accent. It only emerges when he's talking up Debby at Mother's. I nod toward Charles, thinking Rich might earn a scowl or worse from Mr. Smith and Wesson for ogling his wife, but the young husband's face remains fixed in a serious pose. Letting go of the door with one hand, I wave at Donna. She flicks her fingers and ducks further behind Charles. "I'm Curt and that's Rich."

"We just made it up from Baton Rouge," Charles says.

"I hail from Florida," Rich replies. "But I've been living with Yankees the past few years."

"That's too bad, living with Yankees." Charles looks at me. "No offense."

I shrug and renew my grip with both hands.

Charles squints up and down the street. The small lawns are brown except for piles of red and yellow leaves under the barren limbs of maples and elms. The gray sidewalks and street match the dull overcast sky.

"Are there any Baptist churches around here?" Donna asks in a soft tone.

Rich gleams at her. "I go to a Southern Baptist church out on Conklin Avenue. I can introduce you tomorrow morning."

"That would be so nice."

Donna blushes under Rich's gaze. I never heard him mention church before. A chilly breeze blows up from the river, brushing the hair on Donna's shoulders. She folds her arms under her breasts, pulling a few inches of her white blouse from her tight blue jeans.

Charles looks at Rich. "Ain't one of them Negro churches, is it?

"It's about 99% white," Rich says, turning to catch my glare as I shift my weight. I'm still holding the door in its frame.

"Had to ask," Charles squints.

I frown at him and swing my head to include Rich and Donna. Before I can reply, Rich laughs, and Donna's eyes widen with surprise at my expression.

"No offense intended." Charles says, looking down at his shoes. "The agent said we could pick another place if we don't like this one. We just want a place of our own."

"Don't worry, you'll like it here." Rich taps my shoulder and I lean away. "Curt here is 100% Yankee, but he's okay."

"Yeah, welcome to my neighborhood." I return my attention to checking the edges along the door frame.

Over the next few days, I hardly see my new neighbors, which is fine by me. Charles works an irregular schedule, late shift most days. I hear him clomp down the stairs as I'm going to bed. One night after a long day lifting milk crates at Crowley Dairy, I crash to the squeaks of the bed upstairs, achieving a quick rhythm for a couple of measures. Then the weak trickle of the shower.

Later that week I drop a box of pizza on my rusty kitchen table and reach into the refrigerator for a cold Genesee. I barely hear the knock at first, and it persists as I jog to the door. Donna smiles up at me with her bright blue eyes accented by mascara.

She wears a starched white blouse, a pink Dunkin Donuts skirt and matching apron. She smells like a glazed donut. She follows my eyes up to her hair and pulls out a pin behind the pile of curls. With a shake of her head her golden hair unwinds, flowing like honey from a jar.

"I found me a job." She holds up a white donut bag like an offering.

Her smile is contagious, warmed by pick lipstick. I wonder if she shares her husband's attitudes, but I shove that thought into a corner. "Congratulations! I'll make coffee to go with the donuts."

She hops over the threshold. "I don't drink no coffee."

I laugh. "I only have coffee and beer. Unless you drink water."

"Water's fine." She takes a quick look around. My living room is cleaner than usual. I picked up the beer cans last night, though my computer books cover my one worn chair, its stuffing held in place by straining black threads. She trails me into the kitchen where I fill a jelly glass with water.

"Scooby Doo, my favorite." Her eyes glimmer under the yellow kitchen light.

I sweep my hand toward the pizza box spotted with olive oil.

"I'll take a half slice," she says with a sheepish grin.

I retrieve two paper plates.

As I set the table she says, "We went to Rich's church. He offered to fix our shower."

"Nice of him," I nod as I sip my beer.

She lowers her eyes and tilts her head with an artless grace that confirms my read of Rich's intentions. She centers her paper plate and adds, "I dropped out of high school when we decided to move up here. Rich said you'll know where I can get my GED."

"That's right, he just moved here, too." I muse, dissecting a slice of pizza. The knife snags most of the cheese into a white blob. "They have night classes at Binghamton High and Broome Tech. People like Tech better."

She sips her water and smiles. "Charles and I have been married almost three weeks! Our parents said we should wait but here we are."

"He's a lucky man." I slide the least mangled half slice onto her plate.

"He's the Night Security Manager at Agway." She raises her chin with a look of pride. "Same job he had in Baton Rouge."

"But you're not in Louisiana anymore."

"No, and with him working nights I have no one to talk to." She catches my eyes. "Would you mind me stopping by every now and then?"

"No, I wouldn't mind at all." The blood rises in my cheeks.

Her eyes glaze. "I miss my mom." She stands up. "I better go take my shower."

My cupboard fills with donuts over the next week as Donna makes good on her pledge to visit me. I begin sipping more beer to control my blood pressure in her presence, while she sticks to drinking tap water from my Scooby Doo glass.

I see less of Charles given our work schedules, though one morning I find him pulling weeds in the narrow flower bed between the foundation and the parking lot. Judging from the overgrown beds, our cheap landlord hasn't planted anything in years. When Charles finishes his chore there will be nothing but bare dirt.

"We got marigolds on sale at Agway," he says when he reads my doubtful expression.

"There's a water hose around the back," I reply. "But it might be rotted out."

Charles stands and swipes his hands on his jeans. "We got plenty of those, too."

"Marigolds will be an improvement," I grin and unconsciously glance at my watch. Running late again.

"We should pop a beer one of these nights," he smiles expectantly.

"Maybe the weekend."

"I have off Sundays."

I nod and hop into the Dodge, feeling guilty for not engaging him longer, though I'm relieved to have an excuse.

One evening I'm not that surprised to find Rich at the door instead of Donna or Charles. Rich carries a tray of tools, an array of pipe wrenches and fittings.

"Charles asked me to fix their shower." He checks the swing of my door.

"He's working tonight."

"How would I know that?" he laughs and follows me into the kitchen. He looks over my shoulder as I fetch a couple of beers from the refrigerator. "Is that all you eat, beer and yogurt?"

"Trying to stay healthy." I peer at him over my beer can. "Donna's probably underage."

"She's eighteen and she's married." He winks. "And she's hot."

"Eighteen-year-old women are hot by definition."

He slaps me on the back. "You sound so moral. You should go to our church."

"I'm on a different path."

"Yeah, the winos at Mother's say you're seeing a vampire."

I shake my head. No secrets at the dairy or Mother's.

I take a deep swallow of beer as another knock interrupts my thoughts of Angie. When I pull open the door Donna greets me with her arresting smile. She wears fresh makeup and a blue cotton sweater, her hair falling in curves down her shoulders and over her breasts, matched by a thin gold chain and cross. Her eyes find Rich and she smiles wider.

"Hi there, Donna," Rich beams, "I guess we better get your plumbing fixed."

"I'm tired of that drippy shower."

"I'll fix it before Charles comes home, so he can enjoy a nice hot shower tonight." Rich glances at me.

"You're the expert," I smirk as they stomp upstairs.

I drain another beer and try to concentrate on operating system diagnostics, the last chapter in my computer correspondence course. I hear the shower gush and I assume Rich is finished with his repair, though I don't hear him leave. I stand and stretch my arms, trying to remember the differences Angie explained between the UNIX commands in my book and the VMS commands I use at work. I need another of her tutorials.

Friday night I bribe Angie to help me study. After she puts Crowley's PDP-11 computer to bed for the weekend, we drive to Pat Mitchell's ice cream shop in Endicott for a pint of strawberry shortcake. Ice cream takes priority over computers. I set the carton on my chipped kitchen table and offer Angie a chair.

She hears the soft knock before I do.

I shrug my shoulders. "Sounds like Dunkin Donna."

"I've wanted to meet her."

Donna smiles at the door, holding her customary donut bag. She wears her blue sweater and gold necklace with the cross, her eye makeup gleaming deeper than usual under the dim porch light. I wave her into the living room.

"I missed you last night," she says softly.

"We were doing inventory." I point my chin toward Angie.

Donna's eyes swell, scanning Angie's black outfit and her black woven leather necklace with a silver pentangle medallion. Angie stands a few inches shorter than Donna but their necklace pendants ping together as she gives Donna a quick hug after my introduction. Donna blushes and reaches for her cross as if she expects a flash reaction, matter meeting antimatter.

"Angie's helping me with my computer course."

"I'm in it for ice cream," Angie smiles. "But I'm willing to share."

"You know computers?" Donna tilts her head in wonder. "All I know is donuts."

Angie catches her eye. "You can do anything you want."

"Oh, I don't know." Donna glances down at her hands.

"Well, I want coffee," I tell them. "Donuts, ice cream and coffee, a three-course dinner."

The two women follow me into the kitchen where I retrieve bowls and paper plates. I take the broken chair, rocking in rhythm to the stove top percolator.

"My mom had one of them boiling coffee pots," Donna says. She sips water from the Scooby Doo glass.

"I like to think I'm camping."

"You are," Angie smirks.

Under the bright kitchen light, Donna's makeup looks heavier, like layers of paint over a dark varnished surface. I ask, "Are you okay?"

She touches her cheek under her right eye and looks down at her ice cream bowl, avoiding my gaze. "I fell down."

Angie studies the bruise. "Looks like a hard fall."

"I hit the sink."

I don't believe her and neither does Angie. I stand to turn off the stove before the percolator boils over.

"We all fall down sometimes," Angie says with a sympathetic look.

I fill cups of black coffee for Angie and me. Donna looks out my kitchen window at the murky halo under the streetlamp. She exhales with a sigh, raising her chin and reaching for her water. She runs her fingertip around the rim and looks at me. "I'm real clumsy."

I hold her eyes. "If it's ever more than that, you should just come down here."

Donna stares at me, her eyes shining. "I couldn't do that."

"You'd be safe with Curt." Angie points her spoon at my chest and a pink drop of ice cream falls to the table. "Everyone's afraid of him, except me."

We stare at the drop until I wipe it up with my fingers and lick them clean. "Ha, if you ever come down here to hide, I'll be hiding with you."

"Don't believe that," Angie says.

Donna nods with a tight grimace. "That's nice to know I can come here. But I was raised to face my own problems." She looks at Angie.

"That includes the freedom to change." Angie waves her spoon like a wand and slides a bite of ice cream between her lips, chasing it with a sip of coffee.

Donna follows her lead, dipping her spoon in her bowl. "I like your ice cream."

"Curt tells me you're working on your high school diploma," Angie says. "I went back to school to get my degree."

"I wish I knew computers like you do."

Angie winks at me over her coffee cup. "Even Curt can learn computers. It would be easy for you."

I chug my coffee and look inside the donut bag. "Eclairs and donuts, ones and zeroes. How hard can it be?"

Donna gives me her expert expression and replies with a hint of irony. "We call those long ones cream sticks."

Angie stifles a laugh. "Don't worry about ones and zeroes, just start with your high school degree." She pulls a pen out of her black jeans and writes a phone number on a paper plate, sliding it toward Donna. "I can show you around town, not that there's much to see."

"I'd like that." Donna folds the paper plate in quarters. She checks the wall clock and stands up. "Y'all are so nice."

"No, we're not," Angie glowers. She loops a lock of black hair over her ear, breaking into a grin.

Soon after Donna's quick steps climb the stairs, heavier and slower boots follow. I tip my brow toward the ceiling. "Rich is going up to fix her plumbing."

Angie reaches for her coffee cup. "Will you be able to concentrate on ones and zeroes?"

"Cream sticks and donuts. That's all I think about."

Angie raises her cup and traces the wet ring on the tabletop with her index finger, stealing a glance at the greasy ceiling. "Hard to study here. We should go to my place."

"Yeah, I'm ready for my exam."

Late the next day I drop my course booklet and the multiple-choice questionnaire at the post office, glad to have it finished. As I walk home the early winter dusk fades into darkness, and the streetlights come awake, buzzing behind the barren silhouettes of trees.

Back in my kitchen I snag a Genesee from the refrigerator and consider my options for dinner, leftover ice cream, donuts, yogurt, or all of the above.

During my second beer the yelling begins upstairs. I try to block it out, but when I hear the loud smash of breaking glass and Donna crying, I stride toward my front door, intending to check on her. I hear footsteps running down the stairs followed by a loud knock. I snatch open the door.

Charles stands in front of me holding a gun. The barrel points at the floor, his finger on the trigger. He breathes hard, his face burning red.

He squints up at me, tilting his head, his lips quivering. "Donna told me."

I nod my head slowly, glimpsing the gun and trying to keep his eye, wondering how much Donna revealed. He might think I'm the one banging his wife. I recognize the service issue .45 and check the safety latch partially hidden by his thumb. The gun is ready to fire but he hasn't shot me yet.

Charles looks down at the pistol and tilts his head the other way. A tear rolls down his cheek. He breaks into sobs, rocking his shoulders, his hand firm on the .45.

"Maybe you should give me the gun," I say in a soft tone.

He shakes his head. "I can't do that."

He raises the gun to his chest, opening his palm and studying the dull black steel. "I want to know where that Rich is."

"He's not here." I wave him in, pointing toward the kitchen and waiting for him to walk ahead of me. He carries the gun flat against his white T-shirt like a dinner plate, but his index finger remains on the trigger. I pull out a chair for him and he flops down, releasing the gun from his hand like a hot iron, dropping it on the table with a thud.

"I have beer, coffee, and water." I force a smile.

He wipes his eyes on his shirt sleeve.

"And ice cream and donuts."

"Those damned donuts."

I watch his face and his .45 as I retreat to the stove to warm up some coffee. He lowers his head above the gun and shudders with a quick sob. "I'm gonna kill that son of a bitch."

"He ain't worth it."

Charles jumps to his feet. "He deserves worse."

"Maybe. But you need to think about yourself." I hold his bloodshot eyes. "And think about Donna."

Gritting his teeth, he rolls his neck and takes a couple of deep breaths like he's trying to relax, but his shoulders sag back down.

"Is Donna okay?" I ask.

"She's fine. I didn't mean to hit her the other night. I shouldn't have done it." He walks to the stove and stares at the heating percolator. "I hate myself."

I study him for an awkward moment. "The coffee's only a day old," I tell him. "I have free milk from the dairy if you take it that way."

"I should kill myself, that's what I should do."

"Then Donna would have nothing."

"She's got Rich."

"He won't last."

Charles peers at the ceiling like he's trying to probe Donna's mind through the joists and floorboards.

"Coffee?" I hold up my coffee cup, and he sits down. I fill the cups and take a sip. "Less burned than I expected." I point my chin at his gun. "Where did you get the .45?"

"Army surplus." He looks at me. "You know guns?"

"I was in the military."

He pauses for a second and drops his eyes. "I didn't know."

"No one does, except my boss." I smirk. "Take that back. I put it on my application at the dairy, so now everyone knows."

Charles straightens his shoulders. "I'm in the National Guard." He studies my face. I sense him clicking off the difference in our ages. "Did you go to Nam?"

I fetch a bag of donuts from the cupboard. I never talk about the war but I hope I can distract him from his .45. "Yeah, I was in country."

He says, "I wish I went to Vietnam."

"No, you don't."

"Yes, I do." Charles jerks his head up and down. "My cousin told me about it."

"He lied." My chair scrapes the linoleum floor when I sit back down. "He should have told you the war was about staying alive and keeping your friends alive. Nothing else."

Charles squints at me, unbelieving. He watches me empty the bag of donuts, one glazed, one with sugar, and one with chocolate frosting. He raises his eyes, still doubtful. He reminds me of a young private, fresh from boot camp, starched and secure in his beliefs, a lot like me the first few weeks.

"Let me tell you something." I sip the bitter coffee and lean forward in my chair. "I was a Marine. During my last tour we got a new lieutenant who wanted a medal, so he sent us out on extra patrols. He had no idea what he was doing, other than getting us killed. We all hated him."

I chug the rest of my coffee, my fingers quivering at the memory. "During night watch my job was to pick targets for the nightly mortar barrage and give them to the duty officer. One night I put the coordinates of his hut on my list. He transferred the next day."

Charles stares at me like I'm a ghost.

"The company commander was mad as hell and said he would court martial me, but I never heard any more about it. The officers hated that bastard, too." I grab the glazed donut and rip it in half. "Some nights I imagined my coordinates were the old men who sent us there. LBJ, McNamara, Nixon. If I were there now, I'd have coordinates for Ronald Reagan."

I raise my empty cup. "But I didn't kill any of them." I slam the cup down harder than I intend, shaking the steel table. "If I end up dead or stuck in jail, they win." I look Charles in the eye. "If I make it home alive, I win."

Charles breaks my stare, his hand fumbling to pick up the piece of glazed donut, turning it in his fingers. "They don't know you won."

"I know." I stand up to refill my coffee cup. "I don't care what they think."

Charles rolls the piece of donut into a little ball. He pops it in his mouth and gathers the fallen sugar into a pile. "I don't know some of the men you hate, but Ronald Reagan's a good man."

"You're thinking about the movie star cowboy." I shake my head. "Now he threatens war every day, and he only cares about rich people. Wait until they have layoffs at Agway."

"They're talking about it."

"Yup, same with the dairy." I dunk a piece of donut into my coffee and watch the oil slick spread.

We sit there for several minutes, sipping our coffee and picking at donuts. Charles looks up from the table. "Donna's been talking to your girlfriend. They went shopping."

"Angie likes Donna, just don't let her know you called her my girlfriend."

He breaks into a half smile and stands up. His face still gleams pink, though a few shades lighter. Checking the wall clock, he says, "I better get ready for work." He clicks on the safety and slides the gun into his jeans. "Thank you for the coffee."

I show him to the door and retrieve a fresh can of Genesee. I listen upstairs and the rest of the evening is quiet until I hear Charles descend the stairs for his shift.

By that time I'm pacing the floor, walking from kitchen to living room and bedroom and back again. I'm wired from the coffee, but I know it's more than that. I stop for a few breaths and walk some more, trying to shake off the tension of the visit and my unwanted memories of the jungle. Long after Charles leaves, I still see faces and coordinates. One sip of beer and one step at a time, I finally make it home again.

A few nights later I'm looking forward to a fresh six pack when the yelling starts. Heavy footsteps run down the stairs. Pushing open my front door, I hear a siren and I see red and blue lights reflecting off the low fog, a police car turning up the street. I run upstairs and knock.

Donna cracks open her door and peeks over the burglar chain. Her face is red and puffy, her eyes glazed from crying.

I don't see any new bruises. She leans away and says, "Thank you, but I'm okay. I don't know who called the police."

"Do you want me to talk to him?"

"He ain't comin' back." She gazes down the stairs.

"Charles?"

She shakes her head and I back away. She closes the door and turns the bolt.

Through the dirty stairway window, I see the police cruiser idling behind Rich's red pickup. The cops talk to him in front of their open car door. They wave him away and he pulls out.

Back in my apartment I hear slow steps ascend the stairs, but they leave soon after. The cruiser quenches its lights, leaving a thick yellow haze under the streetlights. I raise my green can of Genesee Ale and toast Donna's graduation. But I celebrate too soon.

I'm getting ready for bed when I hear a knock on my door. Charles and Donna smile up at me, holding hands. Snowflakes float in the porch light, catching in Donna's hair. Charles wears a sweatshirt with an image of bullets piled in an ashtray above the words, "Smoke 'em if you got 'em."

He looks his wife in the eye. "We had a long talk with our parents. They want us to come home and have a real wedding."

"A church wedding," Donna chimes in. "We had a Justice of the Peace wedding."

"Congratulations, you'll be warmer in Louisiana."

"No, we're staying here," Charles replies. "After the wedding."

I crack a grin. "If you live up here too long you'll become Democrats."

Charles shoves his hands into the pockets of the khaki slacks he wears for work. "I can't never do that."

"I can." Donna rises on her toes and smiles brightly. Charles jerks his head toward her, squinting into her blue eyes, holding them for several seconds. He finally sighs and reaches up to her face, sliding a golden curl off her brow.

FIGHTING THE WAR AGAIN

My boss Sherman barks like I'm a private in his Army Ranger company, but we're standing on the loading dock at Crowley Dairy, not Vietnam.

I look him in the eye. "No."

His cheeks glow red, bleeding to purple near his ears. Sherman's about my height though weighs twice as much, his former military physique overlaid with folds of padding. He's normally a hard driver but fair.

"I ordered you to move those pallets and crates!" He points at my chest and waves his finger at my forklift and the pile of pallets in the corner of the storeroom. The pallets stay in that corner most nights.

I crack a grin. He knows I worked through lunch to load the trucks ahead of schedule, and I plan to leave a few minutes early to take my friend Artie to the Veteran's Hospital in Oxford.

"Okay, Curt, you're suspended without pay." He extends his thumb like an umpire. "Get out of here."

"You're docking my pay?" I raise my voice.

"You heard me." He turns and walks away.

I scoot around, blocking his path and glaring at him.

"Now you're fired." His purple face inflates like a water balloon. I've never seen him so angry. He takes a step back and pivots around me, striding toward his office on the upper deck.

I rip the day's manifest off my clipboard. I should just walk out but I'm supposed to enter the shipments on punch cards. I care about getting the entries right. Learning computers is my plan for getting off the forklift for good, not that it matters now. I stop in the breakroom for a glass of water on my way to drop the manifest on my desk, simmering with disbelief.

My friend Renee stands in front of the coffee machine, reading my anger with a look of concern. She wears her white apron from the bottling line, and today she smells like buttermilk. Her long blond hair is tied in a bun under a light blue hair net.

I take a deep breath. "Sherman's fighting the war again."

"Everyone heard the battle." The sound from the loading dock echoes like a loudspeaker through the cavernous brick building.

I snatch a paper cup from the aluminum tube near the water tank.

"You know what the problem is." She gazes down the white hallway, toward the accounting office.

"That problem's bigger than both of us." Sherman's heavyweight affair with Julie from accounting is a primary subject of dairy gossip, but I thought their romance was over.

152

Renee shakes her head. "Not that problem, worse." She waits for me to swallow my water. "They're shutting down the dairy for Christmas. Orders are slow."

"Christmas is supposed to be eggnog and ice cream season."

"They're keeping the Poughkeepsie plant open." She reaches into the refrigerator for a carton of milk. "Sherman fought Old Crowley to keep our plant open, but he lost."

"No paycheck." I sneer. "Merry Christmas."

Renee sips her milk. "They're still having the holiday party."

"What a relief." I squeeze my cup and throw it in the trash. "He could have told me."

"Maybe he wants to tell everyone tomorrow. Company meeting. I heard it through the rumor mill."

I stride down the hallway, shoving open the steel paneled door labeled "Accounting," its letters worn by years of handprints. Julie sits with her wide back to me and doesn't look up. She still blames me for a decline in the Richter scale of her affair with Sherman.

After dropping off the manifest, I head outside and chill my anger with the car windows down, scooping the blustery December air as I drive to Artie's apartment, but I can't shake my feeling of dread. If business is bad at Christmas, what about the bleak winter months after the shutdown? Not easy finding another job this time of year.

Artie hops down the front steps of his apartment building, spearing his crutch around patches of ice with the agility of a slalom skier. He slides the crutch into the back seat and grips the front door frame, swinging his thin body onto the seat and pulling his coat over the stub of his right leg.

"Right on time," he smiles. "I don't want to keep that cute young nurse waiting."

His babble lightens my mood. "Your nurse last month looked like a sloth."

"They're all cute to me." He pops three squares of Nicorette gum into his mouth. He forgoes chewing tobacco on hospital days.

"That's a big hit of nicotine."

"It takes a few sticks to get a chew going." He works the gum into a wad, bulging in his cheek like a real plug. "Mind if I turn on the heat?"

"It's your car. You can do anything you want." Artie loans me his car for work and I return the favor by driving him around. He likes having a chauffeur.

"We might get weather," he says as a few snowflakes collide with the windshield. We head north out of town, following the river, white chucks of slush dotting the water.

Artie grins with his remaining teeth. "Beer River."

"I thought the Susquehanna was Beer River. That's the Chenango."

"Same difference. It looks like beer to me."

"You know the rule. No beer until after your appointment."

"It's my rule," he sighs. "Even if I ain't fooling nobody at the VA."

Soon we roll into a small town with one store, crossing over an old steel bridge, tires humming as Beer River pushes its endless flow of suds toward Binghamton.

Artie pulls his jacket tighter. "Glad you got off work early."

"Sherman threw me out."

"Why? You've been staying sober." Artie winks. "Most of the time."

"He had a Vietnam flashback and I refused to play grunt."

"You argued with him."

I turn on the wipers, hoping the defroster still works. Artie watches the snowflakes splash on the window, already clumping on the wipers. He reaches for an empty Styrofoam cup I brought from work.

"You even spit when you chew gum?"

He shrugs and shifts the huge wad between cheeks. "You know I'm worried about you."

"You're worried about me?"

"You argue with your boss and get fired, you beat up Renee's boyfriend, and you chase Debby's fiancé out of town."

"Debby's fiancé was planning to bolt anyway."

"Mike the bartender gets you to back him up whenever there's a fight at Mother's, like last week when you threw out Chad Dixon."

"I help Mike for free beers." I shake my head. "And Chad Dixon's an urban blight all by himself. The mayor should ask for federal renewal money, rebuild Dixon's entire family."

"Well, you have an anger problem, and you resort to violence to solve your other problems."

"You've been watching those morning talk shows again." I pump the brakes and pull over to the side of the road. Grabbing the scraper, I hop out and chip ice off the windshield. I slam the driver side wiper down three times until I shatter a clump the size of a golf ball.

I climb back in the car and Artie says, "You can get help at the Vet's Hospital for your anger problem."

"Was I too violent with the ice?"

"I know you're a veteran, but you don't talk about it."

"You don't talk about it either."

"It's hard for me to hide it." Artie glances at his stump. He likes to show it off for free beers at My Mother's Place, though he never talks about how he lost the leg.

"At least you don't go to the VFW. They'd love you there."

"Heroes go there." The wiper smears a layer of ice across the windshield. "They just want me for Memorial Day photos."

"Yeah, I'm no hero either."

Artie stares ahead. "Days like this make me think about the leg I left in Korea. My missing toes still feel cold."

"Maybe your leg is curled up under a nurse's blanket."

Artie spits into the coffee cup. "I'm thousands of miles from that nurse. But today might be my lucky day."

"When your toes are cold you can think about her stroking your leg."

"I do." He gazes at me. "You were a Marine, right? I was a staff sergeant. Army."

I pull into the hospital parking lot. "I made sergeant, twice. They would have made me staff if I reenlisted."

"They wanted you to re-up even though you'd been busted?"

Shutting off the car, I watch the wipers make a final pass and stop. "I was good at some things."

Artie zips up his jacket for the icy walk to the hospital door. "Well, today's my lucky day. You'll see."

A stern woman in a white smock looks up as we approach the reception desk. Artie points me toward the waiting area and hops up to the counter. He pulls a mass of paperwork out of his jacket and leans over, whispering and glancing at me. With a final nod, he heads into the waiting room and lowers himself into the chair next to mine.

A guy with a burr cut and a khaki tee shirt, tattoo sleeves on both arms, emerges from the back room and calls out a name, roaring like a drill instructor. In the row behind us an old man pushes an older man in a wheelchair as fast as he can move. The orderly glares at them and waits until the last second to help with the door.

"Some guys never get out," I mutter.

Artie ignores me and straightens the brim of his old Mets cap. After a few minutes Sergeant Orderly calls Artie's name and repeats it louder. Artie jerks up and limps to the desk.

With Artie gone I shift my weight on the orange stuffed chair, institutional vinyl, colder than the seat of Artie's car. On the wall hangs a pink and blue pastel painting that looks like the artist crossed out a landscape in disgust, planning to start over. The more I stare at the artwork the colder it looks, reminding me of a desolate northern plain, too cold even for caribou. After an interminable time, I decide to take a walk around the hallways to warm up, following white stenciled numbers on battleship gray walls with no other labels, as if the purpose of the rooms was a military secret.

When I return to the waiting room, I find Artie beaming with good luck. He stands up and drops his crutch to the floor with a thud. His right pant leg is rolled partway up a shiny new beige leg. He takes a couple of uncertain steps and stops, looking down. I pick up his crutch and hand it to him. "Your leg looks great, Artie."

"Just a temporary leg until I get the one they measured for me."

"I always wondered why you didn't get one sooner."

"This here's a new model. The old one itches and gives me sores." He scans the faces watching him standing without a crutch, their tired eyes hoping for their own miracles. "Let's get out of here," he whispers. "Too many sick people."

Outside I steer the old Dodge out of the lot, ice crunching under the tires. Artie's cheek bulges with fresh tobacco and he retains his wide smile, eyes sparkling above his weathered skin like a garden gnome. "My nurse was cute," he says between chews, "but she only stroked my fake leg to show me how to put it on."

Artie spits into the cup and drops it back in the holder, turning his head to watch the snow blowing past the windshield. "I still think you should see someone. The shrink is even cuter; you'd like her."

"Snow's too cold to stick." I mumble, turning off the wipers. "I never should have told you I was a Marine."

"You didn't tell me. You put it on your application at the dairy."

"No secrets in Beer River."

"You can do something with your life. Like learning computers."

"Is that why you want me to see a shrink? Because I like computers?"

He shakes his head. "You can do better. You shouldn't be sitting with us at Mother's."

"I don't want to be better than anyone."

"You learning computers made me think it was time to get a new leg." Artie grabs the cup and spits out a brown stream, wiping his chin with the back of his hand. "And the VA's getting me new teeth."

"You deserve a new leg and teeth. You might have to give up tobacco, though."

He flashes a brown smile. "I'm still Artie."

The snowflakes flare in our headlights like white tracers. Artie leans back and I focus on the lane lines, slowing down a notch. A semi bursts out of the whiteness and blows our Dodge toward the bank of plowed snow on the roadside. I hold our lane with a brief skid, nearly spilling Artie's spit cup.

I catch his worried eye and flash a smile. "You could smuggle drugs in your leg."

"Would you do that?"

"No, of course not. How about beer?"

"It would slosh around."

"Leave it in the cans."

Artie laughs. "Might double my weight."

We stop at an intersection with a small grocery store and two gas pumps. They're out of Genesee Ale, so we settle for a six-pack of the lager. I sip one and leave the rest for Artie. He recovers his gleam by the time I drop him off at his apartment.

Back home I take a shower and change my T-shirt before walking to Mother's. Artie turns the corner on Court Street behind me, carrying his new leg under his arm. I hold his crutch while he straps on the leg, and I pull open the heavy oak door. He shuffles to a bar stool next to Carl and spins it down a few inches, smiling and waving to his friends. Everyone wants to see his leg. I slide his crutch under the bar and ante up for the first pitcher.

"Is this a celebration for getting fired?" Artie grins with his brown, gapped teeth.

I tip my glass in a toast. "To your leg and the nurse who stroked it."

Carl gives me a quick nod when I offer to top off his beer, his eyes centered on the snowy television above the bar with President Reagan's sincere smile fading in and out. He welcomes the Kansas City Royals to the White House for winning the World Series.

"I'd like to throw a fastball at that Old Ranger," Carl mutters.

"It would slide off him, Teflon man." I pour a second glass for Artie and look away when he takes a swig without spitting out his tobacco plug.

Carl frowns under his white mustache. "Fame is power," he says.

We drain the pitcher and I order another as Carl lectures us on his Triangle Theory, sounding like one of his columns in the Binghamton Sun-Bulletin. The three human ideals are sex, money, and power. If you have one point of the triangle you can acquire the other two. Politicians have power, so they can get sex and money. Actresses have sex, so they can get money and power. Rockefeller has money.

"You have fame," Artie says to Carl. "Everybody reads your column."

"Fame in Binghamton doesn't mean much. Debby hardly looks at me." As if on cue, the elfin waitress sways through the bar, and all eyes follow her path between the tables and back to the kitchen. "She likes Curt."

"She liked me for a few days." I laugh. "I don't have any of your three points."

Artie beams, "Your vampire likes you."

"She likes the way I punch input cards." Artie and Carl trade a wink. Angie helps me learn the computer system during night shift and sometimes our sessions extend until morning. But not tonight; she has a list of reports to run for Sherman.

A chair crashes on the floor. Two guys face each other with raised fists in the far corner. Chad Dixon and his younger brother, both drunk. At least they're fighting each other tonight instead of bothering anyone else. Mike taps me on the shoulder, and I follow him across the room.

The brothers dodge around a full pitcher in the middle of the round table, sloshing the beer across the gouged wooden surface and onto the floor. Mike rushes between them and I stand on the far side, across from Mike, my hands on my hips. "Sit down or I'll throw you out," Mike says. "And Curt here will drink your beer."

The younger brother wears a scar on his cheek and a checkered gray flannel shirt, torn at the shoulder. He smirks, breaking the stare with his brother and grabbing the back of a chair. He shrugs at Mike.

Chad turns to me. He's not a bad guy when he's sober, an infrequent condition. We were once on friendly terms until I grew tired of his explosions. Now his hatred radiates like a furnace. He shakes his head, and his baseball cap slides off his greasy forehead, flopping top down in a pool of beer. When Mike and I threw him out of the bar last week I gave him an extra shove and he landed in the gutter. He remembers.

He squares his shoulders. He wants to fight me, but he knows it's a bad idea, having tried it last week. He pushes his dirty black hair out of his eyes and squints, pointing his finger at me. He grins and reaches both hands into the front pocket of his stained sweatshirt. I catch the glint of a hilt and the bulge of a large hunting knife as he shifts the handle to his right side.

I force a smile, holding my palms open. "Why don't you sit down and finish your beer like Mike said?"

He glares and pulls out the knife, eight inches of polished steel. My combat training clicks in my mind. Rule one, wait for the right moment. Then act on reflex. Hesitate and you might be dead. I envision myself grabbing his wrist with my left hand, shoving the knife away, and slamming my right fist into his elbow, breaking his grip. He looks down at his knife. Now is the time.

I pause for a second, flashing back to my conversation with Artie and my tendency for violence. Maybe if I had tried to reason with him last week, it might not have come to this. I could try to talk to him now. Chad raises his eyes and locks mine, ready to slash, tilting the blade forward and cocking his wrist. I waited too long. The knife snaps toward me. Time slows as I follow the blade's trajectory and lean away, not fast enough.

A pinkish blur descends between Chad and me, smacking his arm before the point reaches my gut. Artie's leg. Chad's knife hits the floor and spins under the table. Artie lifts the leg and tries to catch his balance before lurching backward, crashing against a nearby table and sprawling on the floor. Debby screams, her voice echoing from far away, though she stands just behind Mike.

Chad yells in pain and reaches down for his knife. I swing my knee up into his jaw and slam the side of his head with my open hand, propelling him backward. He stiffens, extending his arms, trying to grab the air, falling like a tree. His head bounces off the floor like a chunk of firewood. Mike holds Chad's brother in place. I step around a chair and poke my foot against Chad's shoulder. He's done for the night, knocked out or passed out, breathing deeply. I snatch the knife and hand it to Mike.

Carl helps Artie stand up. A trickle of blood runs down his forehead where he caught the edge of the table. Debby runs up with a damp towel and dabs Artie's wound, telling everyone she called the cops. But Artie's fine and seems to enjoy Debby's soft touch. He straps on his leg and grabs the full pitcher. "I'm getting used to this leg," he says.

Sirens wail and soon two cops burst through the door, red and blue lights flashing through the dirty windows behind them. I step away from the table, hoping to avoid the law. I hate to see anyone arrested, even Chad Dixon.

Carl says, "Wait, I want to take your picture for the paper."

"Take Mike's picture," Artie says.

"Debby would be better," I call back to Carl. "She's the only point of your triangle in this place."

Artie retreats to the bar with his prize pitcher of beer. I accept one more glass in celebration, but I soon head home, planning to get to the dairy early, hoping to talk to Sherman.

I lie in bed trying to bury the events of the day, not happy about how I reacted to Sherman or Chad Dixon. Mostly my mind circulates around concerns about my anger, wondering if I should get an appointment in Oxford like Artie suggests. Thinking about the war doesn't make me angry but being reminded of it does. I never slept well in the jungle. After a few weeks, the sentry fire and mortar shots became hypnotic like white noise, though I always listened for enemy rifles, gaging their distance. When the pings grew closer, I awoke with a start. Some nights I still hear them closing in, even in the relative safety of my dingy apartment on Chenango Street.

I give up the watch around 5:00, knowing it will be a strong coffee day. I brew a thermos of thick mud and bounce Artie's Dodge across the gravel parking lot of the dairy just as the last of the night's shiny aluminum milk trucks drains its load into the holding tank, ready for the first shift foreman to switch on the bottling line.

Halfway through my thermos I finish punching my input cards from yesterday's shipments, leaving me a few minutes to play Asteroid on my monitor. Angie picked up the PDP-11 version of the game from one of her techie friends, but no one else knows it's on the network. She shared the secret with me.

After saving my last spaceship, I top off my caffeine with a cup of machine coffee from the break room and head down the corrugated stairway to the shipping dock. The truckers and warehouse guys in drab coveralls and the line workers in white aprons mill around, murmuring about the company meeting. Each group keeps to itself on two sides of the dock, like two colors of a chess set waiting for someone to load the game board. I pick out my friend Renee standing among the white figures, a queen among the overweight pawns.

Sherman sees me and he doesn't tell me to leave, probably avoiding a confrontation in public. He announces in a loud voice, "We're waiting for the office staff to show up."

I sit on a milk crate by the truckers, cradling my coffee.

The two elderly key punch operators from accounting shuffle through the warehouse door, and Julie sways in to join them. Finally Old Crowley himself steps carefully down the stairway and all talking stops.

He raises his thin voice, "I'm here to tell you the shutdown will last four weeks. We'll start up strong in mid-January and we'll have the best year ever, making up the slack."

The workers stare at him like he's a substitute preacher reading his sermon from a book.

When Crowley steps back, Sherman says, "We tried to avoid the shutdown, but we're hoping you'll enjoy the extra time with your families. I'm sorry it came to this."

Crowley gives him a cold stare and nods his head. He walks slowly to the stairway and the meeting breaks up.

Angie waves at me from the back of the crowd. She wears a black tee shirt and black jeans, unaffected by the frigid air on the dock. Her long black hair frames a pale face accented by deep red lipstick. Her small dark figure creates a wave in the crowd of white aprons heading to the bottling room, as if no one wants to get too close. She watches them pass with an amused smile.

"You're still working here," she says.

"Not officially." I glance at Sherman standing by my forklift answering questions from a few stragglers. "And you're working the day shift." She usually comes in after sunset.

"I want to show you how to run reports." Her intense gaze quickens my pulse more than my morning caffeine.

"Sure, but I can't do it first shift."

"Of course, but I'll be back on second shift tomorrow. Mail me and we'll set up a time." She gazes over my shoulder. "Curt's learning how to run reports."

I feel Sherman's bulk behind me as he says, "I think he's ready."

I turn to face him and Angie glides away toward the computer room.

He catches my eyes and I try to read his mood. My anger from yesterday simmers though Sherman seems okay with me learning reports. It could mean he decided not to fire me, but his somber expression dampens my hope.

"I wish you had moved those crates like I asked," he says in a measured tone.

My temperature rises. I throw back my shoulders and take a deep breath, fighting to control my temper, remembering how he told me I could leave early yesterday, but then he reneged. I hold his stare.

"I was mad at Crowley." He shakes his head.

I glance at my forklift and the pallets lining the cement block wall. "I could have handled it better."

"Don't do it again." He climbs the stairway to his office, pausing halfway to catch his breath.

COLD GOODBYE

Artie waits for me outside My Mother's Place on Friday night, leaning against a parking meter with his crutch tucked under his arm. He pulls a plaster cast out of his pocket and shows me the imprint of his gapped mouth.

"VA's getting me false teeth in two weeks." He spits a brown stream of tobacco juice into the gutter and checks the sky. "Smells like rain."

"I'm happy about your teeth, but you could have shown me inside where it's warmer. What about your new leg?" I glance down at his stump.

"Needs a refit." He shoves the cast into his jacket. "They sent Rich up to jail in Auburn today. Debby's in the kitchen crying."

I turn toward the bar door and Artie taps my shoulder. "Curt, you should forget about it and go home. You got your job back at the dairy. You don't need Debby messing you up."

"I won't stay long."

"Date with the vampire?" he winks.

"She wants to show me reports." I'm meeting Angie when she gets off work, though we're not planning to talk reports tonight.

"You should go to her now," Artie says.

We duck our heads as a cold, wet breeze blows up the street. "Artie, just because Rich is in jail like Mark doesn't mean I'll start up with Debby again. I can't keep up with her drinking and she wouldn't have me anyway."

"I know her. She'll want a big shoulder to cry on."

A thick raindrop splashes on my neck and rolls under my jacket. "How did Rich get busted?" I ask belatedly. For the past two weeks I tried to ignore Rich and Debby nuzzling in the bar like hamsters.

"She didn't say." Artie shrugs and turns up his collar as the spitting rain grows more persistent.

Back inside I order a pitcher of Genesee Ale for Artie and me. Debby's brother Daryl pushes through the kitchen door carrying two plates of burgers and fries, a sure sign Debby's in no shape to wait on tables. He stops behind our stools and taps my shoulder, pointing his chin toward the kitchen. I follow in his wake, ignoring Artie's wrinkled brow.

Debby leans against the stainless-steel refrigerator, her cheeks moist and puffy. She winds her arms around me like a straitjacket, then pushes me away, not far enough. "They took Rich from me," she mutters into my chest. "How can they do that? Take my men to jail?"

I stroke her curly auburn hair, recalling our short fling. She went back to her old boyfriend Mark quicker than a flipped switch when he came home, and I got fired for showing up drunk for work. She and Mark lasted about three weeks, the standard half-life for her romances, igniting with a flash and decaying like spent fuel. But I never felt the full decline, still stuck in that first moment with her, trying to forget it and seal it away. Gathering my willpower, I gently unwrap her arms and step back.

"I'm sorry," I whisper, thinking I should say something.

She stands up on tiptoes, reaching around my neck again, and I don't stop her. She shivers slightly, irresistible. I stare into her wide brown eyes shining with tears, catching a reflection of my own eyes. "Can you give me a ride home?" she asks softly. "Daryl says I can leave early. I'll make it up to him tomorrow."

Despite her normally playful demeanor as barmaid and Mother's prime attraction, Debby always knows what she wants. Part of me hopes it's just a ride home, but my internal voice weakens the longer I stand there. I glance at her brother who nods his assent, though he doesn't look happy about it. Not sure if he's thinking about cooking and serving tables himself or about Debby and me. "I walked here."

"You can drive my car. I don't want anyone to see me like this."

"Sure, I'll walk back."

She plants a wet kiss on my cheek, and I trudge out to the bar to pick up my jacket. Artie tips his forehead, following my route to the coat rack and back to the kitchen like I'm a losing boxer going out for the last round.

At Debby's apartment she lures me inside with a promise of Genesee Ale. One beer and then I'll leave. As soon as we step inside, she drops her damp jacket, and our arms twist together, breath and pulse rising in the same rhythm. She shivers again and I know I'm lost, our clothes falling off like molted skin.

We never make it to the bedroom, making love and lying for hours on her Persian carpet, sprawled on piles of pillows, our elbows and knees knocking the growing scatter of beer cans, until I finally doze off, unable to match Debby's thirst.

I wake up cold and alone, no clothes, no blanket, legs hooked under the coffee table, stiff and thoroughly drunk. I hear Debby's peaceful snores from the bedroom and the soft ticking of her wall clock. Past one. I dress and stagger out the front door, leaving Debby asleep like she left me, but at least she's warmer.

I walk quickly toward the Exchange Street Bridge, icy rain falling heavily and running down my neck. The brim of my Yankee cap provides my only protection, the deluge soaking through my jacket, sneakers squishing. The waterfall below the Park Diner splashes high in the dim streetlights, its current under the bridge dotted with ice, looking like Beer River.

At Angie's door I pause, feeling even colder. Her apartment is dark, though I see a light in her bedroom when I knock. She cracks the door, clutching a black robe around her, hair tussled with sleep, face paler than usual, rinsed of makeup.

"You look terrible," she says.

"I messed up."

"You sure did." She pushes the door open.

"I was supposed to be here at eleven."

"You're frozen." She waves me inside.

I stand on the rubber mat, shaking with cold, as if her words drained the last heat from my wet skin. A puddle forms around my shoes.

"It was Debby, wasn't it?" she asks.

Nothing for me to say.

She strides back to her bedroom, pushing a lock of hair over her ear. I lean against the door frame, not wanting to sit down and soak her chair. Folding my arms against the shivers, I feel deeply tired, hardly drunk any more.

Angie crosses the living room, stopping halfway and throwing a black bath towel at me. I wipe my face and drape the towel across my shoulders.

Keys jingle in her hand when she returns dressed in jeans and a sweatshirt, pulling on a slick black raincoat. "Let's go," she says.

I follow her out to the carport and crawl into her Celica, covering the seat with the towel. She punches the knob of her cigarette lighter and waits for it to pop as the car warms up. We head back across the Exchange Street Bridge, the suds of

Beer River making me queasy. No words pass between us. She's quiet and determined like a deputy driving me to jail.

After she drops me off my hands quiver trying to hold my key steady. I pile my clothes inside the door and retreat to the bathroom, drawing a hot tub and throwing in crystals of the bubble bath Angie left a few nights ago. The bubbles are gone by the time I emerge, drying quickly and hustling to bed.

I spend the weekend drinking coffee in my threadbare chair, staring out at the rain slanting over the parking lot. I try to read a programming manual, hoping it will help me if Angie wants to show me reports. Normally I might walk down to Mother's on Saturday night, but the deep cold lingers in my bones. Maybe my desire for Debby has finally burned out, though I'm not ready to risk it. She'll forget about me when Rich gets out of jail, and maybe Rich will forget about me, too. He was never my best friend and he's more likely to blame me than Debby.

Monday afternoon after my shift on the forklift, loading milk crates onto delivery trucks, I head upstairs to punch computer cards with the shipment details. When I finish, I check my monitor one last time, seeing a message from Angie.

vmpire: gotta minute?

sure

vmpire: come down

on my way

I grab my fresh stack of punch cards and head to the computer room. The frigid air-conditioning wafts out the door as I step up to the raised white flooring. Angie swivels on her chair to watch me, her black tee shirt bulging with her full breasts, her face firm. She wears deep red lipstick, not smiling.

"You look better," she says.

I feel my face flush even in the chilled air. "I've been studying DB2 to learn reports."

"This isn't about reports." She taps the chair next to her and I sit down, staring at the monitor on her table. "I want to talk about Friday night."

I turn to face her.

She says, "We've been seeing a lot of each other."

I glance up at the vent in the ceiling, sucking out chilly air and making the room colder, thinking I hear the beginning of another goodbye. "I know you don't want a boyfriend."

"You have so many demons."

"You mean Debby."

She shakes her head. "Sure, I'm angry about that. But if you have a brain, and I think you do, you'll get over her." She reaches for her cigarettes and flicks her lighter.

Smoke curls toward the vent.

She follows my eyes upward. "You stare at the ceiling in the middle of the night."

"I'm listening."

"Listening for what?"

"An old habit."

"From Vietnam?"

I shrug my shoulders. "I don't want to bother you with my problems."

"There are other little things."

"They don't sound so little."

The air conditioner suddenly stops and smoke billows around her face with nowhere else to go. Her eyes glaze. "I think I'm falling in love with you."

My cheeks feel numb, trying to answer.

Angie leans toward me. "You can't say it, can you?"

"I'm not good with words. It's not you." The air-conditioner shudders on, chilling me inside out. "I mean, it is you."

She cups her face in her hands, her shoulders rocking, her cigarette forgotten. "I can't let myself do this," she cries softly, raising her eyes, black mascara running down her cheek.

I take her cigarette before it burns her fingers, dropping it in the ashtray and retrieving a tissue from the box on her shelf. I snatch one for myself, blowing my nose and dabbing the corners of my eyes. We hold our gaze for a long moment, until we finally shake hands awkwardly like diplomats.

Back home I return to my chair and the scenic view of the parking lot, sipping a can of Genesee Ale and then another. I grab the blanket off my bed, still feeling a chill.

Around eleven the phone rings, shaking me awake. I hear the morgue's air conditioner and the humming computer cabinet fans.

"Hey," Angie says.

"Did my shipping job run okay?" I ask, trying to guess the reason for her call.

"I'd tell you if it didn't." She exhales slowly. "I still want to show you reports."

I glimpse the manual lying face down on the floor. "Yeah, I want to learn reports."

"Later in the week. How about Thursday? Come down after your shift."

"Got it."

"Bye." She clicks off.

I pick up the DB2 book and check the beer cans around my chair. One sloshes and I swallow the dregs, trying to remember where I left off.

Drowning in Joy

Most guys come out of jail looking pale, but Rich flashes a tan like he just stepped off a Caribbean cruise. He saunters into My Mother's Place with Debby on his arm, heading to the bar stool between Artie and me while Debby splits off to the kitchen to prepare for her shift. Her quick glance tells me she hasn't told Rich about our short tryst when he was locked up in Auburn.

Rich stands 5-6, built like a small tank with a wide frame and arms like iron pipes. He has hardly any neck. His shoulder muscles wrap around the base of his head like a thick weld. His red hair is shorter now and his mustache trimmed, his Yosemite Sam appearance lost on the floor of the prison barbershop. He flashes a warm, toothy smile and focuses his steel blue eyes. "Great to see you, Curt," he says to me.

I wave to Mike the bartender for another glass and fill it from my pitcher of Genesee Ale. "Welcome home."

Artie and I catch him up on the news of the past week, every subject except Debby, and I wonder if he'll tell us why they threw him in jail. I order another pitcher.

Around eight, Freddy enters the bar and circulates between tables with a handful of betting slips, balancing a cigar stub between his lips. In his old gray jacket and brown knit cap, he resembles a boulder, but he rolls softly. Everyone gives him space. He passes the bar and hands Artie a slip listing the NFL games and odds for the week. Artie winks and Freddy shakes his head, fishing a pencil stub out of his pocket before he moves on.

"Need to ask you a favor," Rich whispers, leaning toward me. "Well, two favors."

"You always say football bets are for losers."

"Nah, I was hoping you'd lend me fifty bucks. I'm starting back at my construction job, but it's a week until payday."

"Sure." An ace carpenter, Rich is good for the money, and I'm feeling guilty about Debby.

Artie looks up, his radar pinging at the mention of money in case some might fall his way. "Crowley Dairy's shutting down for the holidays," he says to Rich. "Curt will be short of cash."

I shake my head at Artie's fatherly intervention and Rich smiles. "Don't worry, I won't let him starve."

Artie goes back to plotting his football bet and Rich casts his attention toward the corner of the bar near the pinball machine. His voice returns to a whisper. "Is that the Mexican that sells pot?"

"Eduardo. He's a nice guy."

"You buy from him?"

"Sometimes. Is that your second favor?"

"Yeah, can you get me some weed? We could split a bag." He flashes a tight grin. "But you'll have to front it."

I nod. Another twenty bucks, though I'll have smoke for the holidays. I cross the bar and wait for Eduardo to finish his Royal Flush pinball game. He earns two extra balls and gives me a high five. When the last ball drops, he turns to me.

"Having trouble with my car," I say.

"I'll check it out." He heads out the back door near the kitchen.

I wait a few minutes and follow him into the alley, trading him a rolled up twenty for the Baggie.

"You want to try it?" he asks.

"Not tonight. I trust you."

Back at the bar I shove the ounce into Rich's jacket. "Split it later."

Artie pretends not to notice. "Eduardo has a nice family. Cute wife and two kids."

Rich snorts. "Wetbacks breed like rabbits."

I push my change to the back of the bar and chug my last swallow of beer, not wanting to hear another of Rich's racist rants.

He shakes his head. "My wetback boss in Ithaca got me sent up."

"We were wondering," Artie says, filling our glasses as I sit down.

"Sucker had it in for me because I earn white man wages. Everything's my fault. I should have known the cement was too wet. Should have known the frame was out of square. I used too many nails. Shit, I was a carpenter when he was chasing bulls down in Mexico." Rich glances at Artie and me. "Then one Friday, payday, he's avoiding me. I ask another foreman what's up and he tells me Jose's about to fire me. That's why he's avoiding me. Little coward."

He pauses for a sip of beer. "Later I see him walking up the ramp to the first floor just as I'm heading down with a twelve-foot two by four. He looks away like I knew he would, and I swing sharply to the left to avoid a stack of plywood. The two by four smacks him in the side of the head, knocking him off the ramp into a pool of mud." Rich erupts with laughter. "Funniest thing I ever saw. Rubbing his head and trying to stand up. Falling on his ass in the mud."

Rich slaps my back.

"Was he hurt?" I ask. I spy Artie's blank expression over Rich's shoulder.

"Nah, he's screaming mad, fires me on the spot. It was worth it. Then a cop shows up at my door with a warrant for assault. Just like him to send a cop to do his dirty work."

"Sounds like an accident," I reply.

"That's what my lawyer said but the judge didn't agree."

I shake my head.

"When I saw my lawyer this morning, all he did was stare at Debby." Rich grins. "So the guy's not stupid."

"Was it an accident?" I ask.

"He should have watched out." Rich shrugs his shoulders. "He never should have crossed me in the first place."

Freddy steps up behind me, dropping a meaty hand on my shoulder. Turning to face him, I almost bump the unlit stub of his cigar, catching the peat moss aroma. "Can I see you a minute?" he says in his raspy voice.

I slide off my stool and Artie pushes his betting slip and two bucks toward Freddy who shoves the money in one jacket pocket and the slip in another. Eyes follow us to the front door, Freddy's status rubbing off on me like I'm a chauffeur for a movie star.

Outside we duck under the awning of the hardware store next door as fat snowflakes carpet the sidewalk. Freddy lights his cigar with a silver lighter, takes one puff and gives up. "Sorry about the dairy," he says. "I heard about the shutdown."

"Only a few weeks."

"Sure." He waves his hand like he's clearing smoke. "I can use some help."

"Football's almost over." When Freddy was sick in October, I picked up football bets and paid off winners. He threw me a nice tip. "Horses?"

"Nah, the horse game is dying. Betting's legal in New Jersey." He shrugs. "I don't want you to sell cars either. I'd hire you for construction. But I have other ideas."

I nod slowly, not sure what I'm getting into.

Freddy catches my eye. "Big guy like you and smart, there's things you can do. Maybe you stand next to me when I talk to people."

I stare back at him, pondering what to say. I can use the cash.

"You wouldn't have to do anything, just stand there."

"Okay, maybe I'll help you out."

"You won't regret it." He coughs and slaps my arm. I turn to head back into Mother's, but he stops me. "Friendly advice. Stay away from Rich."

"He just got out of jail."

"He didn't go to jail."

"He said he assaulted a guy in Ithaca."

"Maybe he did, but he didn't go to jail. He busted seven people in Ithaca, all Mexicans. You can read the paper, five for marijuana and two illegals. They went to trial this week. Guy's a narc."

I lean back against the widow of the hardware, recalling the news article. "Hard to believe."

"Believe it." Freddy flicks his lighter and his stub smolders. "If he asks about pot or anything else, play dumb."

"I just bought an ounce for him."

Freddy shakes his head. "Don't do it again."

"He could have me on a felony."

"He might be after Eduardo. Word is he's a mean shit but he protects his friends."

I watch Freddy's cigar go out, feeling a chill.

He clears his throat and stares at the butt like a misbehaving child. "I don't think the DA will bother with an ounce."

"Less than an ounce if I split it with him." I shrug. "I gave him the whole bag."

"Might be entrapment anyway." Freddy drops his lighter into his pocket, the one with the betting slips. "I can't help you. Rich is a fed. Glad I'm not in that business."

He slaps my arm again and we head back inside.

I take my stool between Rich and Artie, ears ringing from my conversation.

"What did the boss want?" Artie asks with a wink.

"Offered me a construction job on some apartments he's building in Endwell."

"They look good from the highway," Rich says. "Union job but I'm not a union man."

"Freddy is," Artie says. "You quitting Crowley?"

"Only working for Freddy during the shutdown," I reply. "I want to keep learning computers at the dairy."

Debby drops her empty tray on the bar, and we all turn to watch her. She steps behind Rich and rubs his thick shoulders, swinging her head back and forth, waving her auburn hair, her fingers barely making a dent. Good time for me to leave.

I take a long way home, walking past the closed storefronts draped in tinsel, and across the Court Street Bridge. I stop to stare at the gray Chenango River reflecting streetlights and windows in wavy patterns, a liquid city with shapes joining and separating like dreams or worse. I turn up my collar to the chill and stuff my hands in my jacket.

Maybe Rich is after Eduardo, a dealer and a Mexican, even if he grew up in Scranton and doesn't even speak Spanish. I see the faces of Eduardo and his family, standing like human shields between me and jail. If I warn him, Rich might turn his attention to me, especially if he finds out about my one-night stand with Debby. If he knows what Freddy told me, he might bust me to protect himself. I spit into the water, my wad disappearing in the slush. I wonder who else he threatens.

The current swirls under the streetlights, peaceful for now, but Rich looms like an ice jam upriver, ready to burst any minute and flood our dreary town.

I spend the next few days at home studying computer manuals and preparing for the dairy inventory. When I asked Angie if I could help, she winked over her shoulder and returned her attention to her terminal, not the warmest response though it's all the motivation I need. Saturday night I take a break and walk to Mother's where I find Rich talking and Artie drinking his beer. Artie listens to anyone with a full pitcher.

"The joint serves ground beef every meal," Rich says, nodding at me when I sit down. "Meatballs, breakfast sausage, sloppy Joes, Salisbury steak, anything but a real hamburger. All tastes the same. I draw the line at tacos and burritos. I've eaten enough of that Mexican shit."

"Not much Mexican food around here," Artie says. Mike shows up with a fresh glass and I ask for a pitcher of Genesee Ale.

"Just wait, the Mexicans are coming," Rich replies. "What about you, Curt? You like beaner food?"

"I stick to the four basic food groups--canned, frozen, pizza and beer. And coffee."

"You eat yogurt. Saw it in your fridge along with the beer cans."

Artie purses his lips and shifts his tobacco plug to his other cheek. "Yogurt sounds disgusting."

My pitcher appears and I pour myself a glass, refilling Artie and Rich. Artie hops off to the bathroom, wending between tables on his crutch and one leg like a surfer.

"Been wanting to talk to you," Rich says in a low, serious tone.

Here it comes, the Debby talk. I sip my beer and look up.

He continues, "You think that spic that would sell me a pound or two?"

"Never asked if he sold quantity."

"Would you try for me?"

I shrug my shoulders, heart pounding, remembering Freddy's warning. I search his eyes. He might want to bust Eduardo or both of us. "You don't need me."

"You're right, I can buy it myself. I got an advance from my boss. I can pay you back, too."

"No worry."

"Can you talk to him, though? Set it up."

"Sure, I'll talk to him."

He slaps my shoulder. "You're a great friend."

Artie returns, followed by Debby. She plants a juicy kiss on Rich's cheek, carefully avoiding his mustache. She wears tight blue slacks and a ruffled white blouse. Brass hoop earrings hang below her curly auburn hair and her makeup is fresh. She smells like a spring garden. I glance away.

"I'm going dancing at Pearl's," Rich announces proudly.

"What about me?" Debby replies with a cute pout. "I'm going, too."

"Of course you are. You're my woman." Rich returns her kiss and they hug, caressing one another's back. Their cloying exchange makes me burp.

Soon enough they leave and Artie I and return to our beer.

"Mike washed the windows," Artie says.

I swing my eyes toward the sidewalk where the dim streetlights shine brighter than usual. A silhouette crosses my view and pulls open the door. Eduardo heads back to the pinball machine. I wait a few minutes until he's alone.

"How's your car running?" Eduardo asks, shaking my hand.

"Good for now. How's the family?"

He shows me a new snapshot of his wife and two girls taken at the mall photo booth with its faded khaki curtains.

"The older girl's almost ready for school," I say.

"That's Maria. Our baby's Janet, and my wife Linda. Now you know everything about me." He shoves the billfold back into his jeans and scans the room.

"I know you sell car parts. Got a friend who wants to buy a car."

"Sounds like he should talk to Freddy," Eduardo smiles. Freddy sells two or three cars a year from his used car lot on Chenango Street.

"Freddy doesn't have the car he wants."

Eduardo nods. "Who we talking about?"

"Rich."

"I've seen him. Not very friendly. He's a friend of yours?"

"He talks about you a lot."

"Talks about me?"

"Yeah, and he has other friends."

"What do you mean?"

"Might be time to sell your parts someplace else."

Eduardo stares at me, disbelieving. He cracks a smile and I hold my blank expression, finally turning away.

Back at the bar Artie says, "What was that all about?"

"Doing a favor for a friend."

A few minutes later, Eduardo pushes open the front door and exits into the blowing snow.

Later in the week a suit from Poughkeepsie appears at the dairy. I'm supposed to show him how to enter shipping data into the computer and run my nightly jobs. I feel like a celebrity for about five minutes until I realize I'm training him to do my job. My boss says they're only shutting down the Binghamton plant and shifting the work to Poughkeepsie for four weeks. I don't trust bosses any more than I trust the law.

After work I head to Mother's where Artie coaxes me into buying a pitcher. The bar has a festive air with tiny Christmas lights strung above the dusty bottles behind the bar, and Mike sprayed snowflakes on the outside windows. He even taped a pine branch above the cash register. Eduardo misses his 8:00 round.

Rich arrives late, spinning on to the stool next to me. He glances toward the pinball machine and says to me in a measured tone, "I see the trainer but no monkey."

"Good to see you, too, Rich."

He looks across my chest at Artie, his foul mood drawing attention, drinkers pausing to watch. "Some guys think they do the right thing, but they fuck it up."

Artie catches my eye.

Leaning back, Rich slaps sixty bucks on the bar. "They think they know what's happening, like they have it all figured out. Right, Curt?"

I catch his glare and send it back. "What if I do?"

"You should have known better." He stands and zips his jacket. "Good thing for you I never hurt my friends." He pushes his way across the bar and shoves open the door, sending a cold draft across the room.

Mike appears in front of me and slides the twenties my way. He scans the bar. "Show's over." He grabs his bar rag and wipes the varnished wood until the gawkers return to their glasses.

"I don't think Rich is coming back." Artie spits into a paper napkin.

"What about Debby?"

"Moving up. Someone saw her eating dinner at Morey's with Rich's lawyer, Jensen."

"Has a mansion down on Front Street."

"That's him."

I slide one of the twenties back across the bar and wave for another pitcher.

"Season of joy," Artie croons at my gesture.

"Yeah, I'm drowning in joy."

HEX

THE POET AND THE PRINCESS

A poster taped near the door of Swat Sullivan's pub advertises my once friend Allen presenting "An Evening with Allen Ginsberg." Allen resembles the famous poet, though he trimmed his curly beard and wild locks when he took his teaching job at Columbia.

His move back to the city from Binghamton strained our friendship, and it was further twisted by his shoestring catch of Mona after she and I broke up. I forgave him Mona, but when he started seeing Chelsea, my next girlfriend, I wanted to feed him a few poetry books.

I brush past the poster and head inside to order the dinner special served on Irish Saint Days. Every day is an Irish Saint's Day according to the calendar hanging above the bar, but the meal's always the same: beef and vegetable pie with a crust of mashed potatoes and toasted cheese, cheap and filling. The menu claims the rich gravy is fortified with Guinness, though I doubt they waste precious stout on a shepherd's pie.

Popular among the college crowd for literary gatherings, peaty smell, and old oak, the Irish dive makes the students feel poetic, inspiring the odd brogue you often hear around town, a New York City accent with rolling r's and guttural vowels.

Chewing through my bowl of carrots, onions, and small cubes of meat followed by two pints, I try not to dwell on Allen and Chelsea, having suppressed their memory for the past several months, keeping myself busy driving my forklift at the dairy and trying to learn computers. But their images reemerge from the thick broth like failed saints looking for spare change.

On the night of the event, none of my friends from Crowley Dairy agree to join me. It's not the poetry as much as the cost of beer, inflated by the dark woodwork. The dairy shutdown has everyone worried about money. I decide to go alone.

Staring into the low lights and hanging smoke, I spy Allen with his back to me, sitting at a table of younger folk wearing the fresh clothes of students. I scan the crowd for a glimpse of Chelsea's ever-present red beret to no avail and return my eyes to Allen's table, apprehensive about meeting him.

As if on cue, the woman sitting next to Allen swings her head toward my tall frame, and my ears begin to ring, a warm numbness rising in my arms and legs like I just lowered myself into a bath. Her shiny black hair radiates around her smooth face in the dim light, accenting the high cheekbones of a model with glistening dark eyes, pink lips, and a deep tan. Her poise reminds me of a painting I once saw, an idealistic portrait of a Native American princess, ethereal, untouchable.

When she taps Allen's arm, he jumps up, hand extended. His bushy black hair has grown back, enhancing the Ginsberg-like effect, and the princess follows in his wake. Now I know why Chelsea skipped the trip.

"Curt, it's been too long," he says, wrapping me in a bear hug. His head comes up to my chin, so I grip his shoulders in return.

"Looks like you're thriving in the city," I reply, though my gaze cycles back to the princess. Her aura feels even stronger up close. I wonder how Allen can keep his wits.

"This is Lorraine. My student at Columbia," Allen says with a hint of pride.

She gives me her hand, squeezing gently, hardly extending across my palm. "Allen told me about you. He says you're the strongest man he's ever met."

"He just wants me to move his books."

"All my books are downstate," Allen chimes in.

Lorraine cocks her head. "Your books are everywhere."

"I need a beer," I say, breaking away with a smile and heading to the bar to order a Guinness. Allen waves me to the table with his students and they find me an extra chair. Soon he rises for his performance. Allen's mesmerizing chants are even better than I remember, and he has added a small twanging instrument Lorraine identifies as a harmonium, just like the real Ginsberg.

He ends with a poem about seeing Walt Whitman in a supermarket, wincing and cooing as he squeezes imaginary peaches, very funny. The students encourage an encore before he finally returns to the table. An Irish folk band ascends the small stage, leaving few decibels for conversation. Unable to talk, we stare at one another like statues.

On a whim, I invite Allen to my apartment, though I haven't cleaned it recently. He doesn't care, sounding like the old Allen, but I worry about Lorraine once she states her intention to join us. After spending the evening at the same table, I can now talk to her without sweating, but my apartment might turn her off.

Once there, she hardly notices my shaggy dwelling, drinking her way through Genesee Cream Ales like she just returned from a week in the desert, leaving Allen and me far behind. While I listen to Allen's latest obsession with Kerouac, her alluring eyes glaze over and close. She rocks back in my one armchair, as Allen and I watch from our perches on the floor. She sits up abruptly and I point her toward the bathroom.

We watch her sway across the room and gently pull the door shut behind her with a squeak. The old wooden door needs a new coat of paint. I often wonder if the layers of chipped enamel hide oak panels, but it's not my door to strip. Allen's still savoring his last vision of Lorraine, her scent lingering in the air, when I ask, "What's Chelsea say about her?"

"Lorraine's not what you think. She's just a student."

"Chelsea doesn't know?"

He shrugs. "Lorraine heard I was driving up to Binghamton and asked for a ride." When he sees I don't believe him, he smiles. "She says she's part Iroquois. I think she's an Iroquois goddess, a reminder to us mortals that beauty still exists even in these dire days, a gift from the Great Maker." He punctuates his rant with an index finger jabbed into my forearm. "A gift for you."

"Might be too much for me," I reply, considering her brains as a Columbia student in addition to her striking appearance, but I warm at the thought.

"Well, you know Chelsea's stronger than me. I can't risk making her mad."

"She didn't want to come?" I'm still suspicious.

He shakes his head. "You haven't heard. She's taking care of her sister's teenage daughter, imagine that. With caretakers like us, poor Heather will never get out of therapy."

"Rose, that's her sister, right?"

"She's the stable adult in the mix of that family unit. She deserves a few days in Atlantic City without Heather." He rescues a tiny roach from the ashtray.

"I'll roll a fresh number." I slide my Aja album onto my lap and sweep a few pinches of weed into an unbleached wheat straw rolling paper, my nod to healthy smoking.

Allen takes the joint as I retreat to the kitchen with empty cans and return with three cold Genesee Cream Ales. Our evening feels like the old days, just the two of us, with one exception.

"Wonder what happened to Lorraine?" I ask.

"We should give her some privacy." Allen shifts back and forth on the beanbag and manages to gain his feet. "But she's been in there a while." He totters to the bathroom door and knocks softly. Hearing no response, he shrugs and returns.

"Any smell?" I grin. I can tell Allen's thinking the same thing. Hard to believe the goddess has normal excrement.

"She's young and strong, what could happen?"

I slip Steely Dan out of the sleeve and pop it onto my turntable. "We'll give her until 'Deacon Blues.'"

"Do you think that's wise?"

"You're the doctor."

"Modern literature. If Kerouac were in the can, I'd know what to do."

We soon lose ourselves in the jazzy, exotic ballads, pulling us inward like a trance. I relight the joint and wash my throat with beer, wishing I could play the saxophone. Allen taps the rhythm on the orange crate in the center of the living room, and both of us steal occasional glances at the bathroom.

I stand up with my joints cracking. "It's time."

"What about 'Deacon Blues?'"

"That was 'Deacon Blues.'" I stride toward the door and knock. No answer.

Allen appears at my side. "Lorraine, it's Allen. Are you all right?" He raises his hand, gesturing for me to wait, but it's been too long. She might be in trouble, who knows what.

Nudging Allen aside, I push open the door.

Lorraine sits on the toilet, her head cradled between her knees, one hand clutching a mass of toilet paper. Stepping around her to give Allen room to enter, we stare at her immodest position, unsure what to do. I check for the rise and fall of her shoulders. Her jeans and yellow lace panties lie on the floor around her ankles.

"She passed out," I whisper.

"Do you think we should resuscitate?"

Glimpsing at Allen's knitted eyebrows and intense glare, I burst out laughing. Allen joins in and our snorts fill the tiny room, though Lorraine doesn't quiver. Gaining my senses, I pull myself together. What if she wakes up and sees two men standing around her half-naked body?

"We have to move her."

"Move her?" Allen croaks. I can tell he's echoing my concern. Moving her means we must touch her.

"We can't leave her sitting on the throne all night." With that, we share a brief laugh.

"I've had this dream before." Allen shakes his head. "But it doesn't feel the same."

"Okay, I'll lift, and you pull up her jeans." Reaching around her shoulders, I slide my hands under her armpits and twist her around so I'm behind her back, her head rocking on her chest. As I raise her limp body forward, her sweater rides up her sides. Her curves are everything I imagined. Allen's hands quiver as he lifts her panties and then her jeans, pulling up the zipper and leaving her belt unfastened.

He sighs. "I can't believe she's still out."

"Help with her legs."

Lorraine is heavier than I expected, but we squeeze her back through the door, across the living room, into the bedroom, and onto my bed. I pull the covers over her.

"Guess I'm staying the night," Allen says as we return to our spots on the living room floor.

"Where were you planning to stay?" When he doesn't answer, I add, "Extra blankets in the closet." He claims the beanbag and I get the pile of floor pillows. Our lumpy accommodations are only tolerable because of the beer.

Allen shoots a lingering glance at the bedroom door. "Tell me you're not tempted."

"Of course, but it's illegal," I say, already falling asleep. "Besides the necrophilia."

"Thanks," he chuckles. "Now my dream is a nightmare."

After a few minutes, Allen says, "You shifted closer to the door because you're worried about me sneaking into the bedroom." He groans. "You should be."

"Maybe you should watch me."

"I trust you."

Ever the optimist. Before I can frame a retort, I drift off.

Way too early the next morning I hear water running in the kitchen. I find Lorraine rummaging through my cabinets and refrigerator, searching for food. The coffee pot sits over a flame on the stove. "What do you eat?" she asks.

"Should be some yogurt. Maybe some corn flakes."

She purses her lips and keeps hunting. She looks like she just stepped out of a movie poster, the princess I first saw at Swat's. No hint of a hangover, the blessing of youth or constitution. She even retouched her makeup. I excuse myself for a shower, thankful today is my day off.

When I return Allen's sitting in the kitchen with his head propped on an elbow. Lorraine is rearranging the cabinet above the stove where I keep my baking supplies, most of them prehistoric. In a circle around three unmatched coffee mugs in the center of the table, she placed a cracked bowl half-filled with cornflakes, two cups of yogurt, both blueberry, a jar of peanut butter, and a few slices of white bread in their wrapper. I wonder if she excavated the toaster yet.

Hearing me enter she turns with a radiant smile. "You look better," she says.

Allen shrugs, "Better than me, for sure."

"You're a poet," she replies.

"There's a poem in this somewhere."

"Famous New York professor channels Allen Ginsburg," I chant, trying to sound like Allen. "Wows the crowd at Swat Sullivan's with his Howl."

"Overflowing with Guinness," Allen adds. Usually, he swells with metaphors, but his hangover must have dulled his muse.

Lorraine pours the coffee, extra dark. "Well, I loved that place."

"Swat's is one of the best," I say, curious how much she remembers. I can tell Allen's more worried than me since Chelsea might not believe his tale of altruism.

"Nice of you to let me stay here." Lorraine flashes an unnerving grin, and I scan her clear eyes. She must know some of what happened. She woke up under the blanket with her clothes on. She might remember enough to swear out a complaint.

"My pleasure." I grab one of the yogurts.

"When are we leaving?" she asks Allen.

His eyes shift between her and me. I know he planned to stay the weekend in Binghamton.

She persists, "I have to finish my term paper."

"Your professor will give you an extension," Allen replies.

"You wouldn't do that."

Allen peers out the window. "Guinness drank and curtains drawn, the poet sputters back to New York."

"Should I pack you both a peanut butter sandwich?" I ask.

Shaking his head, Allen says, "No, but now you owe me a visit."

A SURE BET

Distrustful of phones, Freddy summons me through Artie. Most days Freddy works out of his downtown office, the old green Buick in the back of his used car lot on Central, but he's sick. When I stop by Mother's, Artie passes me a verbal invitation to Freddy's house, a red brick mansion framed with dark hardwood from the last century and double stained-glass doors behind a marble walkway and steps.

Wearing my patched blue jeans and sweatshirt, I expect an alarm when I lift the brass knocker.

Freddy answers the door, so pale he could drop dead. A large man, he wheezes and ushers me into an open ceiling living room about the size of a cathedral with a flagstone floor. Just off the atrium an oak door leads to a plush office with tall windows overlooking the brown front lawn and a hedge of bare lilacs. He waves me to a leather chair and coughs into an embroidered white handkerchief.

If this were my parent's house the chairs would be covered with plastic, especially with a guest dressed like me. The contrast with his Buick's cracked upholstery always leaves me speechless. I know Freddy's well off from his various businesses, though he conceals his wealth like the tsar visiting his estates disguised as a serf. One of his trademark cigars rests on an ornate brass ashtray, unlit.

"Curt," he grumbles, coughing again. "I asked if you wanted coffee."

"Yeah, coffee, sure." His voice and his cough are only a few notes apart on the gravely scale of his tortured vocal cords.

A small, elderly woman in a yellow pant suit appears next to me. Her stealthy approach marks her as a servant, not the trophy wife I've heard about. Freddy nods and she retreats as silently as she came.

Picking up the cigar with one hand, he raises his double chin to ask if I want one. I decline more for my health than his. Freddy smokes cigars strong enough to break up a street riot. He pulls a hard cover notebook out of his desk and slaps it on the table. Licking his finger, he flips to the middle and secures the front pages with a rubber band. "Those are not for you," he says.

"Got it," I reply, having gone through this ritual before.

"You know the horses. Now we got dogs. Same as horses, just smaller." His chuckle ends in a deep cough.

"And no jockeys." My weak joke earns a shrug as the yellow pant suit reappears with a tray holding a blue enameled coffee pot, matching cups, saucers, sugar, and cream. She pours our coffee and disappears.

"I heard we're getting competition." Freddy leans his cigar in the ashtray and heaps three scoops of sugar into his cup, stirring with the sugar spoon. He sips and blinks, "Let me know if you hear anything."

Taken aback, I agree with a nod. Freddy seldom reveals any details about his business. I wonder if he's testing me to see how I respond, trying to assess a role for me in the unspoken hierarchy of his empire.

He raises his head and locks my eyes, confirming my suspicion. "You're a good man."

Hearing his usual signal that we're finished, I sit up straight.

"Drink your coffee."

I help myself to the heavy cream. "You have the slips?"

Shaking his head, he rasps, "My brain's filled with snot." He retrieves an old blue cloth bag with barely readable yellow letters: "New York Bank".

Inside I find two wads of betting slips secured by paper clips, last week's and this week's, and a fold of bills.

"Count it," he says.

Two hundred dollars in twenties, fives, and ones. Less than usual.

Freddy taps the notebook. "Should be enough."

Each wager is recorded in Freddy's proprietary code. Recalling the scores for last Sunday, I crack a smile. "Maybe we'll have a lot of losing Jet fans again."

"Take a few extra percentage points for yourself," he wheezes and grins. "Not too much."

"Thanks, I can use it." With the dairy shut down I have no paycheck, not even free milk. I occasionally help Freddy with his business, but his illness is well timed, for me at least. My percentage comes out of the new bets, and Freddy will backcheck my math from the entries in his book. I'd never short him, not my thing, I've heard stories about some who tried.

"We still need to talk about your future."

I take a swig of coffee. Freddy's been trying to recruit me for a full time gig, though he's vague about the details. With the way things are going at the dairy, his request is becoming harder to turn down despite my second thoughts. I keep hoping the dairy will rebound, unusual in the local economy.

"But I'm too sick," he continues. "Damn weather feels like spring." He inserts his cigar in the corner of his mouth. "Too much fresh air."

I leave him staring at his silver lighter, unwilling to snatch it up.

After dark I make the rounds of the joints downtown, and Freddy's comment about competition makes me wary, scanning shadows for new bookies or thugs. Starting with Swat's for the cheap dinner crowd, I pick up a few bettors to pad my increased percentage, but the slips often sell themselves. Just walking into most bars with the New York Bank bag peeking out of my back pocket draws more attention than a TV ad, and my height helps. Everyone feels lucky on Wednesday night, long enough after the disappointment of last weekend and close enough to the renewed anticipation of payday. I violate the dress code at Pearl's with my jeans and sweatshirt, but the bouncer never messes with me, letting me escape with a wink before the live band drowns out conversation.

It's 8:30 when I push open the ancient door of Mother's, reinforced with steel strips. The door has been smashed so many times by drunks on both sides that there's hardly a block of unmarked wood larger than a fist. Daryl, the manager, keeps the door for ambiance.

Artie waves to me from the bar. I work my way around the tables before I slide onto the stool next to him. He wants me to buy a pitcher, as usual, and I don't disappoint. Several of Freddy's regulars in Mother's decline this week, even after I tell them the dogs pay better than horses. Mother's is my last stop so I can drink a few cheap Genesee Ales before I call it a night, and Artie is always my last slip, venturing his two bucks.

Even he declines, though he slurps the beer from my pitcher, always thirsty. I never understood how he could drink beer and chew tobacco at the same time, a well-honed talent, and he spits a brown stream into a spare glass as I turn my eyes away.

"I bought into a new business," Artie announces.

"For two dollars?"

His face clouds for a second. "This is serious."

I take a deep gulp, ears tuned to the hint of competition.

"The Southern Tier Investment Corporation."

"Sounds like a bank," I grin, imagining Artie with his yellow eyeballs and rosy, brown complexion as a bank director.

"You should think about it."

Carl calls from down the bar, "Very risky, my wife would kill me."

"You have to take risks to make money," Artie replies.

Blinking his bleary eyes to stay awake, Carl says, "Sounds legit but risky."

"Sure, it's legit." Artie turns back to me. "You could buy a share tonight. I have the paperwork right here." With his one foot he taps a manila envelope resting on the floor under his crutch.

"Bad time for me." I refill his glass and wave for another pitcher. "I don't even bet on football."

"Might be the best time." He winks at the New York Bank bag.

"You know whose money that is."

"Make eight times your investment in a matter of days." He adopts a serious tone, unlike his usual sloshy banter.

"Some horses pay eight to one." I reply.

"This is a genuine business."

"Okay, what are you selling?"

"Shares." He reaches down and grabs the manila envelope, flipping it onto the bar, avoiding the beer spills. "As my good friend, I want you to benefit."

I lean away. Artie's much too cagey to take risks with money, and his enthusiasm raises my suspicions. There must be an angle I can't see.

"You can make two thousand dollars!" he persists.

He slides out a Xeroxed chart that looks like a basketball bracket on its side, with handwritten names on each node. I notice a couple of blank ladder sheets underneath the top page.

He explains, "I'm supposed to fill one out for each of the next investors. When you buy your share, I give you a chart with this guy on top." He points at one of the two names in the second tier. "Then you make new charts for your investors with the next name on top. That's how it works. When your name gets to the top, the checks come to you!"

"That's you on the bottom line, under Debby?" I ask, trying to parse his explanation.

"Yeah, she already sold her two shares, so she earned her investment back."

"You paid her back?"

"No, half of my investment goes to her, and she forwards the other half to the investor at the top. She only has to sell two shares."

Debby is the fulcrum of everything Mother's. Her sexual allure flashes like a lighthouse, drawing customers to her family bar, always on the lookout for quick money to shortcut her dream of transforming Mother's into an upscale restaurant. She could sell anything to Artie and her magic sometimes works on me, though for me it's not financial. I declared myself immune to her charm, but I wonder who bought her second share.

Artie grins as I scan the investment ladder populated with several people I know. Five levels including the one node at the top, a binary progression, first chapter of my computer correspondence course. My quick math shocks me.

"You gave Debby 250 dollars?"

"Earlier tonight. Now I need to sell my two shares."

Artie pays everything with cash and protects his disability income like a Rottweiler. Occasionally on rent days I spot his roll of bills, his life savings, depleted now.

"I'm counting on you," he says, his voice trailing off. His eyes swerve to the sound of the kitchen door cracking open, and I fill in the blanks. Always inclined to protect Debby, Artie must have bailed her out after she bought into the scheme. Now he wants me to cover him.

"Love to help you, but I can't."

"Okay, will you come to our corporate meeting at least?" He taps the top of the chart. "Tomorrow night at the Radisson."

I glance down the bar to see if Carl's still listening, but his forehead's pressed to the bar. Debby slides by to remove his empty glass and he pops awake, looking around to make sure no one saw him pass out. All conversation stops, and not because of Carl. Debby's rocking gait between the tables is the show they came for.

"Who's the top dog?" I ask.

"You won't like it," Artie replies. "Your buddy, Anton."

"That asshole."

"I don't care. As long as I get my money."

On my way out, I stop to see if Carl needs a ride, but he says his wife's picking him up at eleven. His shift on the Sun-Bulletin news desk starts at seven in the morning. I swing by Freddie's mansion and drop the bank bag and updated notebook into the front door mail slot. The door responds with a slow rendition of Jingle Bells, sounding like a phantom's organ. I spy a light in the atrium and no other signs of life.

The next evening, I show up early at the Radisson Hotel, once the gem of downtown, having since endured many names and owners, most recently Holiday Inn. Inside I smell fresh paint and the ammonia scent of carpet cleaner before I see a black sign with white movable letters: "So Tier Ivest C0—Rm124."

A desk clerk with a red clip-on tie points me down a corridor toward the Garden Rooms, which overlook the parking lot. Passing a row of empty meeting spaces, I enter another hallway. Room 124 looks like a common hotel suite; must be a mistake.

I enter a double room with the beds removed and four rows of folding chairs facing a projector screen and an easel with a large white pad. Renee waves and skips over to brush a kiss on my freshly shaven cheek. As my friend from the dairy and Anton's girlfriend, I should have expected to see her.

Her wide smile gleams under blue eyes, and soft blond hair frames her long face. Anton does not deserve her, but they grew up together. I know their story by heart after the dozens of coffee breaks Renee and I shared, when she smelled like ice cream from the packaging line and I carried a cloud of sweat and diesel fumes from the loading dock. The last time I saw her we stood outside the Crowley gate holding our final paychecks before the Christmas shutdown.

"Are you joining the investment company?" She takes my hand and I see several people in the room staring at me with envy.

"Should I?"

She gives my fingers a quick squeeze and drops my hand, glancing at the faces around us. Her grin retains its radiance, though I detect a bit of strain at the corners. "People choose to join, or they don't. No pressure."

I try to read her eyes, but she turns away as Artie limps into the room. Everyone knows Artie and it takes him a few minutes to work his way down the greeting line to me. "Where's the refreshments?" he asks, but Renee fails to hear him, returning to the front where she piles manila envelopes next to the projector. Carl appears next to Artie's crutch and points to a cooler sitting on a low dresser.

"Can't be enough in there to fill your leg," Carl chants, echoing Artie's standing joke about how the beer he drinks drains into his missing appendage.

Artie leans his crutch against the wall. "We won't be here long then, will we?"

Taking my cue to fetch Artie a beer, I also grab cans for Carl and me, depleting the supply, though I commend

Anton's choice of Molson. Must be a high-class business meeting.

Anton enters through the adjoining room's front door carrying a pointer stick like a football coach. A stocky guy with a smart suit and slick black hair, Anton's thin lips roll into a sneer when he spies me in the back row. He quickly recovers and lifts his arms above his head and calls, "Welcome to the Big Game!"

To applause and a few cheers, Anton's resounding manner stokes the locker room energy. He flips on the projector to a photo of a Cape Cod mansion followed by a cruise ship and then a light blue Cadillac, the color matching Renee's Chevelle. Then a series of messages printed in large black letters on soft pastel landscapes-- Dedication, Perseverance, Honesty, and more--some of them featuring hazy highways and semis. He chants the titles with a clear enunciation like he's addressing the high school varsity. I realize these are probably the same slides his father uses to motivate his truck drivers.

The spell is broken when the door near me opens and Debby squeezes through with a giggle. Always attracting attention, she flashes an apologetic smile which reads more like a come on, and her spicy cologne fills the room like pollen. The woman in front of me elbows her husband to regain his attention, as she might in church. Sliding between Artie's chair and the wall, Debby bumps Artie's crutch and it thumps to the floor.

Once Debby finds her seat, eyes return to the screen, but the projector is off. Anton follows the plug to a yellow extension cord along the side of the room to an outlet near Artie's crutch. His eyes settle on me with an unfriendly glare, as if I unplugged it on purpose. I shrug, realizing I'm closest to the socket. Moving in slow motion, I stand and replace Artie's jacket, which had fallen from the back of his chair, pick up his crutch, and restore the plug after three tries. Bowing to the crowd, I return to my seat, dislodging Artie's crutch again, though this time its fall evades the outlet.

Anton curses as the projector enters its warmup cycle, forcing him to finish his presentation without images. His upbeat message is clear. We all have fun. We all get rich. Don't listen to anyone who says otherwise. They're lying. Listen to the investors who have already made it big. No mention of details like selling shares and their cost.

After one final cheer several investors gather around Anton. I'm the first to leave with Artie and Carl close behind, anxious to top off their beer at Mother's. I want to avoid Debby, especially after Carl admits he bought her second share.

"What about your wife?" I ask.

"I haven't told her yet."

Artie says, "I hope you won't have to."

I spend the next few days on the threadbare chair in my living room, trying to absorb the gist of a DB2 programming manual. When the dairy reopens, I hope to dazzle Sherman, my boss and earn a bit more time running computer searches, less time on the forklift.

I show up at Mother's for Monday Night Football, a sacred Binghamton ritual drawing a larger crowd than most churches. Although Freddy pushes the horses and dogs to expand his reach, football has the largest congregation.

Artie sits at a stool with a sullen expression. Never seen him so down, especially when he sees me, someone likely to stand a pitcher. The whole bar seems quieter than usual for a Monday night. I normally field a few last-minute wagers for the game, but no one approaches.

When the pitcher appears, Artie fills his glass. "I can't sell my two shares," he says with a sidelong glance.

"Wish I could help you."

He stares into his glass and tongues his tobacco wad into his cheek for another swallow of beer. "At this point, I wouldn't let you."

"Can't you sell your share back to Debby?"

"She says she can't. Already paid out. Then she'd be stuck."

I nod my head, knowing Debby's unlikely to part with the money even if she had it. "What about Carl?"

"He's under house arrest," Artie explains. "His wife."

"How's he supposed to sell his shares?"

"No one's buying."

I catch a hint of Debby's perfume and my hormones reflexively pick up. She appears behind us and pats Artie's shoulder like a mourner at a funeral. Batting her brown eyes to give me a clear signal that I should bail him out, she sweeps up an empty glass and sways toward the kitchen. She's smart enough to know her payoff depends on investors continuing to buy. I stay for the football game though there's not much fun in it this week.

Tuesday afternoon I return to Freddy's house after Artie conveys my summons. His cigar smolders in the ashtray, a sign he feels better, but he still wants me to make his weekly rounds.

After I recount the money in the New York Bank bag, I ask, "What do you know about the Southern Tier Investment Corporation?"

"Building outfit? Never heard of them." Freddy's business empire extends to the unions and his commercial construction company.

"Just investments."

"Investing in what?"

"Shares." I describe the scheme, relying more on Artie's manila envelope than Anton's slides. Freddy pushes the lit tip of his cigar around the ashtray like an artist painting a picture.

He waves his free hand to stop me. "Who's running this thing?"

"You know Anton?"

"Trucker boy. Sure, I know him." Freddy shakes his head. "Are you in?"

"No, can't afford it."

"Bad for business. Makes people afraid to bet." He eyes me as the swampish scent of his cigar blows into my face. I try not to flinch. "Someone always wins with football and horses, and you can try again next week. With a pyramid scheme only the first guys win. Everyone else gets hurt."

"Yeah, Artie, Carl…" I name a few others.

Freddy reaches into his massive oak desk for a rolodex and twists the knob. He calls out in his raspy voice, "More coffee please."

By the time his finger pauses on the card he wants, a fresh tray appears, along with a basket of wreath-shaped butter cookies sparkling with green sugar. He gestures me to pour and waves away the silver-haired server in her pink pantsuit. "Let's call Anton," he says.

Must be the trucking company phone line because it takes two requests to get him.

"This is Freddy." He pushes the speaker button, motioning me to stay quiet.

"Oh yeah, Freddy, what can I do for you?" Anton replies.

"How're your boys treating you?"

"The drivers? Good for now."

"I told your father he'd get a two-year contract."

"Good advice."

Freddy chuckles, "You can call it that." He leans back in his chair and takes a long puff on his cigar, rocking back and forth, waiting.

"Is everything okay?" asks Anton.

"Sure, but I've been hearing about this Southern Tier Investment Corporation." Freddy winks at me.

"Just a little side business. Just for fun."

"I like to know these things," Freddy says. "So do my friends in Scranton."

"You saying I need your permission?" Anton asks, beginning to fume.

"Did I say that?"

"It's legit."

Freddy laughs and ends with a cough.

Anton continues, "Are you threatening me?"

"Come on, Anton. I knew your father before he could drive." He takes a bite of cookie, wiping his fingers on a cloth napkin. "Two ways this could go. Now that I know about it, I have to tell Scranton. Or you can shut it down. If I were you, I'd do the latter."

I hear Anton's heavy breath on the speaker box. "Or what?"

Freddy calmly replies, "Come on, Anton, we're talking business here."

"Your friends in Scranton want to take over."

"You should listen to my advice."

"Okay, I heard you."

With that Freddy bids farewell and hangs up the phone. To me he says, "That was fun."

He offers me a Christmas cookie and I take one. He nibbles around the edges like he wants to eat the hole in the middle last.

When I finish chewing, I muse, "I don't believe him."

Freddy slides me a thick white business card embossed with his name in gold letters. "Bring that to Anton, so he doesn't forget." Freddy glances out the window like he's checking the weather. "Wait until tomorrow."

Nodding as I jam the bank bag into my pocket, I stand up to leave. Freddy raises his hand and I stop. He says, "I still want to talk about your future."

My apartment's only a few blocks away, but I bide my time as I pace from one streetlight halo to another, pondering my conversation with Freddy.

The next morning, I pull up to Anton's house at six, a bit earlier than the time I used to pick up Renee for our early shift at the dairy, the favor for her that pissed off Anton. I always admired his two-story ranch house with its lit walkways, aspen saplings, and coiffed lawn, and I miss the rides with Renee and her witty perspective on dairy gossip. Those mornings Anton was gone by the time I arrived, but today his cherry red double-cab pickup sits next to Renee's light blue Chevelle with its daisy decal. I timed my visit perfectly.

"Message from Freddy," I say when he cracks open the wide oak door and the aluminum storm door.

Stepping onto the porch, Anton lets the aluminum door slap closed, and Renee hovers behind the glass panel, wiping her hands on a dish towel.

He frowns as I shove Freddy's card toward him.

"What's this?" he bristles.

"Your contract."

He flips the card away.

"You promised to shut down your phony corporation and refund the money," I remind him. Freddy didn't say anything about refunds, but I bet he'd go along.

"I promised nothing." Anton puffs up and leans closer. He's thick and mean enough to intimidate most people, though he remembers what happened the last time he started a fight with me. "Now you're Freddy's lackey?" he sneers. "I thought he could take a joke. The STIC is just for fun."

"Not fun for people who can't afford it." I glimpse Renee behind her boyfriend, but she quickly looks away.

Anton replies, "People lose that much in Atlantic City every weekend."

"You heard Freddy."

Holding his stare, I smile with all my teeth.

He turns away and stomps his foot. Odd gesture, more like a toddler. Over his shoulder Renee continues to wipe her hands, twisting the towel and rewinding it, her long fingers never pausing as if kneading dough. As her friend, I wish she'd leave Anton for good, not for me—that moment is past—but I still covet her Chevelle. I watch Anton's back rise and fall, waiting for his reaction.

Finally, he twists his neck toward me. "You stay away from my house," he growls like a drill sergeant.

I return his glare. "Your choice."

Wednesday night I stop by Mother's, though Freddy has already passed through with the New York Bank bag, deciding at the last minute to make the rounds himself.

Despite the lingering cigar and cigarette smoke, the air breathes lighter as if Daryl opened all the old cloudy windows. No mention of the Southern Tier Investment Corporation, and Carl occupies his usual stool, released from house arrest. Artie buys me a glass of Genesee Ale for the first time in memory. He reads my somber expression.

"Your old girlfriend Renee came through," he mutters. "For me and Carl anyway. But I heard what Anton said."

"Renee deserves better," I reply.

Carl pipes in, "Rich guys always win even when they lose."

"Does Freddy know what Anton's been saying about you?" Artie's voice drops to a whisper.

I smirk. "Freddy's the one who told me."

"Is there anything you can do, or Freddy?"

"If people think I ratted to the cops about Anton's scheme, my denial only makes it worse." So would my first impulse, to bash my fist into Anton's snide expression. "Good thing Freddy's feeling better so he could make the betting rounds. He missed his hobby."

Artie spits into an empty cup. "Not good for you with the dairy closed."

"Wish there was a job at the newspaper," Carl adds.

"I'll be alright." I wave over Mike the night bartender to order my dinner and a pitcher, while I mentally rerun my talk with Freddy earlier in the evening. He hardly winced at Anton's lies as if he expected and even welcomed the rumors, freeing me from the betting slips. No one will trust me now, but Freddy has other tasks in mind, though vague. My response to his renewed offer of a permanent role was equally noncommittal. I still hope the dairy calls me back.

Carl picks up my tab and the Knicks win for once, further raising everyone's spirits, except for Debby. Wearing a pubescent pout under her dark eyes, she rakes in a windfall of tips to counter the loss of her pyramid payday.

PUNCH THE BUNNY

Over the phone yesterday evening Chelsea mentioned she was pregnant, but the long-legged teenager climbing out her back seat hardly resembles an embryo.

Bounding up the porch steps two at a time, Chelsea's passenger greets me with a bright smile. Her thick dark hair and smooth face resemble Chelsea, and I try to place her in my meager knowledge of Chelsea's family tree. As tall as Chelsea, she's lanky and tan, with a constellation of freckles under sleepy hazel eyes. She wears a tube top and shorts, her clothes so tight she might have pulled them on a year ago when she was a size smaller.

She holds out her limp hand like an actress. "I'm Heather, I so wanted to meet you." In her other hand a well-worn pink bunny stares cross eyed. Heather looks too old for the bunny, though I'm not one to question their relationship. They both penetrate my personal space, making me uncomfortable. Even with the cold December air piercing my T-shirt, I'm glad I took a shower.

I give Heather's hand a quick squeeze as Chelsea appears beside her. She wears her characteristic red beret, but her eyes have a tired glaze. She looks as used and beaten as the bunny after her early morning drive from New York City. From the edge of my vision, I glimpse her torso, but it's hard to discern a baby bump under her red coat.

"It's great to see you, Curt." She pulls down my head for a hug and a sisterly kiss.

"Come on inside," I reply, fighting off a shiver.

Throwing their coats on my threadbare armchair, Chelsea says, "I didn't know Heather was coming until last night. It was too late to call, knowing your work schedule."

"Dairy's shut down." I shrug.

"I forgot." She glances at Heather. "I hope you don't mind."

"My mom's shacking up in Atlantic City," the girl announces. I try to detect a hint of anger or remorse in her voice, but it sounds flat. She kneels in front of my orange crate and thumbs through my album collection.

"Heather's my niece," Chelsea explains.

Piecing the clues together, I recall hearing about Chelsea's older sister living in the East Village, her sister's on and off relationship with a jazz drummer, her acting career, mostly commercials so far, and his trips to rehab. Chelsea must have mentioned her niece. I had the impression that Chelsea and her sister were not close, though that might have changed after Chelsea started her PhD program at NYU.

"Plenty of blankets and a couple sleeping bags," I reply. "You're always welcome to stay here."

"You don't live in my building anymore."

"Doesn't matter, still the same blankets." I reflexively glance toward the closet. "But it seems like an odd time to sell real estate, Christmas week."

"She wants to start a school," Heather chants, sitting back on her heels. "For me."

Chelsea smiles warmly. "Of course, it's about you." She goes on to explain her ambition of starting a private school, that much she told me last night, and how she will finance it by selling her three converted Victorian apartment buildings in Binghamton. Starting with a loan from her father when she was a freshman, she built a mini empire while she earned her BA and MA. "I'm meeting a couple of real estate agents this weekend before my classes start again."

I glance at my guests. "Want anything? I need coffee."

"Tea for me," Chelsea says.

Heather shuffles after me and scans the refrigerator before snatching a Coke and sitting in the broken metal chair with her right leg crossed under her thigh. She watches me light the stove while Chelsea makes a phone call. "Chelsea talks about you a lot, so does Allen," Heather chatters to me and her bunny. "Like the time you lifted the bumper of her Datsun when it was stuck in snow."

"Allen exaggerates," I reply. "Always poetic."

"Yeah, he can't help it."

Spooning coffee into the percolator, I hear her retreat to the refrigerator for another Coke. When I turn around, she's staring into my eyes, recalling Chelsea's heated gaze during the nights of our summer romance. She has the same ironic expression, challenging and inviting. I break away, feeling warm despite myself. Heather must be fifteen, if she's that old.

"I wish Chelsea's baby would look like you, not Allen," she says to my back.

Reaching into the cupboard for my mismatched cups and an open bag of Oreos, I chuckle, "No chance of that." I quickly run the math, not impossible, but Chelsea would have said something. At least I hope she would.

"We're all set," Chelsea announces, hanging up the phone. "We have an appointment with Barbara Unger, Endwell Realty."

"I'm not going," Heather replies.

"You have time to finish your snack."

Heather shakes her head. "I want to stay with Curt."

Catching Chelsea's weary glance, I tell them with some measure of relief, "I have to go to work. Helping with the books."

"I thought the dairy was shut down," Chelsea shakes her head.

"Learning to run quarterly reports." I won't say I'm hoping to see Angie.

"No problem," Heather says brightly, her bunny nodding. "Me and Mr. Wiggy can stay here."

When I bump over the broken concrete driveway and cross the slushy gravel parking lot, my car plows the only tracks in last night's snow. I've worked three days this week, but the dairy still feels creepy with everyone gone. The empty semi-trailer waits at the raised dock for its load of milk crates, and layers of dirty ice cover the pile of discarded pallets near the river. Same annoying hitch in the door lock, same dark hallways echoing with my steel-soled boots. Upstairs the papers on Julie's desk appear glued in place and the last shipments still hang from a clipboard above the keypunch machines. One of my tasks for the day.

As the fluorescent lights buzz alive, I sign into my computer terminal. The usual scroll of green letters threatens jail time if I share any secrets, as if anyone cares how many gallons of milk and cottage cheese we shipped last quarter, other than me and Angie and our boss Sherman. Crowley the owner only pays attention on the infrequent days he shows up.

Judging from the job alerts carrying her codename vmpire, Angie must be running reports. She likes to park in the owner's reserved slot, next to his exclusive backdoor and close to the computer room and its freezing air-conditioning, meant to preserve the ancient computer and its fragile circuits.

When I tap on the glass window of the morgue, Angie swings around on her stool, finishes typing a few strokes with one hand before descending the stairs of the raised flooring. She wears black jeans and a black tee shirt with a scooped neck, and a silver clip secures her long black hair. She rewards me with a reluctant smile, her lips daubed in deep red.

I'm wearing a sweater under my all-weather jacket, a gift from my days in the Marines, but I'm still freezing. The cold never bothers her, but her dark eyes ask me why I disturbed her sanctuary.

"I ran the shipping report yesterday like you asked. Had to fix a few entries and it finally succeeded."

"Good boy." She winks, turning back toward her terminal in front of the blue PDP-11 computer cabinets. "You're learning."

I follow her up the corrugated stairs. "I noticed some manifests hanging by the input machine. Can't tell if Grace entered them or not."

"You need the secret word." She lights a cigarette, smoke curling up toward the vent.

"Please?"

"No, imphist." She shakes her head. "Let me show you." She types the command followed by a couple of familiar acronyms and the line printer rings its bell. A rattling scroll of paper spews from the carriage. I lean over and rip it off. Just what I need.

"Sorry, I didn't remember that command."

"Of course not. I wrote it." She flicks her cigarette. "At least you're smart enough to ask. No one else ever did."

"You mean Julie?"

"I mean anyone who believes the mainframe without checking the inputs."

"Julie trusts her own math. She's usually right."

"She has other problems, like you."

I zip up the neck of my jacket. "Yeah, she still thinks I ruined her romance with Sherman."

"Maybe she does, and you also know more about the accounting system."

"Nice to think so, but I'm a forklift driver in Sherman's eyes. At least he lets me run reports."

She stubs out her cigarette and fires up another with a farmer match. "I was thinking about the Christmas party tonight." She grins. "Almost worth going, just to see Julie arrive at Sherman's house."

I take a breath, turning my head away from the smoke. "I was hoping you'd go."

She shakes her head. "No Christmas for me."

"Conflicts with your pagan beliefs?"

"I'm Jewish." She leans toward me. "That's my excuse anyway."

Taken aback, not by her background but why it should matter, I quickly scan our times together. "You said you were Italian. Lasagna recipe from your mother."

"Jewish Italian."

I shrug. "I'd rather talk to you than Sherman and Julie."

"Are you asking me to go to the party in your roundabout way?" She laughs. "People will think we're a couple."

"No secrets at the dairy. No one'll be surprised."

"One condition." She says in assent.

"You're on."

"I've never had a Christmas tree."

Back at my desk, warmed by my cautious detente with Angie, I recheck the manifest inputs and schedule my reports to run overnight. When I turn off the office lights and scrape my car windows for the icy drive home, one problem remains. I can't afford a Christmas tree.

No sign of Chelsea when I shake the slush off my jacket and hang it in my narrow closet, and I find Heather sprawled in my armchair with a Coke and a bag of Lay's Potato Chips propped on her fuzzy bunny. Squinting in the dim light she raises a limp hand to welcome me home. She looks stoned.

My Aja album lies on the floor with my thin baggie of weed next to my stubby blue enameled pipe with silver stars.

"You're angry," she says.

"Should I be?" I bend over to pick up the album, always wary of the drug police, however unlikely. But it's why I keep my stash in my bedroom dresser.

"You're thinking I'm underage and I smoked dope in your house. You're responsible for me, even though no one asked you."

"Does Chelsea know you smoke?"

"See, I knew it. So typical."

I shrug as I carry the evidence to my bedroom.

"You're not listening," she yells. "Talk, talk, talk, and not listening."

She waits until I return and begins punching her bunny.

"Look, Heather, I haven't accused you of anything."

"Of course, you did." She stops pounding and smooths the bunny's pink fur.

Approaching the chair, I admit, "Your smoking bothers me less than going through my stuff."

"Don't worry, I didn't take your money, mostly quarters, or your rubbers." She winks, trying to look seductive and coming off oddly desperate, even pathetic. She kisses the bunny on its button nose. "Sorry about your dresser. And I'm sorry for hitting you, Mr. Wiggy."

I crack a grin.

"He told me his name one day when I was little." She flops his ears. "He knows everything. Sometimes he blushes."

"Wish I had a bunny to punch."

She hugs him protectively and scans my face. Adjusting the elastic of her tube top, she says in a singsong voice, "If you're nice to him you can sit with us. This chair is big enough."

I shake my head, trying not to smile at her awkward invitation. "I'm hungry. Let's make dinner."

Launching out of the armchair, she beats me to the kitchen. I let her choose the courses but I'm not well stocked. She settles on spaghetti and a jar of Ragu sauce, and she offers to make garlic bread in the oven with margarine and powdered garlic. My white bread is stale but not yet moldy.

While we cook, she rattles about her parents, how her mother could do better. Sticks is so nice but weak. "He can't say no to anything," she explains. "They pay him for gigs just to show up and sometimes he's too loaded to set up his drums. He always keeps the beat, though." Her mom is not as smart as Chelsea. If she were, Sticks would be out on the street.

I refrain from asking about her mother's escape to Atlantic City this weekend. I'm more curious about Chelsea's plan for a private school.

"I'll be her first student," Heather says. "She wants to teach the usual stuff, but she really wants to make us into modern women. Did she tell you it's a school for girls?"

I'm about to say I didn't know about the school until last night, when I hear Chelsea open the unlatched front door and clomp the snow off her boots.

"How are you two getting along?" Chelsea asks cautiously, eyeing me.

Heather replies, "We made you dinner."

"Family recipe," I add, opening the cabinet drawer in search of leftover packets of parmesan from my last pizza.

Over the table we hear how Chelsea's meeting with the realtor was promising though not as much as she hoped. The agent will list her buildings, but the market is slow. Wait until Spring. Knowing Chelsea, once she decides on something, she wants it now. That's how she ended up at NYU and later flipped me for Allen.

When we finish our mounds of spaghetti the kitchen grows quiet. Heather's running commentary faded after Chelsea arrived, and she sullenly grooms her tolerant bunny, picking off bits of lint and dropping them on her plate.

"Let's go to a movie," Chelsea suggests. "They still have a movie theater here, don't they?"

Heather nods slowly, obviously concerned about the movie Chelsea might choose.

"Can't," I reply. "Christmas party tonight at my boss's house."

"They shut down the dairy and they're having a party?" Chelsea asks.

"Yeah, I have to show up, so he'll remember to rehire me when the dairy reopens."

Heather gleams, "I'd love to go to a party."

"We don't have anything to wear," her aunt replies.

I should tell them they're not invited, but Sherman won't care. "You can go as you are."

"I get the first shower!" Heather skips toward the bathroom.

"Your bag's in my car," Chelsea calls after her. "I hope this is all right," she says to me. "Tell me it won't screw up your dairy gig."

I try to read her expression. Before she left town, she tried to convince me to leave Binghamton and Crowley Dairy behind. "When my boss sees me with you and Heather, it can only help," I grin, though I'll have to explain their presence to Angie.

When we pick her up, Angie doesn't take it well at first. As we work our way across the icy sidewalk to my car thrumming at the curb, she mutters, "With you it's always something. Or someone." She slips on a patch of ice and grabs my arm. "At least it isn't Debby."

"I love your dark look, reminds me of Black Sabbath," Heather gushes when we climb into the front. "Where'd you get your blood red lipstick?"

"Charon's Beauty Supply down on Church Street," Angie replies, reaching over the seat back to shake hands with Heather and Chelsea. "She orders it special for me."

"Are they open tomorrow?" Heather glances at her aunt.

"No idea," Angie replies. "This town shuts down on Sundays, but there's only a few days left until Christmas."

Chelsea nods, addressing her niece, "You can find anything in the village." I see her eyes reflected in the rearview mirror, darting between Angie and me. Angie leans against the passenger door, a gesture Chelsea certainly reads.

"I hate the village. You and Allen should get married in Atlantic City," Heather says brightly.

Angie and I return a blank stare.

"Allen's scoping out a jazz club near NYU," Chelsea explains. "Curt, you might get a call to be best man."

I laugh. "He probably wants me to move furniture."

"You'd go to the city?" Angie asks, perking up.

I look the other way, my usual response when confronted by a trip downstate.

That quiets the conversation, but the initial awkwardness has evaporated. We soon arrive at Sherman's two-story blue house on the rim of a hill in Endwell, a much better neighborhood than I'll ever afford. Angie rests her hand on my elbow as we walk up the scraped sidewalk with Chelsea on her other side. Heather hops ahead of us.

Sherman and Gloria greet us at the door wearing matching green Christmas sweaters. Gloria gives me a hug and a surprise kiss on my ear. I know she credits me with encouraging Sherman to give up his affair with Julie, who I spy in the background studying their every move.

"I'm Bill," Sherman says, extending his wide paw to Chelsea and Heather. He voices a warm hello to Angie and asks her how the reports are going. She returns a sad look. They didn't furlough the dairy for no reason.

Sending Angie an aborted half smile, Gloria takes both of Heather's hands. "There's some young folk downstairs, much more interesting for you. Jim Franz is down there."

"Slim Jim," Sherman laughs. "Mr. Basketball."

Heather shoots Chelsea a do-I-have-to look as Gloria leads her to the stairs.

When we escape the greeting line, I ask Angie, "What was that with Gloria?"

"She thinks I'm hot for Sherman because I worked for him at Universal."

Chelsea smirks.

"Yeah, he'd crush me," Angie admits.

We head toward the dining room table piled with cookies, cheese balls, several dips, and three molded wreaths of red and green Jell-O salads. I hear someone whisper,

"Vampire," as Angie passes. She scans the crowd with a royal grin.

Bending over to snatch a beer from a cooler on the floor, I rise to the wide smile of Hank, Julie's husband. She's nowhere to be seen. I recall Hank's a teacher, and he immediately hits it off with Chelsea. When their conversation meanders toward computers in the classroom, Angie joins in and I slip away.

I pass my friend Renee cornered in the kitchen with her boyfriend Anton scowling into his glass of punch like a cat just pissed in it. I nod her way and push through the glass doors to the deck.

Leaning against the railing and inhaling the frigid air, I relax. This is the perfect party. I made my requisite hellos and I got away from them all. Except the cold is creeping through my skin. Not cold enough to go back in, not yet. Angie finds me huddled in my jacket, which I luckily forgot to surrender at the door.

"Something's happening," she says, urging me back inside.

Sherman stands in front of the fireplace in the expansive living room, his head down like he's praying. The couch and all the chairs are filled, so Angie and I huddle near the door. Chelsea stands next to Hank, but I don't see Julie.

"Sorry to disturb the party," Sherman begins. "I'll be quick and let you get back to your food and drinks." He pauses and looks around, his eyes resting on each person briefly. "You are my favorite people and I'm not sure when we'll be back together again. Mr. Crowley says two more weeks, but there isn't a firm date."

Someone replies, "We'll be back in the grind soon enough." Some of the revelers raise their glasses.

Sherman's not finished. "I didn't know this would happen when we first planned the party, and it's been the hardest decision of my life. For family reasons Gloria and I have decided to move back to Washington. This has nothing to do with Crowley. I expect the dairy will reopen stronger than ever, and with such a wonderful group of people, it will certainly be successful."

Silence spreads through the living room like nerve gas. Angie whispers, "We're doomed."

Behind me I hear a soft moan and I turn to see the door to the deck sliding open. Julie. Angie doesn't seem to hear her. I follow Julie outside where she leans against the railing, crying with deep gasps. She must be freezing in her thin silk blouse.

"I don't want your jacket," she says.

"You don't want the others to see you."

She nods, dabbing her eyes in a tissue and forcing a grin. "Can't blame you for this one."

"I had no idea." I stand there watching the Christmas lights next door reflect off the snow.

"Thanks, I'm okay now," she says, but she still won't take my jacket.

Once I leave her, Angie meets me in the kitchen. "That was nice of you. But let's get out of here." She heads for the stairway to locate Heather, and I spy Chelsea in the living room among the crowd pressing around Sherman, who appears in danger of falling into the fireplace. Someone calls out to him, "Wish we were going with you."

Off to the side, her shoulder against the gray stonework, Chelsea studies a shelf display of porcelain Santas standing, sitting, and waving in front of a green and purple crayon child's drawing of a Christmas tree, though it could be a mountain. Chelsea's the only one not fixed on Sherman's words and his obvious discomfort. I finally catch her eye, not wanting to shove my way through the milkers.

"What a rock star," Chelsea says. "Very impressive. I can see why you like him."

"Not really."

"Very heavy," she whispers. "Must be two Meat Loafs."

Not finding Angie or Heather in the kitchen, we descend the stairs into a dark canyon lit only by black lights and souvenir Day-Glo concert posters, except for the far corner where a dim pole lamp shines down on an old pinball machine and a throng of children, some standing on Crowley milk crates. I'm drawn to the pinball machine, but Chelsea points me toward the couch.

Heather and Angie are locked in a conversation, unaware of our approach. Chelsea eyes them with a smirk, and I wonder if I have time for a quick pinball game. As if reading my mind, Angie tilts up her head and says, "There you are."

"Where's the basketball star?" I ask Heather.

"Cute, but such a bumpkin."

"You'd beat him one on one," Chelsea grins and then adds to Angie and me, "She has moves."

"Don't make me sick." Heather grimaces.

At the door I congratulate Gloria on their upcoming move to Washington, and she rewards me with another peck on the cheek. Outside Chelsea says, "Her husband didn't look that happy about it."

I reply, "Just a show."

"Yeah, they're getting out," agrees Angie. "Very timely."

Chelsea shoots me a lengthy grin, her eyes saying, "You should have listened to me."

She's the first to notice when I miss the turnoff for home. I only drank one Genesee. I have no excuse.

"Getting Angie a Christmas tree," I explain.

Angie says, "I was just kidding. I've never had a tree but it's no big deal."

"A promise is a promise."

"Curt, it's midnight," Chelsea reminds me. "Everything's closed."

Heather leans forward. "You never had a tree? This is so cool."

The Agway parking lot is empty, though it's plowed and well lit. I choose a spot just outside the chain link fence across from the Christmas tree lot.

"They have security guards," Chelsea moans, decoding my intent.

"Not after midnight on Saturdays," I explain. "My upstairs neighbor works here. God protects the store on Sundays so the watchmen can go to church."

"That sounds worse," Chelsea replies.

Angie adds, "The sooner we get out of here the better."

"I'll climb the fence!" Heather offers.

I nod toward her excited face washed by the parking lights, acknowledging she might climb better than me, but I worry about the barbed wire at the top. I have experience. Scanning the lot, I find a pile of shipping pallets. Dragging two of them over, I lean them against the fence, one behind the other.

"I'll climb the fence and choose a tree," I explain. "Heather and Angie stand on top of the pallets, they're the lightest, and I hand the tree down to them."

"What about me?" Chelsea asks.

"You watch for police."

"Good, I'll be the first one arrested."

The climb up the fence is harder than I expected with the freezing wire and the toes of my boots too wide to grip the square holes. It takes even longer to disentangle my jeans from the barbed wire. With a wrenching motion, I slip and sway until I catch my balance, smiling down at the women to show my confidence, which I hardly feel. Too late now.

Once over, I leap to the ground. After a quick appraisal of the first row, I hold up a tree for Angie's perusal.

"Something smaller," she says. "What about that one?"

Too scrawny. We finally settle on a 6-foot spruce, according to the tag.

Now to get it over. One hand gripping the tree, I ascend the chain link barrier and pause at the three strands of barbed wire at the top. "Can you hook the tree until you get over?" Angie asks, sensing my dilemma. Clever idea. With a grunt I swing the tree up and catch it on the barbs. Scaling the last two feet, I extend my leg over the top, careful of my crotch, and rest straddled on the wire. From there I pry the tree loose and lower it down to Angie and Heather.

My reach is not long enough and when I release the tree, it falls to the left of Heather. She leans too far and sprawls to the gravel along with the tree, raising screeches from Angie and Chelsea.

Heather remains motionless as I scramble down the fence. Chelsea gets to her first while Angie waits to give me a hand. We gather around Heather, who still clutches the tree. She looks up at us, her eyes scanning us one by one. Finally she laughs. "I'm fine. You look so worried."

"Me worried?" Chelsea says.

"My fault for not bringing Mr. Wiggy."

To Angie's questioning glance, I add, "Her magic rabbit."

Angie nods. "We need a magic rabbit."

"You need a tree, too," Heather says to me.

"No room."

The tree fills the trunk of the old Dodge Dart and peeks out after I tie the lid down with a strand of twine. But we're not free yet.

Just as we pull out of the parking lot, a patrol car approaches and slows to let us turn. The cops follow us for several miles, even when I detour down a side road.

"What's he doing?" Chelsea asks. "He must see the tree."

"Calling in my license plate to the FBI," I muse.

Angie turns toward me. "Is this car still registered to Artie? He has more DWIs than teeth."

"The VA gave him new teeth," I say, slowing for a stretch of ice. "Besides, the car's registered to me now."

"Oh good. I feel so much better," Chelsea moans.

In the reflection of the trailing headlights in my rear-view mirror, I see Heather smiling.

"They're just burning time until their next donut break," suggests Angie.

Chelsea glances into the rear-view mirror. "I hate stealing."

"In a couple days they'll throw away the leftover trees," I reply.

"Not this one." Angie grins.

After I turn back onto the main road, careful to come to a full stop and flick on my turn signals, the patrol car peels off in the other direction. We all exhale, and I resume my route to Angie's apartment to complete our mission. She reads my intent and says, "Let's drop them off first."

Pausing at my place, I give Chelsea the key and tell them to help themselves to the stale bread, yogurt, and corn flakes. When we pull away, Angie says in a wry voice, "Heather's quite a fan of yours."

"She thinks I'm a rabbit."

Angie punches my shoulder, so softly I hardly feel it. "She told me to give you another chance."

"But you never care what anyone says."

"Of course not."

THE JOY OF HEX

The new General Manager of Crowley Dairy disappears as soon as Old Crowley, the owner, introduces him at a company meeting. His new gray Mercedes remains parked in the official GM slot when I arrive in the morning and when I leave after dark. Either he lives in his office or he died there. Everyone has a theory.

Three weeks after his brief appearance, I'm one of Ray Matucci's first visitors, summoned by his secretary Marge who speaks in whispers like she's serving the Pope. He smirks behind the oak desk my former boss Sherman seldom used. Sherman preferred to mingle with his workers on the bottling line and the warehouse.

Matucci wears a clean, pressed gray suit, white shirt, and red striped tie. Younger than me by several years, he looks like a freshly minted college grad, but I can't read the diploma centered on the wall above his head. He rests his right hand on a leather football balanced on top of a pile of printouts next to his computer terminal. I help myself to the upholstered visitor's chair.

"Must be your day on the loading dock," he says, studying my blue jeans and T-shirt as if he's counting the stains seeping into his chair from my sweaty morning driving a forklift and hefting crates of milk.

"Every day." I hold his glance, suppressing my apprehension. Sherman allowed me to learn computers on my own time, inputting the shipping manifests and running reports.

He nods and taps his football, the only clutter on his desk. "We've been studying our organization for efficiency," he says.

He expects me to respond. "Yeah, Crowley wants to automate shipping and accounting," I offer, assuming the worst. I wonder how much Crowley matters any more given the rumors of his pending retirement.

"You have an interesting role, really two jobs." He releases the football, laces up, and folds his hands in front of him. "You don't look like an accountant."

His eyes scan my long frame and thick arms, and I shift my weight self-consciously, hanging my elbows over the armrest, trying to look relaxed, how an accountant might look.

"I met with Angie, the computer operator, this morning," he continues, cracking a half smile. "They call her the vampire. She's very impressive. You know her?"

Everyone else in the dairy considers us a couple, though Angie would never admit it, especially to me. With Sherman gone, she's the brains behind the operation. "Angie trained me to run searches and reports."

"She mentioned that when I asked about her automation project." He looks up at me. "She's almost finished."

That's one of the reasons I'm worried. Sherman gave me a chance to get off the forklift eventually, but the dairy has no real need for a part time junior operator. I might as well glue my butt to my forklift.

"I also talked to Julie," Matucci adds. He pauses to retrieve a poster sized organization chart covered with yellow sticky notes from his desk drawer.

My mentor when Sherman first let me keypunch the shipping manifests, Julie blames me for undermining her affair with him, though he made the decision to break it off himself. She probably thinks I moved Sherman and his family out to Washington.

"Julie says you argued with Sherman."

"We had our moments."

"Sherman didn't mention any moments to me," Matucci says with a tight grin. "He said you're too smart to be happy driving a forklift for long. I should either promote you or fire you."

He lifts the poster board so I can see it better.

I search in vain for my sticky note in the shipping department column. Maybe our little talk will end worse than I thought. His finger tap draws my attention to the accounting column where I see my name above the keypunch operators, dispatchers, and accounts payable specialist.

"What do you think?" he asks. "Julie hasn't seen this yet."

"You want me to move to accounting?"

"I want you to take over accounting." He smiles. "Sherman said you know the accounting system better than anyone. Except Angie, of course."

Suppressing my excitement, I lean forward for a closer view of the chart. With Sherman, moving off the forklift was always a vague *someday*. "Where's Julie?"

"Oh, she'll be working for you."

My elation dissolves into a suspicion he's playing me, or I didn't hear him right. I stare at yellow stickies, wondering how he could leave Julie's off the chart. She ran accounting when I first started at the dairy, and she's been there as long as anyone remembers. Crowley says he can't run the business without her.

"She doesn't like computers," Matucci explains. "If it were up to her, we'd still be counting pebbles in a bag. We need someone with more computer savvy."

"She keeps it all in her head and in her books."

"Not anymore. The real books are on the mainframe."

"Have you told her?"

"That will be your first management act." He slides the chart back into his desk drawer. "You might need her for a while."

I sway back against the chair, my T-shirt even wetter now. "When do you want my answer?"

"Sherman told me you wanted to get off the forklift, and it saves a position on the dock." He laughs, his voice higher than I expect and conveying I have no choice if I want to keep my paycheck.

Feeling light-headed, I stand and thank him, but I don't agree, not yet. He doesn't press me for an answer.

In the outer office Marge asks me how it went. When I shrug my shoulders, she whispers, "Congratulations."

I head to the lunchroom where I'm late for my morning coffee break with Renee, a ritual since I started at the dairy. My best friend at work other than Angie, she stares at a pastoral painting of cows in profile floating above a solid strip of grass. No flowers, no manure. Renee's not the only one who believes one of Crowley's grandchildren painted the scene in their elementary school, one that doesn't teach perspective. Renee wears a white smock with her blond hair swept under a net.

"Sorry, I had to meet with Matucci," I explain.

"So, he exists."

She waits while I feed a quarter into the coffee machine and watch the muddy instant brew spit into a Styrofoam cup. Renee's cup is already empty. I continue, "He wants to make changes."

"No more ice cream." She extends her arms to show me the lack of Neapolitan stains, and I can't detect the sweet telltale scent. "Can't say I miss it. They moved the ice cream line to Poughkeepsie."

Not surprised. Our sister plant stayed open when they shut us down for a long holiday over Christmas. "I bet Matucci didn't come down and tell the crew."

"Heloise told us."

Ken Helmut, the line supervisor, earned the nickname "Heloise" for his tidiness, often demanding extra cleanup after shifts and never offering overtime. Sherman should have done the line a favor and canned Heloise when he left.

The loudspeaker bursts with scratchy melodic bells signaling the end of our break. She waves and shuffles out the door, leaving her empty cup on the aluminum table. Unlike her.

I'm still blowing on my coffee when Julie clacks into the lunchroom on her high heels. A large woman, she is sexy in her way with voluptuous curves and jiggles under her pink polyester blouse and black slacks with her elastic panty bands clearly visible. She carries her white ceramic coffee cup with a faded image of her two children. After depositing her quarter in the machine, she waits for the cup to drop, quickly discards it, and slides her cup under the stream of instant coffee.

She sits down across from me with a warm smile and a suggestive leer, taking me by surprise. I planned to spend my coffee break prepping for her cold manner of late, but this is the old Julie, the accounting expert who willingly helped me learn the ropes, along with an occasional flirt.

"You met with frat boy," she says. "Everyone hopes he'll put you in charge of shipping. The line hopes you'll replace Heloise."

I stare into my cup, surprised my name is floating around. Some days Sherman liked me, even when I stood up to him, though he also fired me twice. "Matucci's announcing his reorg next week."

"So which one will it be?"

Clearing my throat, I face her expectant stare and fumble for the right words. "Just between you and me."

"You know me."

"He wants me to move to accounting full time."

"There's more," she says, reading my eyes.

Angie says I can't keep secrets because my eyes betray me, not to say I don't try. I steady myself to tell her the rest, knowing she'll hear the details on the dairy floor anyway. "He wants me to manage accounting."

"That little prick." Her face reddens, extending down her neck and up the foothills of her heavy breasts. She grips her coffee cup like she might throw it before taking a deep breath. "Old Crowley won't stand for it."

I feel my pulse quicken, reacting to her anger.

She growls, "Crowley would never let him fire me."

"You're not fired." I assure her, though her comment recalls the missing yellow sticky note.

"Matucci doesn't have the nerve to tell me himself." She sits back, the legs of her aluminum chair squeaking on the floor. "Oh, I get it. You're telling me because you're my boss."

"I didn't ask for the job." I try to sound diplomatic but it's too late. By telling her Matucci's plan I effectively accepted the position. No going back now. "I'll need your help."

"Sure, you will."

I get up to grab another cup of metallic tasting coffee and give her time to stew. My first cup is only half finished, but today will be a high caffeine day. When I sit back down, she's sipping her coffee and staring at the portrait of floating cows, her posture relaxed.

"Not your fault," she says in a softer tone. "You're not even qualified. Crowley knows that."

From the perspective of her business degree, she's correct. Not the time to bring up her disdain of automation. "We have to work together," I say.

"You're right. I shouldn't talk to my boss like this." She stands up and pivots to leave. "You can tell frat boy I'll be a good girl."

"Don't forget your cup."

She reaches down with a quivering hand and fixes her eyes on me. "There are things only I know, but don't worry, I'll never quit."

I watch her sway out the door, relieved the confrontation is over and wondering what secrets are hidden in her loose-leaf binders. She might soften and show me herself, return to the mentor she once was, though I doubt it.

Gulping both cups of lukewarm mud, I follow Julie to the accounting office where I grab the shipping report I ran early this morning. Julie doesn't look up as I pass.

Out of habit I carry the printout as a prop in case anyone wonders why I'm going down to the morgue to see Angie. Sherman might have cared; not Matucci since he's unlikely to abandon his pet football to walk the halls.

When I ring the bell and she opens the door, strands of her long black hair wave free above the fans in the raised flooring. She looks great and I wish I could hug her, but not at work.

"I met with Matucci," I say as we take chairs in front of the blue computer cabinets.

She lights a cigarette and smirks, "Frat boy."

"He said he talked to you about accounting."

"He asked about my project." She exhales smoke into the updraft. "And Julie, though I didn't say much about her."

"He wants me to manage accounting." I shove my hands under my armpits. "I already told Julie. She's going to talk to Crowley."

"It's about time someone made a change."

"I don't know anything about accounting."

"You know more than you think. You know the accounting system and most of the reports. And you have me." She flashes an elvish grin. "Besides, Joyce is a CPA. That's more accounting than we need."

I seldom talk to the accounts payable clerk though her desk sits near mine. She exudes a quiet confidence in contrast to Julie's boisterous manner. "I said I wanted to think about it, not that he'll let me."

"You'd rather drive a forklift?"

"Julie helped me a lot. She's run accounting for years."

"She's smart." Angie nods. "But no one can read what's in her head."

"She has shelves of loose-leaf notebooks."

"That no one else understands."

"She's not the only one they don't understand." I smile. "Some accuse you of black magic."

"Frat boy picked up the new system pretty fast. So did you." She lights another cigarette from her stub and says, "This place needs all the help it can get."

I watch her smoke disperse and escape through the ceiling vent. "I didn't see a sticky for Julie on his org chart."

"Ding." She takes a long drag and stares at me. "You shouldn't think you have to protect her."

We agree to meet after work, though Angie says she'll be home late. "I'm running another pile of reports for Matucci. Tell you about it later."

I spend the intervening hours at My Mother's Place. Angie won't be pleased but a glass of Genesee Cream Ale might improve my mood. I tell myself I should be celebrating.

When my friend Artie pumps me for news, hoping I'll spring for a pitcher, I mention my move into accounting. He knows my ambition to learn computers. "That's worth two pitchers," he cheers, slapping my shoulder. Carl and a few other regulars slide closer to my stool at the bar and extend their glasses.

Mike the bartender sets down a frothing pitcher and holds up his hand. "On me," he says with a swipe of his towel. We both know little of the beer is destined for my glass, but he always treats me well.

Artie spits a stream of tobacco juice into an empty glass. "You earned it, Curt. I'm proud of you." He glimpses the other drinkers like a father at graduation. I remember all the times he pleaded with me to drop my computer manuals and drink with him instead, but he's supported me more than most.

"I earned something, I guess." I raise my glass and give everyone an excuse to lift theirs. Mike arrives with another pitcher just in time.

Carl takes his cigar stub out of his mouth and looks at me sideways, as if examining my eyes for cataracts. "You don't look happy."

"He never looks happy," Artie says for me.

Blinking his eyes like he might fall asleep, Carl adds, "I wrote a column today about how people are unhappy because it's a habit. When something good happens they deny it or think it's a sign of worse things to come. At least to their inner selves. I call it 'The Joy of Hex'."

"Too deep for my inner self," Artie says with a smile at me. "Maybe your girlfriend, the vampire, knows about the hex part."

Carl replies, "You missed my point."

As usual, the other customers slide away when Carl explains his Sun-Bulletin column, leaving him with me and Artie.

"Joy of Hex, maybe." I agree when I pour myself another beer. "New job, new boss."

"You get promoted and it's not what you expected." Carl furrows his brows like a psychoanalyst.

"Something like that."

He clears his throat. "There's an opening in the accounting department at the newspaper. I could put in a word for you."

"No more milk and yogurt," Artie says with enthusiasm. He hates anything that sounds healthy.

"Sure," I reply. "Why not?"

The next morning, I call the number Carl scrawled on his used napkin. Milly, the Sun-Bulletin recruiter, schedules an interview late Friday afternoon to accommodate my work schedule. According to Angie I need a backup plan. The numbers at the dairy look dire even with the recent shutdown factored in.

When I arrive on the loading dock, I hop on my forklift as usual. Never has driving the forklift given me this much pleasure, knowing I must give it up. I think of every pallet that needs to be stacked and every milk crate precisely positioned for the bottling line, wanting to leave the shipping floor in perfect order when I hand over my keys. Heloise waves me to a stop.

"The shipping department works for me now," he calls out over the idling tractor trailers lined up outside the open bay doors.

I give him a thumbs up, but he motions me down to the floor.

"I wish you worked for me," he explains. "You've been transferred."

"Matucci said he'd announce it next week."

He shrugs and stares up at me. "He said you know about it already."

Upstairs the accounting office is quiet, everyone bent over their desks. Since Heloise is already implementing the reorg, I figure I should follow. I decide to meet with them one by one. No one seems surprised. Julie even allows me to crack open her loose-leaf binders, but I find nothing unusual other than several inconclusive charts tracking drivers and milk crates, as if Crowley suspected loss or theft. If these are the secrets Julie's protecting, she doesn't say.

My interview at the Sun-Bulletin starts like a field trip, following a throng of sixth graders touring the newspaper, though I have a guide all to myself. Bart Spenser, the operations manager, shows me the Linotype machines still used for last minute stories and changes. Operators with ink-stained hands and aprons pick type faster than pocket thieves. Most stories go through a machine that molds the type in blocks, a wonder of technology according to Bart. Assemblers fit the blocks into large flat trays, including engraved photograph negatives. Another machine embosses the trays into plastic molds, which are injected with lead, and the lead sheets are bent onto half cylinders, ready for the presses.

Bart proudly describes how they melt down the used lead for reuse. Only about one fourth of the lead is new. He points down to the lower level where two men wrestle lead ingots and huge rolls of paper off the pallets stacked nearby. "You look like you could do that job," he yells cordially over the din and squeal of the presses.

"Rather drive one of those," I reply, glancing at a forklift the size of a small tank.

"Me, too," Bart admits. "They won't let me near them."

Everyone always sizes me up for manual labor, but Bart hardly fits that role. Small and thin with wire-rimmed glasses, a tidy black suit, starched white shirt, and narrow blue tie, he looks like an accountant, one you could pick out of a crowd, unlike me.

Back in his office with my ears ringing from the presses, Bart cross examines me about ledgers and reports, asking for full disclosure of the computer system at Crowley Dairy. After a half hour my throat dries up and I rasp more than once, but he keeps going as if he's on a timer. Finally he sits back and runs his index finger through his notes.

"No degree," he says, "But you have a thorough understanding. Only a year on the job." He looks at me like a sideshow freak.

"I took some computer correspondence courses," I reply, trying to remember if I scribbled them on the application.

"I never put much stock in those." He stands up and I follow his lead. "Our bookkeeping is all pen and paper. We're talking about automation, though there's no telling when or if it will happen. Does that bother you?"

"No, but I'd be interested in working on automation," I reply, hoping my voice sounds sincere enough, masking my disappointment.

He walks me back to the recruiter and says he'll be in touch. Millie asks, "Did Mr. Spenser want to know if anything bothers you?"

I nod and unclip my temporary badge.

"That means he likes you."

Two weeks later I get a call from the Sun-Bulletin as I'm finishing my dinner of Kraft macaroni and cheese in my apartment. Angie stayed late in the morgue to run another stack of reports for Matucci.

"Can you come in for another interview?" Millie asks in a rising scale. "I think Mr. Spenser's going to make you a job offer."

"How about tomorrow after my shift?"

"Sorry, it will have to be next week."

We agree on Friday, over a week away, and after she hangs up, I wish Angie were here to share the news. Plenty of time to tell her tomorrow.

When I arrive at the dairy the next morning, several workers in their white smocks are already gathered on the shipping floor, alerting me to something amiss. They should be punching their timecards and heading for the bottling lines. Holding large manila envelopes, their eyes follow me to the stairs. Up in the accounting office, Julie and Joyce have already arrived, and Julie sits with her back to me. Joyce catches my eye and whispers, "Heloise just laid off half the production crew."

Unsure how to respond, I wonder why Matucci never told me anything. Maybe I'm getting the boot. After our one meeting he stayed behind his closed door. The only sign of his continuing presence was a slight bump in my last paycheck. Now this.

Marge appears at the door and summons me to Matucci's office.

His football rests on a stack of manila envelopes, just like the ones I saw on the floor. His organization chart is spread out on the desk, and I already see changes. Many of the yellow sticky notes have slanted lines drawn through them. My sticky appears unmarked. Are the slashes good or bad?

Matucci follows my eyes. "Don't worry, you're still here," he says in a somber tone. "You probably heard we decided to reduce expenses."

"Why didn't you tell me? I'm the accounting manager."

"You still are. You can update the books later." He hands me three envelopes marked for Julie, one of the keypunch operators, and one of the dispatchers. "What do you think?"

My head spinning, I try to respond logically. The keypunch operator makes sense because Angie programmed the shipping and accounts payable reports, and I never understood why we have two dispatchers. But Julie?

I reply, "They all have families."

"Very unfortunate. However, we're running a business." He opens one of the envelopes. "Two weeks' severance, medical to the end of the month, and they're eligible for unemployment and COBRA. You can tell them that."

"Generous," I say with an edge of sarcasm.

"Industry standard."

Shuffling my envelopes, I bring Julie's to the top. "We're sitting here because of people like Julie."

Matucci shrugs and a pink tinge rises up his cheeks. "She already talked to Crowley. You know what he said? He said she should rip off her rear-view mirrors. Forget the past."

I smirk and look away. He'll respond to anything I say with another cliché, whether Crowley said it or not.

"Look, Curt," he resumes, lowering his volume. "I need you to keep the automation going. If you want to save Julie, you can make up her salary with the others."

I glance at the chart. Accepting his challenge would mean laying off Joyce and the remaining keypunch operator and dispatcher. I could absorb some of their work, but I can't expect help from Julie. I scoop up the envelopes and head back to accounting.

Grace, the keypunch operator is ecstatic. She was planning to retire anyway, and now she has a few extra weeks of medical insurance. The dispatcher blames Sherman, our former boss. Dory saw it coming the day he quit. When she leaves the lunchroom, Julie appears without a summons, clutching a box of Kleenex. The rumor channel got to her faster than I did.

Her mascara running, my former mentor's face appears to have doubled in years. She takes the chair across from me and sits sideways, leaning her elbows on the aluminum table. When she catches her breath, she blurts, "My husband's a teacher. How will we pay our mortgage?"

"You're smart and you have a great resume," I say, though I don't think she hears me. When I describe the severance package as Matucci instructed, I might as well be talking to the coffee machine. Before I can finish she raises her hand like a stop sign.

"I thought you were leaving," she murmurs, blinking to clear her eyes and shooting me a deadly look of accusation.

I break her stare and glimpse the floating cows. No one other than Angie and Carl knew about my interview. Maybe the Sun-Bulletin called Julie for a back-channel reference, unaware of our delicate working relationship. Such contacts are supposed to be illegal, but it happens all the time, especially in Binghamton where everyone knows what you ate for dinner.

Turning to face her, I reply, "I haven't decided yet."

TERRY TIERNEY

"Must be nice." She stands abruptly, anger filling the crevices in her face. She crumples up her soggy tissues and dunks them in my empty Styrofoam cup. Pressing her manila envelope against her breasts, she glares at me. "Don't do me any more favors!"

I watch her slap open the Accounting door and it scrapes on the warped floor. Through the doorway I hear Grace and Julie cleaning out their desks, so I give them space and invest another quarter in a cup of thin metallic coffee. Someone left a Sun-Bulletin on the table, but I don't read it. I feel like recast type, only about one-fourth fresh. Or worse.

I'm still studying the cows when Angie peeks in. She never ventures upstairs except after hours when everyone's left except me. I'm glad she came. She takes the same chair Julie used and places her hand on mine. I try to ignore the neckline of her T-shirt as she leans forward, but she notices with a slight smile.

She pulls a crushed cigarette pack out of her back pocket and drops it on the table between us. She slides out a crooked smoke and doesn't light it. "Bad day." She pats my hand. "So, Julie failed to seduce Old Crowley."

Even in my subdued state, an image of Julie's plentiful curves and the geriatric owner raises a slight grin. "She'd kill him."

"Yeah, we would have heard."

"Half of Operations got canned. I didn't see Renee." I realize we're whispering like survivors after a disaster.

262

Angie lights her cigarette. "She has a rich boyfriend. Don't worry about her."

"Is this why Matucci wanted all the extra reports?"

"Today surprised me." She shrugs. "But like I told you, the reports remind me of my last job. Sales trends. Profit-loss stuff. Doomsday scenario."

"Maybe the layoff will help."

"Wouldn't it be nice." She leans back and inhales. "What are you going to do about the newspaper?"

My eyes skim the discarded Sun-Bulletin on the edge of the table. Last night Angie and I hashed out the pros and cons of taking the job, leaving me undecided, though wishing I could maintain my trajectory toward computers. Angie reads my expression and shakes her head.

"You passed your contact to Julie, didn't you?"

"No," I smirk. "Someone called her about me."

"That would piss me off." Angie taps her cigarette in my used cup, leaving ashes smoldering on Julie's wet tissue.

"Now she can fill the Sun-Bulletin with loose-leaf binders, and I can concentrate on computers. Better her than me."

Angie cracks a suggestive smile. "Well, she's better at pushing lead."

"You're thinking about her and Sherman."

"Given his weight, she must have a way with pulleys and rope." Angie's voice trails off and she gazes beyond the floating cows, as if she's imagining the knots and positions Julie might have applied.

I find myself wishing our workday was over.

WAKE

PARTY CRASHER

Eleven on a Monday morning, and I know where to find Artie. He sits at his bar stool, third from the left in My Mother's Place. He holds an empty glass between his hands like he's praying for someone to fill it. Impressions in the wooden bar perfectly match his bony elbows.

Although I paid him for the Dodge, he still expects me to ask his permission when I drive the heap out of town. He bought the car for me to use after my old Ford died and I was out of work. A favor I'll never forget. He always approves my request, and I stand him a Genesee draft in return, sometimes joining him, especially now that the dairy has shut down for good. I'm not drinking today.

Daryl slips the glass out of Artie's hands and pops the spout as soon as he sees me, letting the foam run over the top the way Artie likes it. Licking the glass, Artie taps a celebratory rhythm on the bar, sounding like a syncopated Irish jig. He flashes a gap-toothed smile and offers me a seat next to him.

Smiling at my friend, I say, "You're not wearing your new teeth."

"They need to be refitted," he complains, twisting his jaw. But I know the real reason. The false teeth interfere with his robust tobacco chewing, and no adhesive can withstand the corrosive juice. He chews even when he drinks

"I'm driving up to Norwich, if it's okay," I announce. "You could come along. We can stop in Oxford to get them checked." I doubt he'll take my offer.

"Seeing that cute VA shrink?" He sips his beer, and Daryl appears with an empty glass.

"No, but I promised you I'd make an appointment." Artie worries about my tendency for violence. His diagnosis.

"Sure, you will."

"How do you know she's cute, or even she?"

"I know things." Artie spits a brown stream into the empty glass. I look away. "What's the vampire say about you checking out for Oxford?"

"We're almost done closing the books at the dairy." I glance toward the wall clock and the spiderweb crack from a well-aimed beer bottle years ago. "Angie runs reports and I slap the line printer when it jams."

"Sad story," Artie muses.

"Weird the past week. Angie and I are the only ones left." Her doomsday prediction played out sooner than either of us expected, just two months after the big layoff.

"Sucks," Daryl calls from down the bar. "People losing their jobs. Crowley Dairy has been here forever."

Artie taps my elbow and I assume he wants me to spring for another beer. His red-rimmed eyeballs stare up at me. "You didn't answer my question," he says.

"Angie knows I'm going to Norwich. An errand for Freddy."

"You're keeping the shrink secret," he winks and drains his beer. I signal for another.

When Daryl returns with the full glass, he leans toward me the way he does when he wants to speak privately. I can't help cracking a smile because Artie will hear everything, and there's no other ears in the room.

"Some guy stiffed me for a catering job," Daryl confides. "Couple hundred bucks."

I shake my head. Big money for Daryl who owns Mother's with his sister Debby and their dreams of expanding the dive into a restaurant.

"A rich guy lives on Front Street," Daryl continues. "He ordered a spread for a wedding party."

"Front Street," Artie interjects. "Where Freddy lives."

My eyes glide between them. Daryl and his night bartender Mike occasionally ask me to help them break up fights. His expectant stare echoes those nights, but this is more serious. "Have you talked to the cops?"

"The asshole's tight with the cops. They won't do anything."

That means Daryl's appealing to my connection with Freddy. Other than a few harmless betting slips, Freddy never admits anything illegal, and he never asks me to do

269

anything illegal. A large man with a calm demeanor, Freddy imbues more respect than the mayor.

"Maybe you could talk to him," Daryl persists.

"Talk to who?" I stand up from my stool. If I had any sense I'd walk out now, though Daryl's backed me up more than once through the months of my deepest drinking bouts and my destructive pursuit of his sister. Destructive to me, not to her.

"Buford's the guy."

The name pokes an old scar, but I never met him in person. "Can't promise anything," I reply.

Daryl breaks a grin and I try to ignore it, wondering what I just signed up for. Artie tips his glass in a toast, almost empty, but he waves Daryl off and fixes his crutch under his shoulder, announcing his intention to join me. He follows close behind as I head for the door, pressing into a sheet of wet show.

"Won my bet again," Artie announces.

Every year he bets all comers that it will snow in May. Weary of winter and encouraged by the first tardy hints of spring, the bar patrons figure they'll make a few bucks off a goofy drunk. Artie puts on a good show.

This year he should have doubled his wagers. A thick quilt of white ice and sloshy gray pools cover the road, challenging the bald tires on the old Dodge Dart. I hope I can hold off replacing the rubber until fall given my shaky job prospects, especially if I decide not to go all in with Freddy.

As we cross the river and head north through Chenango Forks, the sun punches through the overcast, flashing white reflections on the hillsides like a stack of brand-new appliances, though the snow still falls in huge flakes the size of moths.

Artie shoots me a worried look. He knows the state of the tires. "Do you know where we're going?"

"Turn off at 23, might be closer to Sherburne than Norwich." I replay Freddy's oral directions by rote, nothing in writing. Artie retrieves a well-worn Chevron map from the glove compartment and turns it like a puzzle wheel searching for our route. He drools an asymmetric brown Skoal stain that lands on the map southeast of Norwich and resembles a military reservation.

"I wanted to talk to you in private," he says, dropping the map in disgust.

"We already talked about the shrink." Artie must have a reason for venturing beyond his stool at Mother's.

"No, it's Debby. She's getting married."

I suppress a smile. Her last engagement imploded in less than a week.

Artie reads my thoughts. "This one's for real. Her lawyer Jensen gave her a fat ring."

We turn off Highway 23 down a dirt road, skidding and shuttering on the washboard surface between potholes the size of duck ponds and throwing up puffs of dirt despite the spitting snow. I hope the Dodge holds together. "He's lasted longer than most."

"I worried about how you'd take it."

I laugh, but it's more of a dusty cough. "She hates me for trying to help her. She says I treat her like an airhead."

A deep rut throws Artie against his door. After a few quick chews he adds, "What does the vampire say about Debby?"

"She doesn't have to say anything." I stop at a side road, scanning the muddy bushes for a road sign. None to be found. This could be the turn I want or a driveway. "Why doesn't Debby's lawyer help Daryl?"

I risk taking the corner and the road further degrades into a two-track with dried weeds tickling the Dodge's undercarriage. If the flurries mature into steady rain, not uncommon this time of year, we'll be doomed to wallow in mud.

"Jensen works for the DEA," Artie replies. "Not his specialty."

"That means he declined because there's no money in it," I reply cynically, swinging into a shallow turnout in front of a dented yellow mailbox. "Here we are."

"There's no name or address."

"Look for the red butterfly, Freddy said." Just below the mail flag, a butterfly decal soars in place with the tip of its right wing worn off. I slip a manila envelope into the box and skid the car back and forth through a three-point turn.

After we navigate the succession of gravel roads, we finally bounce over the lip of the paved state highway. The Dodge rides oddly smooth and quiet like we're sitting on a plush sofa. Filling the silence, Artie says, "That guy Buford has a nasty rep."

"Yeah, I worked for Buford Construction." Wet snowflakes dot the windshield, though not enough to switch on the wipers.

"Same guy. You never talk about the job."

"Before I started at the dairy. I fell into a hole and got fired."

"They fired you for falling in a hole?"

"No, they fired me for shoving the guy who put the hole there. He thought it was funny."

"I don't get it."

"It was slushy like today, and he left a board unnailed. He thought I'd trip, but I fell into a stairwell."

"They fired you for fighting," Artie surmises, shaking his head. He fishes into his pocket for a fresh pinch of tobacco.

I shoot him a sidelong grin. "Don't bring up the shrink again."

Artie shifts his load to his cheek for a muted reply. "Nah, I just wish we brought some beers."

After dropping Artie off at Mother's and fronting him a fresh pitcher, I head back to my apartment and change into my best blue jeans and a clean sweater for my visit to the Buford mansion. The afternoon sun has melted the snow by the time I head out. Might be Artie's last bet for the season.

The cedar shakes and white trim of the old pile with its multiple peaks and windows remind me of photos of

Newport, Rhode Island, estates from the Kennedy years. Artie was right about its location. The back lawn abuts thick shrubbery separating the Buford expanse from Freddy's. I wonder if the two families ever barbeque together, but given the manicured forest surrounding each house, they might not know the other exists.

An older woman with bronze, wavy hair answers the clang of a brass knocker. She wears a white silk blouse under a blue wool blazer unbuttoned to reveal a large Celtic cross on a gold chain. Peering over a glass of white wine, her brown eyebrows arch above hazel eyes. "I don't recognize you," she says with a practiced smile.

"The caterer sent me." I return her smile.

"We're having a party." She tips her head toward the living room filled with well-dressed revelers.

"Thank you." I take a step forward.

She looks me up and down, holding her position.

"I'm supposed to make sure you're enjoying the refreshments," I say.

"We are." Her smile remains fixed in place. "Now you can leave."

"Not until I say hi to your husband."

"He's busy."

"I can wait."

She stares at me, obviously hoping I will give up. She finally turns and I expect her to close the door, but she leaves it open. A fit man with thinning black hair and a pencil mustache appears on the threshold. He sneers through a pock-marked face, holding a scotch glass. A thick silver choker chain dips under a pale blue cashmere sweater.

"Gregory Buford." He holds out his hand, soft and cold like a dead fish. His eyes are bright and predatory.

"Curt."

"Is this your business, Curt, crashing parties?" He flashes a smile with oddly bright teeth.

"Mother's Catering sent me to collect payment for a party you hosted last month."

"You can come to my office tomorrow. I have an office in the back."

"I'm here now."

"The food was bad." Buford grimaces.

"Daryl says there wasn't any left."

Buford's wife tugs his elbow. People inside are starting to notice, all well-heeled like a Ronald Reagan fundraiser.

"You need to leave now," he says.

"So you can stiff us again?"

A large guy, rental security, lumbers up the steps behind me, panting like he ran the long way around the house.

"I'll be back," I grin, raising my voice a few decibels. I brush past the rent-a-goon, and he follows me to my car. A bulky sweater drapes his folds of flesh bouncing in rhythm with his steps. He wears a grim expression, taking his gig seriously.

When I open my car door, he gives me a little shove as I lean over. I spring up and smack his hand away with my closed fist. He stares at me and steps back, trying to ignore the pain.

I drop my Dodge into drive and pull away from the curb.

The next morning the Buford driveway is clear of luxury guest cars, so I drive up the curved pavement. The surface is finished with asphalt, so the Dodge's oil leaks won't show.

The rent-a-goon meets me on the walkway wearing a gray windbreaker with a Litton Security patch. He keeps his distance and leads me back around a rose garden to a small house with the same cedar siding as the mansion. It looks like a servant's abode, where they once stashed their domestic slaves.

I enter an office paneled in oak with a carpet deep enough to plant cotton. Buford stands in front of a picture window with his back to me watching the sprinklers whip large drops in overlapping circles. Two cycles, three, before he slowly turns to acknowledge my presence.

Pulling a copy of Daryl's bill from my back pocket, I extend my hand. Buford snatches the paper and reads the damages. Behind me the Litton guard blocks the door as if I might try to escape.

"Where are the clams?" Buford grumbles. "He never brought the clams."

"You didn't order clams," I grin.

"Why should I pay for the wrong food?"

"You got what you ordered, and you ate it."

"What's this extra 20%?"

"Late fee." That was my idea in case he wanted to bargain. A bill for $200 should mean little to him.

He stares up at me. "I know about you. You worked for Jerry Shepherd."

"Mutt," I reply, recalling my construction gig a few years back and the site foreman. "We called him Mutt."

"He likes you, too. He says you're a loser." Buford shoves the bill into my chest. "Jerry works for me."

"Congratulations." I take the invoice and slide it onto his desk. "You're as bad at hiring as you are paying your bills."

"Get out of here!" he spews.

"Or what?"

I glare at the goon who trips in his haste to clear my path to the door. Waving my hand at the invoice, I pivot to catch Buford's cold eyes. "If you don't pay by Friday, we'll add another late fee."

The guard follows me out the door, but he stops when I pass around the corner of the mansion. He pulls out a cigarette and throws his spent match in the petunia bed. I find my car on my own; no oil spills that I can see.

That afternoon I stop by Freddy's downtown office, an old green Buick Riviera in the back row of his used car lot on Central. He conducts most of his business there rather than the plush office in his mansion as if no one knows how much money he has. He must enjoy the visage of decaying buildings and the scent of air tinged with diesel exhaust from the Greyhound terminal down the block.

He leans against the Buick's fender with one hand resting on the hood ornament and the other flicking his cigar when I walk up. With the dairy closing for good, I check with him most days to see if he has any jobs for me.

"I saw your Dodge visiting my neighbor," he says. His voice sounds like gravel in a mixer. "He's also my competitor. Not changing sides, are you?"

"He stiffed Daryl for catering."

Freddy sniffs. "Buford's a crook."

"Besides cheating his vendors?" I sprout a grin. Many say Freddy's connected with the upstate mafia, but he's never shorted anyone. I spy the untidy piles of betting slips on the Buick's cracked dashboard.

"He's that kind of guy." Freddy reaches through the open driver window to snatch his silver lighter with a raised Masonic crest. "Is Daryl paying you?"

"Never asked." I smirk.

Firing up his cigar stub, Freddy shakes his head. "Thought so. Just like you're helping out at the dairy for free."

I lean back against the rear panel, upwind from his caustic cloud, expecting Freddy to turn this into another teaching moment, how I'm too willing to help people with no reward. His lecture is never about squeezing anyone, just making sure I have enough to eat. But that's not what he's thinking today.

He stares up at a busted streetlight, its bulb jagged like a tulip turned upside down and dirty. "Maybe you can check out Buford for me."

"He cheat you, too?"

"Buford underbid us on that county office building." He pauses to pick an errant piece of tobacco from his lip. "Numbers don't add up. Labor cost is way below what it should be, and he's not overrunning his budget. Hard to find good construction workers, but someone's raising that barn."

"Out on Vestal Parkway across from your apartment site?"

"That's it. Perfect job for us. Two construction sites close together."

"Union job?"

"County jobs are." Freddy nods. "I think he paid someone off."

"Daryl says he's tight with the cops."

A rumble erupts deep in his gut as Freddy twists his thin lips into a smile. "More likely he's fucking the mayor."

I share a grin, imagining Buford in bed with our pudgy mayor, Georgia Swan, nicknamed Gorgeous George after the professional wrestler with a similar taste in coiffed hair. "Should I plant a camera?"

"Not yet." Freddy's eyes shine, still savoring his joke. "Check out his site. You might know some of his crew."

I finger the invoice in my pocket. My favor for Daryl has grown in complexity. But Freddy never expects me to work for free.

"If you stop by my site, bring a hammer. We're short-handed." He flicks his lighter. "Maybe you'll get the bug again. Go back to construction."

"Rather use my brains." This is another topic we've touched before.

"Big guy like you." He checks his watch. "Very rare."

His next appointment, a shiny black Suburban with Pennsylvania tags pulls up next to the Buick, and I leave Freddy fishing a fresh cigar out of his shirt pocket.

I head down Vestal Parkway and turn onto the gravel shoulder near the Buford Construction sign. Across the four lanes of traffic, I spy a similar sign but bigger, featuring I-Beam lettering, Granite Creek Steel, Freddy's outfit. Few know he's the owner.

Pulling on my old work boots to look the part, I climb down and up the drainage ditch and enter a gap in the chain link fence surrounding the Buford site. I duck behind a sand pile to evade the windows of the office trailer propped on cinder blocks. I recognize the trailer from my last construction job, guessing it houses Mutt, the foreman who fired me.

A lanky figure strides across the graded dirt surrounding the bare frame of the new building. I expect someone's coming to throw me out until I recognize my old friend Will. He played the practical joke, causing me to slip and wrench my knee, though that was not his intent. Mutt saw me shove him and overreacted.

THE BRIDGE ON BEER RIVER

"Curt, are you coming back to work?" Will asks. I detect a hint of residual guilt for his role that day. I never looked him up afterward, so I also feel a tinge of regret.

"Mutt would love that."

Will glances at the trailer. "He knows he made a mistake. He said so later."

"He still the same?"

"Busting us for untied shoes and shit? Of course." Will smirks. "But it looks like he's out someplace. You could leave him a note."

"You bet."

"I should warn you," Will's voice drops to a whisper. "There might not be any jobs."

My eyes are drawn to the skeleton building and a few men in full coveralls crawling the girders and mounting floor joists.

"They brought in all those spics." Will shrugs.

His derogatory description grates. "Your family is Mexican."

"Before I was born."

The complaint about Mexicans taking jobs and dragging down wages is common on building sites, but I only cared that they knew what they were doing. And I felt safe. The same criteria I applied to everyone. Freddy would sanction my attitude. "It's a closed shop, right? They make the same wages and pay union dues like everyone else."

Will looks away, stealing a glance at the office trailer.

"Does Walt work here?" I ask. Walt's the Buford union steward, or at least he was in my day. Might be worthwhile to talk to him, though he always protected union business like a nuclear launch code.

"Walt says he's quitting." Will starts walking back behind the unfinished building. "Him and Mutt aren't getting along."

"What a surprise, Mutt pisses everyone off."

Will shrugs to let me know he wants to end our conversation. I hazard one more question.

I catch up with him and ask, "You speak Spanish, right?"

"Some, but we're not supposed to talk to them. Just work stuff."

I shake my head, and Will reads my displeasure. Back when we were working together, he should have warned me about the loose board. He's too good at keeping quiet.

"Look, Curt, I have a wife and kids. I can't take chances." He flexes his hands.

"Mind if I look around?"

"When Mutt's away." Will smirks. "But be careful. You know how he is."

"I'll leave a note."

After a lap around the excavated pit and rising frame, I don't see anything unusual nor anyone one else I remember. I decide to try my luck across the road, exiting through the same hole in the fence and staying clear of the office trailer and Mutt's vigilant eyes in case he's returned.

After I retrieve my Dodge and dash across the busy parkway, I enter the Granite Creek site through the main gate in a chain link fence a couple of feet taller than Buford's.

Some of Freddy's crew know me from earlier errands. I return a few waves as I stride toward a group eating lunch on a pile of lumber behind a row of pickups, hoping to find Mark, knowing he'll give me a straight answer if I ask him the right question. Another of Debby's exes, Mark was cooling in jail when I had my initial Debby fling. The danger of him finding out added to her appeal, though the pending confrontation between Mark and me never happened. She threw me over before he made it home.

I finally find him around the back of the structure sitting in a small circle of diners. He clutches a dented green thermos and watches my approach. Hard to miss, Mark resembles a professional wrestler without the makeup, his face settled into a natural scowl. A nice guy when he isn't drunk, Mark and I carry on a wary acquaintance.

"Did Freddy send you?" he asks. He glimpses his two buddies and picks his canine tooth with his thumb. His jaw drops into a grin, but his eyes are steady. "Tell him I'm doing an excellent job."

I return a quick smile. "He knows." My word with Freddy got Mark hired. Now I hope he'll return the favor.

"You should get a real job. We need the help."

I nod and glance around, settling my gaze on the Buford site across the way. "What about that county building?"

"You want to work there?" Mark scoffs.

TERRY TIERNEY

"I worked for Buford once upon a time." I lean my hand on a sawhorse, careful not to apply my entire weight. These guys would love to see me lose my balance and land on my butt. "I hear they're full up anyway."

"You mean the Mexicans." Mark scans his lunch mates.

One of them shrugs and chomps into a roast beef sandwich on white bread. Mayonnaise oozes between the crusts. "They'll make you live in those trailers," he jokes between bites.

"Behind their site," Mark adds. "I heard they look like dog kennels."

That draws a smirk from the lunch crew.

"I didn't see any kennels," I reply. "Guess they're hidden from the road."

Mark winks at me like he's trying to smile, but it comes out a sneer. "You're better off working here. Freddy would hire you." He takes a swig from his thermos and shakes his head. "But you're already working for Freddy, aren't you?"

I flash a grin. "Guess I forgot my hammer."

As I bounce out of the Granite Creek parking lot and head east toward the dairy to meet Angie, I wish I had packed a lunch. When Crowley shut down, I stocked my cupboard with bread and peanut butter. Too late to go home for a sandwich. Along Vestal Parkway fast-food franchises emerge like beacons, neon burning through the heavy mist. At least I won't be pounding nails outside in the wet afternoon. I spring for two cheap double cheeseburgers, no fries, diet Coke. Angie lectures me about my dietary habits, though I never gain weight. I'll be finished eating by the time I see her in the dairy's frigid computer room where she's closing out the books, Crowley's last paid employee.

The burgers congeal in my stomach like drying cement as I drive across town, replaying what I learned about Buford Construction. Freddy says they underbid a union job. Will was furtive in his responses, the way he acted when his misguided prank almost killed me. The union steward is unhappy and knowing Walt it's not because of the Mexicans. Or maybe it is. How much can I trust Mark's description of their living conditions? Large jobs often provide temporary housing, but their units typically rank higher on the comfort scale than military barracks and certainly better than dog kennels.

After a few hours running reports for Angie, I return to the Buford site about the time the crew begins retreating to their cars and pickup trucks. I duck through the gap in the fence and take a wider route around the office trailer. Several men keep working as the darkness deepens under persistent clouds, and I overhear splashes of Spanish. In the back of the yard behind a row of scraggy blackberry bushes, I find four old camping trailers. One looks like an aluminum-skinned Airstream, and one rests on the bed of a rusted Chevy pickup with flat tires. Each of the trailers features screened windows with bars and an air-conditioner on the roof along with streaks of rust and years of use. Not as livable as a barracks but better than a kennel.

I perch in the shadows, recalling my Marine training, silent and invisible. A rusted VW bus and an ancient wooden fence overgrown with ivy tell me no one has ventured into this corner of the property for years. Leaning back on a damp stump I have a clear view of the trailers, but no one under the yellow halo of the security light will be able to see me.

After seven, a rent-a-goon like the one from Buford's mansion appears with a cardboard box which he sets down on one of the three picnic tables in front of the trailers. A file of men lines up and he distributes dinner on paper plates before disappearing for a half hour. When the guard reappears, the diners peel off one by one and enter the trailers. The goon extinguishes the lantern centering each of the tables. He checks his watch and approaches the first unit. He slides a bar over the door, and I hear the faint click of a lock.

Several minutes after the guard leaves, I retrace my steps back to my car, careful not to stumble on random rocks and discarded stubs of wood. As I pass behind the office, I spy a light inside and Mutt's unmistakable silhouette. If I wanted, I could meet him in person. I have things to say, better left unsaid. I creep around a cement mixer and drift too close to a security beam, my military training rustier than I thought. Mutt sees me through the window and reaches for the phone. I hear his door open, and a flashlight scans my path. But I'm already through the fence by then and sprinting along the shoulder to my car.

I decide to wait until morning to report to Freddy, rather than arriving on his doorstep after dark, and a late hamburger plate at Mother's calls me, though I can hardly afford it. Daryl grills his specials on Tuesday nights, not to be missed.

Only two bites into my cheeseburger, a real one this time, with its pile of pickles and ketchup when both Artie and Carl jerk their heads toward the bar door, following Daryl's glance. Artie mumbles in my ear, "Trouble heading your way."

I peek over my shoulder, then take another bite.

Raising squeaks in the old floor planks like a bowling ball, the rent-a-goon from Buford's mansion lumbers across the floor. Debby veers out of his path, balancing her tray, but he doesn't break stride. I hear him panting behind me but not too close. "Mr. Buford wants to talk to you."

"I'm eating."

"He can't wait."

"You drove him here to talk to me," I reply between chews. "He can wait." Sipping my beer, I pause to admire my burger.

The goon sighs in desperation, exhaling a breath of stale cigarette ash and garlic past my ear, sucking away my appetite. I set down my burger and napkin as his wide paw extends past my elbow. I flinch, expecting a blow, and Daryl gathers himself. Not our first bar fight together.

But the goon holds a check. "Mr. Buford said to give this to you."

Unfolding the check, I read the typed amount and pass it to Daryl. His invoice plus my late fee and a little extra made out to Mother's Catering. Daryl nods and snatches up the bill for my dinner and throws it in the waste bin. Artie looks a bit jealous, but he rewards himself with a refill from my pitcher.

"Now will you talk to Mr. Buford?" the goon asks.

"I'm finished." With one last wipe of the napkin, I push away the remaining half of my burger and follow the goon outside. Under the yellow glow of failing streetlamps, a light blue Lincoln hums at the curb. The backseat passenger window rolls down. Just like the gangster movies, except they usually film somewhere warm like Los Angeles.

"You got your check," Buford says.

"Do you want me to thank you?"

He chuckles, throwing a foggy cloud in the chill air. "I see why Freddy likes you."

That gives me pause. The catering bill had nothing to do with Freddy.

"Just stay away from my job site," he continues.

And the catering bill had nothing to do with the county office building. "Just visiting some old friends." I shove my hands into my jeans pocket, wishing I had grabbed my jacket. "No crime in that."

"You heard me."

The goon takes a baby step closer but brakes when he catches my glare.

"Sure, I heard you."

"Freddy can't protect you forever."

I force a grin. I never expect Freddy to defend me, though there's no doubt he could. "He just wants to know how you underbid him."

Buford's ire drains from his face, and I realize I made a mistake, admitting Freddy sent me to the job site.

"You're a smart guy," Buford says. "Those wetbacks living in my trailers make good money to support their families back home. They could get deported."

"Is that why you lock them up at night?"

"For their protection, so they don't wander off and get caught by Immigration." Buford grimaces. "They don't complain."

"How could they?" I study his fixed expression. He said good money, but I bet it's not that good, not union wages. Men desperate for work will take anything.

The goon steps closer. Buford shakes his head. "This is business; everyone wins."

"I'm not looking to win." I turn to leave and raise my hands to push the lumpy goon out of the way."

"Wait," Buford calls. "I was wrong about you."

Facing him, I shake my head. "No, you were right."

"Calm down. We can all win." He waves me back toward the car, but I don't move. "I need a new foreman. Pays better than your old dairy job and more than Freddy."

No way I'd work for Buford, though I refrain from telling him that.

Buford misreads my pause. "I'll make it worth your while, but all the stuff you learned today stays in the family."

The Mother's front door opens, spilling two businessmen and a waft of warm air. A shiver creeps up my legs.

"Sleep on it," Buford says, his voice returning to command mode like he's already won.

Back inside Daryl offers to grill another burger. I decline and check the clock behind the bar, counting my beers to make sure I keep to my limit and anticipating my escape to Angie's apartment. She still works late at the dairy, keeping her customary schedule.

As my blood begins to thaw after my cold encounter with the blue Lincoln, I decide to hazard a phone call to Freddy. He hates telephones as much as he hates being disturbed after dinner. Daryl lets me use the phone in the kitchen, away from the barroom chatter.

Freddy sounds annoyed, especially when I ask if I can stop by his mansion.

"We're talking now," he growls.

"You asked me to check out Buford Construction."

"Can't it wait until morning?"

"I don't trust Buford." He might move the workers or the trailers overnight, though unlikely.

"Good call."

I recount my conversations and what I saw behind the site.

Freddy grunts. "Not enough to make the county rebid the job."

"Buford says the workers could be deported."

"What do you care about a bunch of beaners?" He pauses, his chuckle descending into a cough. I imagine him inhaling one of his acrid cigars. "Sorry, I forgot who I'm talking to."

"Either they're not on the union books, or they aren't getting scale."

With a subtle change of tone, Freddy shifts to his role as union president. "They should earn union wages, even as laborers."

"That would explain his low cost." I wait for him to mull it over.

He moans, one of his negotiating skills, make the other side think they're hurting you. He smells me leading him toward a request, even if he hasn't heard it yet. "Just spit it out."

I tell him my plan, hoping it appeals to his desire to help the little guys, especially when his reputation benefits, if not his wealth. "You can tell Buford you're sending the union auditors, and you already have evidence. Tell him it's too late to deport the Mexicans. He has a choice of paying them or letting you hire them. You need the help."

His heavy breath fills the line like a billow of static. "I get you. If he stonewalls, threaten him with the county, and if he pays scale, he overruns his contract and loses money" he skeptically replies. "Hard to pull off."

I force a laugh, spinning my suggestion like a joke. "Buford offered me a job."

"You going to take it?" He sneers. "If we go through with your wacky idea, he'll never hire you."

"I could tell my story to Carl instead."

"Carl from the Sun-Bulletin?"

"He's here tonight."

Freddy coughs. "Don't do that."

I give Freddy a minute to ponder the implications.

"Carl could cause a scandal," he says. "The damn county might kill the office project. Or worse, bring in the Feds."

"Yeah, I only want Buford to lose."

"So, you're not taking his offer."

"Not yet." But Freddy's right--no way Buford will hire me after what I told Freddy, even if I was so inclined. Another bridge collapsed into Binghamton's relentless river.

"You're learning." Freddy's laugh rumbles like an old muffler. "Okay, we'll try it your way. No guarantees."

As I hang up the phone, I wonder how far Freddy will go. If his negotiations with Buford go sour, I wonder how much he will risk for the laborers.

That night Angie expresses little interest in my adventures chasing down Daryl's wayward check, but she pumps me for details about my excursion to Norwich, probing if I stopped at the VA Hospital. She ignites the oven and pulls a small pan of her family recipe lasagna from the freezer.

She wears a black sweater to complement her black jeans and straight, dark hair. She replaced her normal dark lipstick with red to signify a date night, good omen for me. My hormones glow along with the stove.

"Did Ms. Shrink ask about me?" Angie asks. We carry on a running joke about the VA psychiatrist Artie recommends, even though Angie knows I never made an appointment.

"She has a deep interest in the PDP-11 computer and anything I can tell her about DB2."

"Get serious," she smirks. "What was she wearing?"

"Gauzy white blouse just like the last time."

"And she sat in front of the window like a Playboy silhouette."

"Her voice was so low it made me dreamy." I suck a hit from the roach and balance it on the edge of the ashtray.

"Poor boy." She stands up to check the oven. "Will you be done with Freddy by Friday?"

"Should be done tomorrow morning." I start to tell her more, but she waves me off. She treats my work with Freddy like he's CIA.

"We're getting an inspection at Crowley on Friday. The new owners want to see the books."

"I'll be there."

She exhales her cigarette and inhales the roach. "Such a waste. They only want the brand name, a computer dump, and some of the trucks."

I heard this before, one of our common rants about the sad loss of the dairy. "And they want you."

"Can't have me." She grins but her eyes carry a serious glimmer. "I have something else to tell you."

Never good with surprises, I stare at the dark shadows of refracted streetlights outside her kitchen window.

"I have an interview at Sphinx next week. In California."

My head spins. Angie can get a job anywhere they have a computer. I never expected California. "The database company?"

"They want me to stay the week, maybe longer so I can look for an apartment." She furrows her brow, reflecting my expression. "Assuming they offer me the job."

Leaning back in the rigid steel chair, I replay our past conversations about how she doesn't want a boyfriend, though lately I've tried to appear like I'm applying for the role.

"This is not about you," she says in a whisper. "No decent jobs here, or there won't be for long. IBM, Endicott-Johnson, Universal—they're all struggling. This place will look even more desolate in a few years."

She's right. Jobs occasionally pop up, but there are more rumors of layoffs than expansions unless you want to work retail or construction. The decaying houses and buildings around the old town create work for builders like Freddy for now at least. "I could put in a word for you with Freddy." I paint a smile.

She shakes her head, reaching over to take my hand, and I softly squeeze her small fingers. "I don't want you working for Freddy either."

I unconsciously gaze at the oven as she gets up to rescue the lasagna. With my nascent computer skills, I doubt any techie company would hire me in California any more than they would here, even with Angie as a mentor. I wonder if Freddy has contacts out west, but Angie has not invited me to join her.

Watching her carve the lasagna into equal squares, I joke, "I have a lot to tell Ms. Shrink next week."

Angie cocks her spatula like a catapult, though I know she'll never risk flinging tomato sauce and gooey cheese across her tidy little kitchen.

Friday morning on my way to Crowley, I stop by Freddy's Buick office a couple of blocks from my apartment to ask what happened with Buford. We share the rundown neighborhood with an empty lot of debris across from his used cars. He once told me the collapsed building and refuse along the curb deters tourists and keeps his office quiet for business. The city promises to clean it up in the spring, but we're already halfway through May.

When I turn into Freddy's, crunching the washed-out gravel, the black Suburban with Pennsylvania plates rumbles near Freddy's pale green Riviera. Freddy leans on the Suburban's shiny hood chatting with two dark suits. Not wanting to disturb him, I take a wide turn to go on my way. He spies me and waves me over.

I park and follow his strides to the Buick's passenger window. Reaching inside and twisting open the glove compartment with a key, he retrieves an unmarked white envelope and passes it to me in his cupped palm. After I shove the envelope between the front buttons of my shirt, he raises his hand, commanding my silence, and pivots back toward his guests.

I refrain from checking the envelope as I walk away, but I know its contents. Hundred-dollar bills emit a unique scent even through folds of stationary.

CONFLUENCE CITY

The homeless camp extends along the riverbank under the Memorial Bridge. With flood season waning, the tents and tarps have crept closer to the water, and the perimeter has overflowed the shadow of the bridge. Most of the sites cling closely to the pylons, their residents aware the police will clean them out if motorists complain about the eyesore.

The Reagan economy has swelled the camp. As always, it fills me with sadness and apprehension. Since I left the Marines, I have been living one paycheck away from moving in, and now without a steady job, I feel that much closer. I can see myself dwelling in one of the tents.

Judging from the rotting piles of garbage and decaying blankets on the edge of the camp, the Binghamton city council has adopted an attitude of leaving the smell to deter the residents. No garbage trucks on this route, though there are piles of garbage bags around the overfilled dumpster, and most of the trash has been moved away from the tents. Once past the heap the camp resembles a small town with no stores and no wooden or brick structures. Only nylon and canvas with occasional cardboard.

Each campsite maintains a personal boundary of a few feet often marked by grocery carts and trash barrels that double as fire pits. Figures zipped in winter jackets and rolled in sleeping bags or blankets line one side in an uneven row, and a cluster of five tents occupies the center of the damp underpass.

This time of day many of the residents are out working, some at K-Mart or queued up outside Chenango Lumber where contractors and homeowners pick up day laborers. Some clean rooms at the Ramada. Others collect cans and bottles. The faces who follow my steps are those on night shift or too sick to work. No children around.

A tall guy rises from a bent picnic chair, his plume of red hair sprouting like a Roman candle above his familiar toothy grin. Justin lived in the basement apartment downstairs from me before I moved to Chenango Street. A Vietnam veteran, he was in a bad way.

He shakes my hand and I stare into his eyes, clear for once.

"Curt, I never expected to see you here." He echoes my thoughts about him. Justin was getting disability, which should have kept him housed and fed unless the checks went elsewhere.

"You look good, Justin."

"Much better, thanks." His eyes circle the camp and his cheeks redden. "Sorry about the clutter. It rained last night."

"We've seen worse," I reply, recalling how we talked about Nam when we shared joints a few times as neighbors.

We riffed on the rations and the weather, but he was usually so slammed that I avoided him.

"I never thanked you for defending me after I fucked up."

Shrugging, I glimpse up at a semi crossing the bridge with a loud rumble like a 747 landing in a storm. The concrete shivers and holds steady. I recall how I caught Justin breaking into my friend Allen's apartment. Chelsea, our landlady, wanted to call the cops or at least evict Justin until I dissuaded her. A few weeks later he left anyway.

"Dumbest thing I ever did," he continues.

"We all have our moments."

"I was strung out, but that's no excuse." He describes how he drifted from one shabby place to another, depending on how much money he could squeeze from his disability check. Until two assholes kicked in his ribs one night and he landed in Binghamton General. Then the VA hospital and a treatment program.

"Oxford?" I ask. "My friend Artie thinks I should see a shrink there."

"Yeah, good people. They got me clean." He winks. "I had a couple of back flips, but good now."

"Not easy." I recall my back flips with Genesee Ale. They're not as bad I tell myself.

"So, why am I here?" Justin asks rhetorically. "Government cut off my disability after the program."

He doesn't ask why I'm here. Last night at Mother's Carl offered me fifty bucks to gather inside details on the camp for a column he's writing. The Sun-Bulletin maintains a slush fund for news tips, and he wants to do me a favor because I lost my job at the dairy. "Reagan's tough love."

"No bucks for drugs, they say, even if I'm clean. Even if the Army scrambled my life." His face goes dark, but he wipes it away with an invisible squeegee. "So, fuck them."

"They make the rules. We don't have to follow."

His head bobs with enthusiasm. "I'm better off without them. I started a new job at Boscov's. I'm a janitor for now, but I should have enough for an apartment in a few weeks."

"Show me around?"

Justin scans my dirty T-shirt and jeans. "You asked the right person," he says, his energy unabated. "They call me the mayor."

I follow his quick steps back up the path.

"You already saw the waste management zone." He shakes his head. "Over here is the kitchen." He points at a small aluminum table with a propane hotplate in the center and two coolers underneath. "Dining room." A circle of logs and overturned buckets surround a steel waste bin. "And the rest room." Nods toward the river confluence where a tarp hangs between two branches and a smaller twig spears a roll of toilet paper. "Parking lot." Three bikes tied with ropes around an old oak. "We've had a problem with that lately."

"With the parking lot?"

"Several bikes have been stolen, and tarps. I'm worried my stove might be next. Or my new bike, that blue Schwinn.

I bought it used." He turns to me. "Hard to watch everything with people coming and going all night."

"Your thief must be a low life."

"He only takes the good stuff."

Justin leads me to his green nylon wall tent in the rear of the cluster. The flaps are rolled up and neatly tied. Through the mosquito screen I see a pile of folded blankets, one red plaid, a couple paperbacks, sleeping bag, and a Coleman lantern. "They call it the mansion. Eureka Tents had a sale before I lost my checks."

"Better than the Army."

"Except for the noise." He points above his head like he's addressing heaven: the traffic gods with screeching tires, bad mufflers, burning brakes, and insistent horns.

"No mortars and machine guns." I pause and shroud my comment in a self-conscious smile, recalling his foxhole nightmares, why they gave him disability checks.

He ignores my words as his eyes scan the cluster of blankets and gear inside his tent. "Sometimes we hear gunshots."

"Sorry, bad reference."

"Don't worry. You're good." Outside he recovers his mayoral aura with a quick grin and drops into a nearby camp chair. "I heard about the dairy. Bad deal."

I take a seat near him, a large flat rock pushed up the bank by one of the floods.

His voice drops to a whisper as if the Viet Cong might be listening. "If you ever need a place to stay."

I shake my head, but a damp thought oozes up my frame like the mud clotting my boots. I look like I belong here with my old jeans and T-shirt. Angie's out of town for the week, maybe longer. I can use some distraction. Rather than trying to interview the residents as Carl requested, I can join them for a while. I'm also curious about the mysterious bike thief. Finding him would help Justin and provide great content for Carl.

"I know you're proud," Justin continues. "I was the same. Just saying."

"How about we start with dinner. I have a few bucks."

"Sure, we can take it from there." He pulls a strapless watch from his pocket. "Folk should be coming back soon. We eat early, the sunlight and all. And I work tonight."

Picking my way past the mud puddles and the sanitation department, I head up the path like Justin was sending me out to hunt game. After I pick up a modest assortment of hotdogs, buns, baked beans, pickles, molasses cookies, along with six-packs of Coke and Genesee Ale, I stop by my apartment for my old Marine jacket, sleeping bag, and a small vinyl tarp. My supplies fit in a cardboard box with the sleeping bag slung over my shoulder, and I heft the box out the door, leaving my car in the gravel parking lot. The weight of my supplies seems to expand from ten pounds to twenty as I retrace the streets back to the camp.

A red and white checkered plastic sheet covers the aluminum table when I arrive. Two gray river rocks secure the tablecloth, but the underpass deflects the wind. Justin introduces me to Daisy and Dell and their two straw-haired girls Hope and Future, calling to mind a family rock and roll band. Hope wears a daisy in her hair like her mother. The girls show me watercolor paintings from Washington Elementary, while Dell grunts his exhaustion and helps himself to a beer. I learn he spent the day piling shards of concrete after a roadway foreman picked him up in front of the hardware store. Daisy cleans rich people's houses on Front Street.

Before I finish unpacking my box, Daisy lights the propane burners and retrieves a large pan of water for spaghetti and a smaller pan for Ragu sauce.

"Where do you get water?" I ask Justin, eyeing the plastic jugs under the table.

"Faucet behind the Ramada." He winks at me. "The gardeners forget to turn it off at night."

Two older men in coveralls join the table. From their callused hands I guess these men are the water's source. They each accept a beer except for Justin who waves me off. He drops wads of newspaper and splintered scrap wood into the barrel, topping it off with a shoebox he lights with a farmer match. Soon dark smoke billows under the highway roof.

Like a censer calling vespers, the fire attracts more campers. Most hover in the periphery of tents as the evening descends, but one wraith emerges from the shadows with an old army blanket flung around his shoulders like a monk. He rummages through the cardboard box, though Justin already removed the food, leaving just an old can of lighter fluid, a couple books of matches, can opener, and a deck of cards. Justin lays a hand on the guy's shoulder and produces a small Hershey bar. With a nod of thanks, the blanket slinks away.

"Could be me," Justin says, with a slight shiver. He sits in his camping chair, and we send the girls into the brush to hunt for hotdog sticks.

I help Hope and Future trim green twigs and spear hotdogs. With the water slow to boil, their dogs will be ready before the spaghetti. And the beans must wait for the stove.

A battered tan Plymouth stops on the road near the path to the camp. I only notice the car because two of the peripheral campers jump up and meander toward it. Out of curiosity I follow them part way to get a better look, and the Plymouth only hovers long enough for the occupants to exchange something through the passenger window. As it pulls away and the two campers descend back beneath the overpass, a red double-cab pickup stops on the street. Anton's car. Two men emerge from the backseat. I take a step forward. Seeing Anton rekindles my outrage. I owe him for spreading the lie that I ratted him out to the police and brought down his pyramid racket.

"Hey, Curt!" he yells. "Nice place you got here."

"You should come down and have a look."

"A threat? You should be asking me for a job like your roommates."

"You pay them to kiss your ass?"

"You'd like that. But it's warehouse work. Honest labor." He cracks a donkey grin. "You should try it."

"Not that desperate."

The window motor whirs and the glass glides up. With a middle finger and a muffled curse, he skids away.

Back at the camp, Daisy declares the spaghetti done, and everyone lines up with paper plates. She fishes the strands out of the pan to preserve the water while I start the beans in another pan. With the table overflowing, I return to my rock, and Justin lowers himself into his chair, balancing his paper plate like a king on a throne.

"I saw you up on the street," he says between mouthfuls. "You should stay away from that guy in the Plymouth. Bad blood."

I nod my head as the mayor sucks up a strand of spaghetti.

"He cheated me more than once," Justin confides. "The other guy in the red pickup, he's alright."

"Anton?" I choke.

"He gives people work. Cheap but better than nothing."

After we finish dinner, I help Daisy scrub the pans in the spaghetti water, and we gather the paper plates into a plastic bag. Justin retreats to his tent to get ready for work. He waves me inside and marks off a strip near the far wall for me, saying he won't be back until midnight or later.

Perched outside on my rock, I watch the girls chase fireflies while their parents and the gardeners play poker for matchsticks under the Coleman lantern. I decline a hand and scan the edge of the dim light around the dying trashcan fire and the flickering lantern. The persistent noise and damp air carry me back to my nights in Nam, though it was much warmer there and the enemy wanted to kill me. Out of habit I study tree limb shadows in case they mutate into figures with rifles. Soon Daisy gathers her brood into two side by side tents, and the gardeners retreat into a small eight-sided tent with a center pole flying a blue paper streamer.

As the camp grows quiet and the overpass traffic thins to an intermittent moan, I find my thoughts focusing on the bicycle thief. After two hotdogs, a pile of canned beans, and a beer, I'm nowhere close to a solution. My initial list is scant. I rule out the residents. In their desperation one of them might grab something to sell, but they live here. Magpies steal from other nests, not their own. Could be the Plymouth, though whoever drives the wreck obviously profits from the camp the way it is. Why take the chance of attracting heat? I wish the thief were Anton, but he's too rich to care about a few bucks for used bikes. That leaves just one more name that I reluctantly consider: Justin, the mayor. Despite his rehabilitation, I can't ignore that day I caught him breaking into Allen's apartment. With his new job, he must be close to escaping the camp, and his relative affluence might have other sources. The best tent, the best chair, extra bedding. The three bikes tied to a tree. He says he bought the shiny blue Schwinn. What about the other two? I try to dissolve my suspicions; I hope he's truly working.

Thinking about Justin pulls my attention to his chair, and my body soon follows. I might as well be comfortable on my watch. While I tap my feet to stay awake, my mind wavers on the edge of dream, hatching an elaborate scheme starring Justin as the mayor of a bicycle underground, lifting Schwinns from the nearby community college campus and high schools, wheeling them here overnight. Or to other showrooms in homeless camps throughout the city, each camp with its tree and nylon rope. No lock on the rope, which makes sense if the bikes belong to different owners or if there are multiple gleaners and salesmen.

A figure separates from the shadows along the street and descends the path. At first, I assume it must be Justin returning from Boscov's, but it's much too early. Maybe a late-night arrival looking for a campsite. I rise from the aluminum chair and duck under a cascade of ivy hanging from a weathered oak. With the drone of bridge traffic and the dearth of light there's little chance of alerting the newcomer, though I creep anyway, dipping into my old wartime habits.

Dressed in a dark fluffy jacket like Justin's and about his height, the figure walks in a slow two-step, pausing to study the darkness. I make out a knit cap and black gloves, but I can't discern a face. After passing the waste management zone, he picks up his pace, pausing again at the cluster of tents. He circles like a delivery van on a bypass route, checking each tent.

With a shudder I see Justin's prize camping stove left out on the table, though the intruder passes it by on his way to the corralled bikes. I lurch out of the ivy but he's quicker than me, sprinting up the path to the street. To reach the path I charge behind Justin's tent, tripping on a guy line and sprawling on a tuft of grass. By the time I scramble up to the street, the figure is gone.

When Justin returns from work, I stand up with effort, my muscles aching from my awkward fall, my joints molded into his aluminum chair.

"You stayed awake?" he asks.

I bend back and crack my neck. "Someone sniffed your bikes but I wasn't fast enough. Might be nothing."

"Probably a tourist. We get them sometimes." Justin shrugs. After a moment he sprouts a grin. "Now I get it."

"What do you mean?"

"You're here to find the thief."

I don't correct him. My mission for Carl has evolved and I owe Justin an explanation. But even with the runway echoing above us, I can hardly keep my eyes open. "Let's get some sleep."

The next day I retreat to my apartment for a change of underwear and T-shirt, returning for another late vigil while Justin sweeps the floors at Boscov's. Nothing happens. My goal of snatching the thief feels more quixotic when yet another night drags on. By Thursday I excuse myself to prepare for a meeting with Freddy, unsure if I'll return to the camp or not. I should have enough fodder for Carl's typewriter.

Freddy often asks me to stand nearby when he signs contracts. My tall frame lends unspoken protection, which Angie translates into "mob enforcer," her gibe satirical and tinged with concern for my role. Freddy pays well, much better than the newspaper slush fund.

Though he'll excuse my lack of an unstained tie, Freddy prefers my one sport coat, white dress shirt, and cotton slacks. No blue jeans. When I arrive at his mansion in the late afternoon, three well-groomed men are already seated at the oval table in his office. Two wear tropical wool and one a light blue leisure suit like he's on his way to the Governor's Country Club. I identify the woolen suits as lawyers based on their cologne and slick hair, but one also emits the distinct odor of Kentucky bourbon. The country clubber gives me pause, and I tense my face to conceal my reaction.

Gregory Buford shoots me a quick sneer and follows my progress across the room with a blank stare. In front of Freddy's desk I stop for instructions, and Freddy waves me to the side of the room facing the lilac bushes outside his tall windows. I take my place a few feet from one of Buford's rent-a-goons, who avoids my glance and adjusts his clip-on tie, black like the ones the servers wear at McDonald's.

Freddy emerges from behind his polished desk, the size of a small boat. When he takes his chair and sips a glass of water, the formalities begin. The lawyers sit next to Freddy and Buford like translators at the UN whispering to their clients. Freddy's lawyer is the sober one.

I'm not supposed to listen, but the presence of Buford piques my interest. Staring outside at the lilacs struggling to bloom in the chill of late spring, I piece together the gist of the transaction. I hear the county mentioned several times, though no one from the county is present. I already know Buford holds the contract for the county office complex out on Vestal Parkway where Freddy sent me to snoop around.

At one point Buford slides a paper across the table for Freddy's signature and says, "Here you go, partner." Buford's voice sounds grudging rather than congratulatory. Freddy doesn't flinch, concentrating on relighting his cigar stub. But the comment resonates with me.

After the ceremony I wait for everyone to leave. Freddy returns to his desk and rummages for a fresh cigar. "That's it," he says to me with a smile.

"I heard something about the county complex," I reply.

"I thought you'd want to witness." Freddy nods. "Buford just sold us a piece of the action."

I glance down at a glass sculpture of a penguin, must be worth a fortune, my suspicions simmering. I want to ask what happened to my idea, using my discovery of Buford's exploited Mexican workers to squeeze out a deal, which Freddy just signed, but my plan included an agreement to give them union wages. Freddy would have told me if my ploy survived his negotiations. He reads my expression and clips the tip of his cigar.

"You did what I asked," he says calmly. "It came out better than I expected."

"Okay, then." I straighten my shoulders and return his gaze, trying to swallow my displeasure. He knows what I want to say, though he's my only real source of income until a steady job pops up.

I'm still fuming several hours later, lying awake in my bed despite its relative comfort after my nights in the tent. A beer stop at Mother's tempted me as I drove home from Freddy's mansion, but I passed by, knowing Carl would be poised to interview me. Not tonight.

When the phone rings in my living room I dash across the apartment and snatch it up on the fifth ring, hoping it's Angie. She must wonder where I've been. But I hear Justin's voice skimming the tinny background of a pay phone.

"Curt, is that you? I saw the thief."

I glimpse the wall clock, past midnight. "Where?"

"I followed him home. He looked like a kid." Justin pauses and I hear the receiver clunk against metal. "I'm at the Sunoco on upper Front Street near the freeway."

"On your bike?"

"He has my Schwinn. But yeah, I rode here on a bike."

"Can you meet me at the camp? You have another bike, right?"

"Not a good one. Should we call the cops?"

"Maybe later."

Justin beats me back to the camp on a yellow bike with splotches of pale green. I grab a balloon-tired relic with bent wheels, the only bike left, and follow him back up the path. He rides standing up for greater momentum, forcing me to pedal harder. He has gears and I don't.

At the curb he turns toward the Chenango Street bridge along a pot-holed street lined with abandoned warehouses. As I pump harder, my bike's tires wobble like sled dogs fighting for the lead, denying my direction. I track fast enough to follow him over the bridge into a neighborhood of three-bedroom ranch houses with flat lawns and geometric shrubbery lit by humming streetlights. He wends through the development, never looking back, until he reaches an old county road ascending the hills.

Lucky for me and my broken bike, he stops near one of the first driveways, an asphalt semicircle in front of a low-slung white house with stucco trim. A spotless green Mercury sits in front under a security light. Must be five acres at least, including the sculpted juniper. I wheel my wreck behind the shrub row and Justin parks behind me.

I study the spread for lights, first the garage, then an adjacent room, must be the kitchen, living room with large windows, bedrooms extending out the far wing. Spurred by the threat of detection as much as the pungent and deadly haze of weed killer, we lay down our bikes and jog along the bushes. I lead Justin in a wide loop around the garage. Through the glass in the back door and the refracted security lights, I see dim images of two more cars and a row of five bikes. Another bike rests upside down on a workbench with its front tire removed.

Justin taps my shoulder and points at his blue Schwinn leaning at the end of the row. Our recon mission completed, we retrace our steps and retrieve our rides. The route back to the camp is mostly downhill, so I let the bent wheels roll as fast as they can, even if they make me seasick. I recover with the last beer from my cardboard box, warm and refreshing.

Popping a Coke, Justin whispers, "Now we should call the cops?"

"Not yet."

"We know where the thief lives."

"The cops might keep your bike. We can't depend on them." Wiping my mouth on my sleeve, I stand up and stretch. "I have another idea."

By the time we crawl out of the tent in the late morning, Daisy and her family are gone, along with the gardeners and the laborers.

While we munch on stale hotdog buns for breakfast, Justin and I follow our route back to the thief's house, deciding to go on foot. For once I'm grateful for the cool weather on our trek, but I wonder if Binghamton will ever see summer.

With its vast lawn and thick shrubs, the low ranch house appears even farther from the street than it did in the dark. We stalk through a string of backyards, leaping fences and avoiding dogs. As I hoped, the Mercury is gone from the long driveway.

Creeping around the back of the garage, I confirm the two car stalls are empty, but the bikes remain. Under slants of sunlight we can see much clearer. A pile of neatly folded tarps rises alongside an array of camping gear. I step aside to give Justin a peak through the door pane.

"Another one of my bikes," he whispers. "And more of our stuff."

I motion for him to stay as I survey the back of the house, ducking under each window and scanning for sound and movement. Satisfied the place is abandoned for the day, I return to the garage.

Wrapping my hand in my T-shirt, I twist the doorknob, locked. But it's one of those cheap models. Always amazes me. Hundreds of thousands for a place like this and two bucks for a lock. Gripping it tightly, I jam the knob side to side, more give with each pass. With a firm jerk, the short wood screws strip out of their holes, and I remove the internal latch stem. The inside knob thuds to the floor. I pause to make sure no one heard it.

Justin stares at the broken lock like a magician snatched it out of the air. "You never said we'd break in," he mutters.

"He stole your bikes," I reply. I twist the stem hole with my jackknife and push the door open.

The rear of the garage resembles a bicycle shop and a second hand camping store. Tools line the long workbench, and wall pegs hold spare tires and chains. Tucked in a corner a thick nylon rectangle tops a pile of tarps and tents. I glance at Justin. "Enough for another city, Mr. Mayor."

The door to the kitchen is unlocked. Justin scowls as I enter. Stainless steel appliances, cherry cabinets, ceramic floor, a kitchen from my mother's dreams. I pass under an arch to the living room with Justin close behind. A long hallway links a series of bathrooms and bedrooms, the largest in the far corner away from the road. Across the hall we find the kid's room.

Inside are Black Sabbath and Janis Joplin posters, a Yankee pennant, and a signed football on the dresser next to a row of framed photos. One picture each with an awkward dad, two different men, same mom a bit older.

I pull open the dresser drawers one by one.

"What are you doing?" Justin gasps.

The lower drawer holds matched socks and a shoebox. Inside I find rolls of pennies, three blue cardboard holders with a nickel collection, and an old cigarette box stuffed with a wad of bills. Ignoring Justin's plea to put the cash back, I shove the bills in my back pocket.

We return to the garage and wheel Justin's bikes out the back door. Under his arm he holds a tarp he says is his, and he asks me to carry a stolen lantern. I replace the lock as well as I can. Should stay in place until someone touches it. We pedal away.

Justin is adamant. "You shouldn't have taken the money."

"Sending him a message," I say between breaths. Justin beats a fast pace. "Otherwise he gets off free."

"He could call the cops."

"Bring the heat on himself? We have the evidence. I bet there's more in the garage." Justin has a point. The cops will always side with a rich kid and his family. But I wonder how much his parents know about their son's side business. It's unlikely they'd condone his thievery or look the other way, not in this neighborhood.

TERRY TIERNEY

Justin's mood recovers by the time we coast down the trail to the camp. He soon excuses himself for a shower at the YMCA before his work shift. With a grin, he says, "I better pick up a lock for the bikes."

After he leaves, I find a pencil stub near Daisy's tent and wrap the bills in a section of newspaper. "To the Mayor." Enough for a security deposit on a dry apartment. On second thought I add Carl's phone number and a note to call him. Justin can use the Sun-Bulletin's fifty bucks more than I can. I stuff the wad into his sleeping bag and gather my stuff.

With my cardboard box lightened of the drinks and groceries I carried to the camp, my slog through downtown feels shorter but not short enough. A patrol car pulls up as I cross the sidewalk to Court Street. I recognize Anton's brother Karl through the driver window, pointing and alerting his partner. Any other cop would ignore me.

He flips on his flashers for show, and a female officer exits the passenger door, blocking my path while she waits for her partner to lumber around the hood. Tan and athletic next to his stocky pose and loose uniform, she sports a tailored fit, pursing her lips like a drill sergeant.

"Where are you going?" she harps.

"Home."

"What's in the box?"

"Sleeping bag, matches. Might be some dirty underwear."

She smirks and glances at Karl.

"Always the comedian," he counters with his usual scowl.

Shifting the box, I cock my hips for comfort. I know how to play this game.

"We had a complaint about a break in this morning off Chenango River Road. Then the woman called back later and said she was mistaken." The cop sputters. "Do you know anything about that?"

Karl cracks a grin. "And last night we had a report of some tall bozo riding a circus bike."

"I don't own a bike," I reply.

"Well, my brother says someone stole bikes from the homeless camp under Memorial Bridge."

When I fail to respond, Karl taps his nose and says, "You need a shower."

I gaze at his partner whose grimace hangs in place until an urgent bleep from the dashboard pulls her attention.

Karl waits until she swivels away, waving for him to follow. "See you next time," he mutters.

WAKE

Angie offered to loan me her car, but she never left me her keys. Which means I'll pick her up at the airport in my old Dodge Dart, assuming it survives the trip. I worry about her arrival, whether it will be one of the last times I see her after her job interview in California, and whether the Dodge and I are both headed for her personal junkyard.

For now, the pockmarked sheet metal still adheres to its steel frame, whistling in the hot wind. The car shudders in its airfoil as if it were flapping extended wings.

In their wisdom, the Binghamton airport planners built on a shaved hill outside the city to lift the runway closer to the sky. Supposed to be better for landing and takeoffs, though the road to the terminal demands the driver's skill, especially in winter when it resembles the Lake Placid bobsled run. Even in today's summer heat, the twisted pavement challenges my bald tires.

The view over each crest explodes with interlocking green hillsides slung with pine and hardwood, quilted with patches of orchards, pastures, and cultivated fields, some overgrown with scrub brush and wild blackberry thorns. The land takes back its own, old farms sinking into forest, hardly visible except for ragged lines of stone walls. Near the road, resilient planks of an old farmhouse and barn lean in gray majesty like a medieval ruin, squire long gone, cows mowing the front lawn.

Local lore says the westward expansion attracted many of the best families to leave the New York hills behind, but the abandoned farms appear as green as the prosperous newer spreads. To my eyes the spirits of the old farmers never left, guiding the transformation back to forest, gentle husbandry like the Onondaga before them, who never left the land either.

A billboard for Binghamton International Airport confirms I'm on the right road, the only road. Travel agencies advertise the international connectivity even though the most frequent international flights are Canadian geese returning home for the summer. Terminal parking is never a challenge.

Easy to spot among the white-shirted businessmen in their dark suits and overcoats, Angie saunters through the gate in her puffy black jacket and black jeans. She wears dark red lipstick to complement her straight black hair and pale complexion. Today she resembles a vampire on a ski trip, but the outside temperature hovers near eighty in the quickening dusk. Her jacket is more air than down, cooler than it appears. She likes the cold.

Her eyes lock mine, and she maintains her pace, suits flowing around her. A small woman, she hardly reaches my chest, but I'm taller than most, my head poking above the crowd.

I read her expression from afar, both expectant and leery. In the months before her trip to California, we patched up our relationship, but it never attained its former luster. The impasse was my fault, a drunken night backsliding with my old flame Debby. Climbing back into Angie's trust was like the old Dodge slipping gears up Airport Road.

Soon she jumps into my arms, dropping her briefcase on the floor, and nothing else matters. At least for these precious seconds. I set her down before any wing-tipped shoes trip on her briefcase. At the carousel I spot her bag—dull black. We hardly talk until my car rocks out of the parking lot.

Rolling down her window, she pops in the lighter. I offer a joint but she declines for now. Nicotine takes priority.

"Tell me everything," she says, firing up a Newport.

"Not much happens here." I shrug. "One of the reasons you want to leave."

"I was gone over a week," she chants through smoke. "Did you see your shrink?"

I open my window and ponder my response to our running banter about my fictitious psychiatrist. "I canceled."

"I should be glad, I guess. She's hot for you." Angie pokes my arm. "Why did you cancel?"

"Someone stealing bikes from homeless people."

"And you fixed the problem?"

I crack a smile and catch a glimpse of Angie's pursed lips and the dark strands of hair flowing behind her seat. "The shrink would approve. Just deduction. No Watson. No violence."

Angie rewards my lame joke with a sidelong grin, tapping her cigarette in the ashtray. "Was this for Freddy?"

"He doesn't know about it." I watch her extend her smoldering cigarette out the window. "You must have more news than me."

"Sphinx offered me the job. For twice what I can make here." She breaks a smile. "If there were any jobs here."

"The database company, perfect for you." I try to radiate enthusiasm though it means she'll be moving west.

"What about you? How goes the job search?"

"Nil for junior computer operators."

"You ran accounting at the dairy."

"Only a couple of months. No degree and not enough experience."

"That's not as important out west." She glances out her window. "What about Freddy?"

"He offered me a job again."

"I was afraid he would."

"Last week I earned two hundred for a few hours work. All I had to do was stand behind him when he negotiated a contract." My voice hides my displeasure over how he handled the Buford situation. I'll tell her about it later.

"You're better than a goon."

"He wants me to computerize his accounting."

"Cook his books."

That stiffens our conversation. Angie exhales out the window. The humid summer air thickens into mist but neither of us complains.

At her apartment we agree on dinner tomorrow, but she doesn't invite me up as I hoped. Our words hang like stale smoke, echoing the plans we tried to share before she left for her interview. She thinks I should follow her to California, not as her boyfriend, but for my own good. She won't ask me directly even if her hints ring like the dairy's old PDP-11 computer before it spits out accounting reports. She wants me to ask her.

My Dodge clunks into gear and plods through the gloaming streets like an old stallion seeking the stables after a day of stress, channeling his rider. The dive bar on Court Street, My Mother's Place. Cheap beer and empathy.

Artie welcomes me to my usual stool with his gap-toothed grin and holds up his empty glass when I order. Daryl the bartender slides the foamy pitcher between us and draws me a glass of seltzer. The beer's for Artie and the fizzy water reflects my best intentions if I have any chance with Angie, at least until she leaves for good.

The crowd seems sparse, particularly when I realize Carl's white mustache and wispy crown is not leaning over the bar next to Artie. The last time Carl missed an evening was when his wife committed him to house detention for investing in a pyramid scheme.

"Wow," Artie hoots, nearly swallowing his tobacco plug. "Who's that?"

THE BRIDGE ON BEER RIVER

A large, voluptuous woman pushes through the door and struts toward me in her high heels. She wears a light blue nylon blouse with an extra button unclasped, and her ample cleavage quivers with her steps. Behind her bright red lipstick, she carries a solemn expression, eyes wet and gleaming in the dim lights.

"I knew I'd find you here." She looks me up and down as if she's appraising a horse.

"Julie," I reply, surprised to see her in a place like Mother's. Once my mentor in the accounting department at the dairy, she never forgave me for calling out her affair with our boss, though I was innocent of causing their breakup. "How's the newspaper?"

Her eyes squeeze with tears rolling through her makeup. One of the few dairy alumni to land a job, she runs the accounting department at the Sun-Bulletin.

Snatching a napkin off the bar, she dabs her eyes and cheeks. "It's Carl," she stutters. "He's dead."

All voices stop and a chair screeches as someone twists toward us.

"Carl dead?" Artie echoes.

Daryl shoves a box of Kleenex to me, and I hand her one. "What happened?"

"He passed at his desk. Heart attack."

Her soft words resound like cannons, impossible to ignore. I seldom saw Carl outside the bar until the past week when he wrote a feature on the homeless and asked me to check out the camp under the Memorial Bridge. Carl kept my name out of the paper, dubbing my friend Justin the Mayor of Confluence City. I hope it helps Justin land an apartment.

I shiver under my T-shirt with a flash of guilt, though the river of beer flowing through Carl's silver mustache and his soggy cigars more likely clogged his heart than my recent investigation. He loved to write, and I found it amazing how his column and stories hit the deadline every morning and he made last call at Mother's every evening. Invincible like my Dodge. Until now.

Julie stares at me with her tissue squeezed in her fist, but unlike Carl, no words flow from me. I reach over her broad shoulders and her head collapses against my chest, forgiving me, at least for the moment. Artie and Daryl stare at us, frozen in disbelief.

Trying to offer comfort, I reflexively pat Julie's back until she straightens up with a jerk as if she realizes where she is and who she's leaning against. She clears her throat and whispers, "His wife is making arrangements." She reaches for another tissue. "I should help her."

"I can help," I offer, though I doubt either Julie or Carl's wife will accept. I only met Margaret once when I gave Carl a ride home, and I was hardly in better shape that night than he was.

Artie perks up. "We should do it here."

Swooning as she twists toward him, Julie shoots a look of disgust. She drops a hand on the bar to steady herself.

"That's not what I meant," Artie replies, glancing between me and Daryl. "We should have a wake."

"Yeah, we could have a wake for Carl." Daryl scans the dim room, already counting chairs and tables.

Julie's not won over, but I like the idea.

Two nights later My Mother's Place fills with Carl's friends along with the ever-present Court Street winos who smell the possibility of free beer like mosquitos swarming human sweat. Several newspaper types line the outer tables sporting loose ties and tired suits, among them Julie in a well-filled black blouse. The bar regulars gather around Artie offering condolences as if he were Carl's only son. I scan the room for Carl's daughter but I doubt I could pick her out unless she wore a white mustache and Einstein hair like her father. Carl's wife Margaret cautiously slips through the door behind me, gathering her black dress above the floor. I guide her to a free table near the bar. No sign of Angie.

Debby sways through the crowd with a tray of beers, most of which land in front of the news crew, and her passage deadens the conversation. Always the center of attention, dressed in a shorter black skirt than usual and a silky gray top, she passes by me with no sign of recognition as if the wake were mine and I was already six feet under. Just as well. Though I have no intention of rekindling our erstwhile romance, which was really a drunken tumble, her attitude chilled when she learned I spend time with Angie. She would rather see me die alone. I follow her to the bar where I retrieve seltzers for Margaret and me.

Soon after I sit down, Daryl clangs a spoon on an empty pitcher until he gets grudging attention from the congregation. He briefly expresses his appreciation for Carl and pauses, glancing toward the press table. With none of them willing to offer, the silence drones like an exhaling organ. Someone should speak.

Daryl shoots a look toward me, not unlike his appeal when he wants me to help break up a bar fight. I shift my eyes to the dirty windows along the sidewalk, but Margaret taps my arm. Now all heads turn toward me. I have no choice. I stride to the bar and stand next to Artie who keeps my customary stool free along with Carl's.

Leaning back against the bar, I hitch up the lapels of my dark gray sport coat, my only sport coat. I clear my throat, unsure what to say. Never one for speeches or even long sentences, I find myself conjuring Carl from fumes of beer and his lingering cigar scent. As I begin to speak my voice wavers and I hope no one notices.

"Carl was my friend. He taught me many things. Like his triangle theory with its indices of sex, money, and power. If you have one of the points, you can get the others. Raquel Welch has sex appeal, so she gets rich. Congressmen have power, so they get strippers. We all know money leads to power." I pause. "Carl said Ronald Reagan is an ideologue with no ideas." A clap rises from the news table. "And the cross-county flights destined for New York City flush their toilets over Binghamton."

I swallow a breath, glimpsing his wife and a young woman now sitting next to her. "He always said his wife and daughter were smarter than him, but he was pretty smart. He left us more ideas than most men. I miss Carl already."

With that I plop down on my usual stool and Artie claps my shoulder. Daryl slides me a fresh seltzer just as one of Carl's newsroom buddies gets up to add his stories. A small, shadowy figure slips onto Carl's old stool. Angie.

With her petite figure and luxurious long hair, Angie attracts as much attention as Debby until Artie shoots a cold look at all the inquiring eyes. He acts like my father figure, and I signal another pitcher for him in appreciation. Although Angie has never appeared in the bar before, her vampire reputation precedes her. "I can't miss a wake." She catches my eye. "And I know Carl meant a lot to you."

Her hand rests on my forearm as Daryl produces another seltzer. I wonder if she wants a glass of red wine, her usual choice, but I'm too surprised by her appearance to ask. Artie leans away to give us room.

"Nice of you to come," I stumble but I mean it.

"I'm glad I heard your speech." Her dark eyes burrow under my untrimmed hair, deeper than they have during the past couple of days when I helped her pack boxes for her move to California. We avoided any mention of our purpose as if we were working together at the dairy and she was not leaving town. When we finished each day, I returned to my apartment, still under a cloud of awkward abstinence, craving her touch while satisfied with helping her. Now her glance implies more. Odd that the smoky dive bar, hardly romantic, draws us closer.

I force a smile. "I didn't say how Carl always took off his glasses when he passed out, just before his forehead thumped the bar. Great reflex."

"I never saw him do that," a soft voice responds. Carl's daughter appears between us. "But I loved your eulogy. Very moving and appropriate." She stares at Angie with wet eyes. "He was a good father."

I nod as she extends her fingers behind her back to me, giving my hand a quick squeeze, continuing to focus on Angie. "I'm Leslie."

"He thought highly of you," I reply. "I'm Curt."

"Of course, you are," she says, casting her voice to me without moving her eyes. Angie shifts on her stool, appearing uncomfortable.

"My friend Angie," I say, trying to fill the tight space.

"The vampire," Leslie concludes. "He wanted to write a column about you, but he didn't think Curt would allow it."

Angie smiles. "Ever helpful."

Before I can respond, Artie jabs my shoulder and points to his crutch under the bar. I retrieve it for him, and he stands on his one leg with the crutch pinched in his armpit, clapping loudly. Soon the bar is clapping in unison, evolving into a jig beat. Artie drops his crutch and begins to dance. He spins and snaps his fingers. A few others join and Artie taps Leslie to be his partner. She reluctantly agrees and he twirls her toward the center of the room, somehow keeping his balance.

I wonder if he will pass his old Mets hat for tips afterward like he does most nights.

Over the din I say, "Leslie's hot for you."

"Good luck. I'm irrepressibly heterosexual." Angie takes a sip of her seltzer and I follow her lead. Daryl rewarded us with extra wedges of lime.

"One of the things I like about you," I reply over the rim of my glass.

"But not enough."

"You mean California?"

She fishes a cigarette out of her beaded black purse. "It's not that."

"Then what is it?"

"You can't fix everything for everyone."

"I'm good at repairs." I reflexively glance at Artie who is beginning to tire. "People depend on me."

"And Freddy?"

"I don't need Freddy to be a repairman."

"Only if you want to get paid."

"There's that," I agree. "But I can be a repairman anywhere."

She suppresses a smile. "I never asked you to come with me."

"What if I just showed up?"

Angie lights her cigarette and carefully blows the smoke behind her, leaning against my shoulder and nipping my ear lobe. Her eyes glisten in the dim light. "That would depend on the situation."

AUTHOR'S NOTE

Although *The Bridge on Beer River* is fiction and all the characters are imagined, I refer to several real place names. Binghamton, of course, is an actual town redrawn from my memory of living there, and I altered the details to support Curt's story. Crowley Dairy is based on a historical dairy, but I never stepped inside. The operations, history, and floorplan are all invented, including the morgue inhabited by the vampire, though I did freeze in similar computer rooms. I visited Swat Sullivan's before it was torn down and even tried to rent an upstairs room one wayward night, but I recast the bar as more of a classic Irish pub and literary venue. Pearl's was inspired by a real country western bar with a huge bucking stallion on the bar, and local lore did say the horse will fly away when a virgin graduates from Binghamton University. Confluence City is imagined, though such urban encampments are unfortunately common. My Mother's Place, alas, is an invented dive, though you can find many like it in Binghamton and other American towns. You might even see Artie waiting for you to buy him a Genesee Ale. If you do, tip one for me.

ABOUT THE AUTHOR

Terry Tierney was raised in Minneapolis and eventually migrated to the San Francisco Bay Area. After serving in the Seabees, he completed his BA and MA at Binghamton University, and earned a PhD in Victorian Literature at Emory University. He taught college composition and creative writing, and he survived several Silicon Valley startups as a software engineer. He lives in Oakland with his wife, a Librarian from the University of California, their two Persian cats, and their enthusiastic Golden Retriever. He is the author of a poetry collection, *The Poet's Garage,* and the novel *Lucky Ride,* both published by *Unsolicited Press.* His work has appeared in many literary journals and anthologies. More can be learned at http://terrytierney.com.

ABOUT THE PRESS

Unsolicited Press is based out of Portland, Oregon and focuses on the works of the unsung and underrepresented. As a womxn-owned, all-volunteer small publisher that doesn't worry about profits as much as championing exceptional literature, we have the privilege of partnering with authors skirting the fringes of the lit world. We've worked with emerging and award-winning authors such as Shann Ray, Amy Shimshon-Santo, Brook Bhagat, Kris Amos, and John W. Bateman.

Learn more at unsolicitedpress.com. Find us on twitter and instagram.

CPSIA information can be obtained
at www.ICGtesting.com
Printed in the USA
JSHW020725090523
41296JS00009B/20